D1534714

# SPECIAL RISK

*By*

# SANDY NORK

For New Cumberland Library - Thank you for supporting local authors! Enjoy the journey! Sandy Nork

*For Bill*

# PROLOGUE

*Paoli, PA*
*August 1984*
*10:30 P.M.*

**A MOONLESS NIGHT. A STEADY, DRIZZLING RAIN.** A two-lane highway bisects the horse farms and stands of maples. The road is slick with mud and stones. A car rests against the limbs of uprooted trees, bent sidelong from the pressure of metal and plastic, the light from the headlamps shocking against their leaves. The car, a small one, is twisted and partially buried in mud in the deep gulley. Steam rises from the hissing engine, and fluids leak from places under the hood. Some of the windows are shattered, sprinkling the mud with tiny points of dark glitter.

A beautiful Asian woman, dressed for dinner with a friend, is crumpled at a severe angle and jailed by the steering wheel against her chest. A piece of metal from the car pierces her side. Her forehead is sliced open above one eye. She, like the car, is losing fluids, but she is still conscious.

*I was afraid,* she remembers, *but I am not scared now.*

She hears a car, and then men's voices. She strains to listen to them over the hissing of the car and the muffling drape of rain.

*I should be relieved,* she thinks. *Maybe they will help me.*

But she is not relieved. She is frightened, but also angry. She hears the voices speak in the language of her ancestors, the language she has tried all her life to forget. She thinks in English, not Japanese, so it takes her time and concentration to make sense of what they say.

They are discussing her, she knows. She hears them say her name. But they also say she is no longer important. They will find what they need without her. They are not going to help her. They are leaving her to die.

She hears their steps, fading now. A car starts and drives away.

She knows this with certainty: *They are right. I am dying.*

*Minaru,* she thinks, *what have we done?*

*Liam, I am so very sorry.*

*Valerie! Who will take care of my sweet Valerie?*

# CHAPTER ONE

**VALERIE SLOAN BENT OVER THE VIOLIN BOW** she was rehairing on the worktable. She combed the loose hairs into a flat ribbon, gathered them, measured them against the frog, and cut them a couple of inches longer. She was about to tie them off with a piece of wire when she heard a car pull into the stone driveway.

Glancing out the window, Valerie saw a black truck, dusty and dented on the back panel, park by the shed her dad used as a garage. A slender woman with dark brown curly hair got out of the passenger side of the truck.

Grabbing a flat metal hair clip, Valerie gathered the ribbon of hair she was working with to keep it from flying away. She placed it next to the bow for later. The customer was far more important than this repair.

Her father rapped on the door of the workshop, then stuck his head inside. "I think Sylvia is here. Should I show her in?"

"No, that's okay. I'll meet her at the door."

Valerie stood up, dusted herself off as a matter of habit, and draped a piece of flannel cloth over the bow and ribbon of hair to hide the repair from sight without having to move the pieces. She made sure the violin that Sylvia was coming to see was handy on a stand on the table, along with a bow, then made her way out of the workshop to the front door of the house she shared with her dad. She tilted her head, sniffing the air, fragrant with the smell of baking bread.

"Sylvia!" she said as she opened the door, not waiting for her to ring the bell, "Welcome. It's good to see you."

"Hi, Valerie." Sylvia smiled as she stepped into the house. "Ooh, it smells good in here!"

"Dad's baking." Valerie gestured to her father. "You remember my dad."

"Of course. Hello, Mr. Sloan. I told some of my friends that I was coming here today. They still speak highly of you. I wish I had the pleasure of playing with the orchestra while you were there."

"Thank you, my dear." Valerie's dad blushed with pride, his Irish complexion giving him away. It made him look younger than his seventy-plus years. "I miss them, too, but I'm enjoying retirement. Well, if you'll excuse me, my bread is almost done, and I believe the two of you have business to attend to."

Valerie's dad headed to the kitchen to pull his loaves out of the oven while the two women moved into the workshop. Sylvia had been at the house before, so Valerie didn't feel the need to show her around. The basic layout was easy to see, anyway. When her dad remodeled it ten years ago, he made sure it was open and bright. Inside the front door, visitors saw the living room and could easily look into the kitchen and dining room.

Turn forty-five degrees, and they could see what Valerie thought of as the heart of the house: the music room. The midnight mahogany baby grand piano resided here, along with four tufted chairs upholstered in the same tasteful blue print as the piano's bench cushion, all for the comfort of her dad's string quartet cronies on practice nights.

A glossy hardwood floor and large windows framed with sheer white curtains enhanced the room's openness. The sheers were pushed back, and the windows opened out onto the side and back of the house, where the tulips and peonies now faded and the first of the summer's rosebuds started to swell. Only the orange daylilies bloomed at this point, but in a few weeks, the garden would be an artist's palette of colors.

Valerie didn't conduct business in the music room. Instead, she led Sylvia to her workshop and gestured to the violin on the stand.

"Ready to take it for another spin?" she asked.

Sylvia nodded, her dark curls bouncing. She pulled the violin from the stand, along with the bow Valerie had placed alongside it. Sylvia drew the violin to her chin, laid the bow on the strings, and played some quick scales that segued into an étude.

"What do you think?" asked Valerie when Sylvia stopped playing.

Sylvia pursed her lips. "I don't know." She looked at the violin, stroking the finish. "It's beautiful and plays well, but... I think I'm going to pass."

Valerie swallowed hard. She needed this sale. She had thought it was a done deal, and now it wasn't.

"How about if I bring down the price a bit?" Valerie asked. She didn't like the idea, but if it meant sealing the deal, she would chip a little off.

"No, it's not that." Sylvia paused, looking for the right words. "I saw another violin, and I'm sure now that I'm going to go with that one. I wanted to play this one a second time to be certain."

Valerie could see the firm decision on her face. "Ah, well then."

Sylvia held out her hand. "Thank you for letting me re-test this one. I'll keep you in mind for my next one."

"Of course. I hope I can help you in the future."

Valerie showed her to the door and watched as she went to the truck. It turned around to head back into Philadelphia. Valerie closed the door and stood next to it, her forehead pressed against the wood.

Behind her, her father said, "Don't worry, honey, you'll make a sale soon."

She faced him. He looked almost childlike, his tousled white halo of hair topping his oval, expectant face and pink cheeks. She forced a smile. "Of course I will."

Her father held out a small piece of paper. "Walter called."

She took the paper and looked at the number. She could hardly focus on it, but said, "I can't figure out why Walter doesn't call my cell number."

"He did. When you didn't pick up, he called the house phone."

"Oh, okay." She shoved the paper into the pocket of her jeans. Walter Nakamura was the last person she wanted to talk to. She knew that her dad wished that she was more social with Walter—he was the son of old family friends, and she had known him for years—but he irked her.

He irked her because he was Japanese. Well, half Japanese. Like her. The difference was, his goal was to become all Japanese.

Her cell phone buzzed in her jeans pocket, and she looked at the display. She didn't recognize the number, but immediately thought it might be another customer.

"I'd better take this, Dad."

"Sure, go ahead. I'm working on dinner."

Naturally. Cooking was her dad's hobby and had been for almost two years now.

She slipped back into the workshop and discovered that she had missed the call. She called the number back, and it rang twice, then a familiar voice said, "Hi, Valerie. It's Harry."

So many times she had heard the phrase, "you could have knocked me over with a feather," but she always thought the idea was laughable. Hearing Harry Zimmer's voice on the phone made her feel otherwise.

"Hi, Harry." She tried to sound aloof. She felt anything but.

"I heard that TransReliable laid you off." As in, TransReliable Insurance Corp, her previous employer. His, as well.

"Three months ago." The anger in her heart hardened her voice.

"I didn't find out until last week. If I had known, I would have called you sooner."

She let his comment hang in the air. What could she say? That he should never have left the company? That he was their best field man? That the stories about him weren't true? That she needed him?

Ah, there it was. Without Harry there, Valerie felt like half a person. Worse, she became redundant to the company. All her research skills, all her organizational skills, all her knowledge of when and why and how to get things done in a timely fashion so that the insurance megalopolis could move their cases forward went out the door with

5

her. She was replaced by newer, younger, cheaper agents with no idea of how the company operated before they stepped in the door and no interest in learning anything about its history. Or if they did want to know, they didn't want to hear it from her.

When Harry left, TransReliable didn't reassign her to another partner. Valerie filled her days with writing reports, filing, and tying up the loose ends of the cases Harry had pending. The company asked her to turn over the ones she couldn't complete to other agents; then they let her go.

She and Harry had been unceremoniously dumped. Twenty years of knowledge and loyalty walked out that door with her, fifteen years went with Harry. She still didn't accept why.

"Valerie? Are you there?"

"I'm here."

"You know, I wanted to talk to you ever since I left."

"Why didn't you?" she asked.

"When I left, TransReliable forced me to sign an agreement saying that I wasn't allowed to talk to any of their agents while they worked there, so I couldn't call you and explain. I ran into a guy who was laid off after you were and he mentioned that you no longer worked there. Now that you don't work for them anymore, I thought we could talk."

"Sure, we can talk," she said, keeping her voice as level as possible.

"Do you have time now?"

"Now? No, I... let me... I..."

"Would it be better if I call back later? Around seven?"

"Yes. Yes, that would be better."

Over dinner, Valerie explained to her father that an old friend had contacted her and that she was expecting another call from him after dinner. Her dad knew the rumors about Harry, so she avoided any mention that he was the old friend she planned to talk to.

"How was rehearsal last night?" she asked her dad.

"It went great," he said. "We stumbled a bit here and there, but that simply means we'll be on our toes for the show. I wish it was a paying gig.

Valerie was pleased that he was playing because he enjoyed it so much, but she, too, wished he was getting paid. Since he retired a few years ago from the position of Violin Master of the Philadelphia Orchestra, he had been at loose ends, filling his time with gardening and learning to cook. He even renovated the kitchen two years ago, a project that Valerie never questioned until TransReliable laid her off. At that point, she took a look at their finances and learned the hard truth.

Her father was a lovely man with many skills and talents, but money management was not one of them. In all the years she lived here with him, she never sat down with him to go over the bills, thinking that, as her father, he would tell her when he needed more money than she gave him. She underestimated almost every bill and never took all of the home renovations into account.

When she saw the situation her father was in, her heart sank. Paying off the loans would take years. He was retired and depended on social security and his pension for income. When she was employed, she shared part of the money she earned at TransReliable with her dad. But now she had no job, some temporary benefits from being laid off and what little income her violin repair and restoration hobby/ business could bring in.

If that wasn't enough to worry about, there was one more factor that Valerie didn't want to think about: next year would be the twenty-fifth anniversary of her mother's death.

Valerie planted a smile on her face while her dad talked. Inside, she fought the urge to cry after losing the violin sale. There was no point in discussing the loss of a paying customer. Her dad was deep into talking music, and there was no room in his monologue for financial discussions.

After dinner, she helped her dad stack the dishwasher and was about to excuse herself when her phone buzzed. Her dad nodded at her phone and said, "Get going. I'm sure you have lots to talk about."

If only he knew.

"Hold on, Harry."

"Harry?" she heard her dad say behind her. Valerie took the phone into the workshop and closed the door.

"How are you doing?" Harry asked when she indicated she was ready to talk.

She didn't want to make small talk with him. She had too many questions and too much anger to be social or smooth.

"I'm fine. But what happened? Why did you leave? Even though the company was laying off people, you and I were golden – we knew they wouldn't lay us off because we had seniority. They trusted us! So what on earth happened? Why couldn't you talk to me, tell me why, or at least let me know where you were?" The words tumbled out, months of anguish unleashed.

"I told you. The agreement."

"Before that!"

"I was too embarrassed. I knew you'd be angry with me."

"They said you weren't trustworthy anymore."

It was, to her, the ultimate insult. Harry had worked for TransReliable almost fifteen years, but "untrustworthy" was what they called him when they told Valerie they were taking him off the roster of outside agents. She had worked with him daily for fourteen of those fifteen years, and it was unthinkable.

"I... got involved in something I knew I shouldn't. I started seeing one of the clients."

"Oh, Harry."

Valerie's heart finally broke. The rumors were true. She wasn't shocked because it was the only thing she could think had happened, but all along she hoped that it wasn't so. She heard stories of agents taking payoffs, looking the other way when a deal went down, getting in the middle and becoming part of a case themselves. Those agents were gone instantly.

Harry was around for a week or two after the initial meeting with the managers, but he wasn't allowed to explain anything to anyone. Not even to her, his inside partner, the one who did his research and wrote reports from his notes and helped him clarify the minutia involved.

"I'm sorry, Valerie. If I could have told you, I would have."

"Couldn't you have taken me aside and..."

"Valerie. Think about who we worked for and what we did for them. It was easy for them to assign agents to keep tabs on their own employees."

Valerie bit her lip. One more issue niggled at her, now that she knew for sure what the problem was.

"So why did you do it, if you knew what would happen?"

"I don't know what I was thinking. I was so hooked on this woman..." Harry sighed. "It's not like dating a co-worker. I would have

9

thought twice about the fallout from something like that. With this, I stupidly thought no one would find out. I didn't think it would get back to the company."

"But it did."

"Yes. Which is why I know TransReliable can and will watch any of us."

"Even their best agent. I'd love to know who turned you in."

"I have my suspicions, but it doesn't matter. The bottom line is that I was wrong and they called me on it. Then they fired me. In the process, I signed away my ability to stay in touch with anyone in the company so I could retain a clean record of my history at TransReliable. I needed that if I wanted to continue to be an investigator."

"So you're still an investigator?"

"Yes. I opened my own office. That's why I wanted to talk to you. You have no idea how happy I was to hear that you didn't work for them anymore."

"Excuse me? You're happy they laid me off?"

"No, that's not what I mean. I mean that now that you aren't working for TransReliable, I can talk to you."

"Oh." Rather than being hurt or offended, Valerie felt elated that he was about to confide in her. Finally.

"And I can ask you to come and work with me," Harry said.

She was glad he couldn't see her with her mouth hanging open.

# CHAPTER TWO

*Upper Darby, PA*
*June 15, 2009*
*9:00 A.M.*

**THE DOOR WHISPERED TO A CLOSE BEHIND HER,** its miniblind rustling. A shiver snaked up her back, a trick of the air conditioning. The room smelled of air freshener.

"It's good to see you, Valerie." Harry met her at the door, blue eyes twinkling and lips curving into a smile.

"It's good to see you, too."

Valerie had almost forgotten that smile. She remembered how he usually got favors granted with that smile.

Moisture coated Valerie's upper lip, and dampness tickled the small of her back. She dabbed at her face with a cotton handkerchief and told herself that she wasn't nervous. *Must be the humidity.*

"How've you been?" he asked. "You look great."

"Thanks, Harry."

Harry moved to hug her, a gesture she avoided by putting her attaché on the floor. He stepped back as if stung.

"Before I called you, it crossed my mind that someone else might have snagged you," he said.

"Funny, I don't seem to be popular among insurance companies these days. Guess I'm damaged goods." Heat spread into her cheeks, and she brushed back her bangs with her fingers, dislodging them from where they stuck to her damp forehead.

"They don't know what they're passing up. But if you're not working for an insurance company, what have you been doing? Working that side business of yours? Repairing violins?"

"Yes, but business has been pretty slow. I'd like to get back to work. Insurance work. After three months of sending out resumés I wasn't sure anyone would hire me."

Harry rubbed his face with his hands as though washing the unpleasantness away.

"Forget about TransReliable, Valerie. Look around you. This is my new reality. TransReliable booted me out, so I opened my own business. And now, they've booted you out, too. I can use you here."

"You make it sound so simple."

"It is simple." *That smile, that pirate, we're-in-this-together smile.* "What, the money I offered isn't enough? I thought you were happy about that."

"Your offer was and is very generous. I accepted because it is, and because I want to get back to work."

"So what's the problem?"

"What you did broke rules. I don't want that to happen again."

"It won't." Harry's eyes met hers and held them.

"Okay," she said. "Let's get to work."

"Great," he said. Then, suddenly, he was all business, tapping his fingers on the desk next to him. "But I also need you to be able to get around town."

"I can do that. I've been riding public transportation all my life. I got here this morning by bus. I can get anywhere in Philly that way."

"I know you believe that. But since you don't drive, my biggest concern about you is transportation. You have to see clients and interview people whenever you can catch them."

"I can do that. Really, I—"

"Look, this isn't TransReliable where you spent most of your day sitting in a cubicle. I need you to be mobile. Our clients are not always in the city. If you work for me, you have to be flexible and ready to move. I don't trust SEPTA trains and buses for that."

Valerie's throat constricted. "I can't drive, Harry. I can barely tolerate riding in a car, much less driving one. Maybe you think I'm silly, but I cope the best I can. I can't afford a chauffeur."

Harry's fingers stopped tapping. "I think I know a way to make getting around easier for you. Rocky would be the perfect driver."

"Driver?" Valerie asked.

The door opened, the miniblind banging against the glass. A buxom woman with strawberry-streaked blonde hair entered the room. She wore a turquoise blue jacket, buttoned snugly across her ample chest, with a matching skirt that ended nowhere near her plump knees.

A lime green shoulder bag that looked like its contents would tumble out at any moment was slung across the woman's shoulder. She wore high, chunky heels in a green that was close to, but not quite, the color of the bag. Even in those heels, the top of her head only came to Valerie's chin.

"Well, at least it's not raining yet," the woman said into the cell phone in her left hand, rummaging in her shoulder bag with the right. "I swear this is the rainiest June we've ever had. Some days I wonder if summer's ever going to..." She stopped short, looking up from her bag, blinking her kohl-lined, heavily mascaraed eyelashes.

Harry said, "Valerie Sloan, meet Raquel Russo, your new driver."

"What?" both women exclaimed.

Valerie stared at Raquel. Raquel stared back, her mouth open. Finally, Raquel said into the phone, "Gotta go. Talk later."

Harry continued, "Rocky, Valerie's our new investigator. I want you to pick her up in the morning and bring her to the office. You'll be her wheels and her assistant. Valerie, Rocky will see that you get wherever you need to go. And she'll help out wherever you need her."

*This is my driver? Oh, boy.* Tamping down her disbelief, Valerie held out her hand. "Hello, Raquel."

Raquel's face exploded into a smile as she pumped Valerie's hand. "Call me Rocky. Everybody does. My dad wanted a boy. He was a huge Stallone fan."

They shook hands longer than usual. Valerie noticed how Rocky's green eyes set off her olive skin, both at odds with her hair. *Mediterranean, probably Italian.* She had to consciously remove her hand from Rocky's grip.

"So, you're Valerie. You don't look like a Valerie," Rocky said.

"My mother was Japanese."

"But your dad wasn't?"

"No, he wasn't."

"Oh," Rocky said. Then she added, "You're so tall!"

"My dad is tall."

"So, if your mom is Japanese and your dad isn't, that makes you half-Japanese, right?" Rocky said. "There was a band in the eighties called Half Japanese. I didn't like them much, but my brother Joey was into them. They were kind of punky. I like Poison, Ratt, and Bon Jovi. Who do you listen to?"

"Classical music, mostly."

"The Beatles? The Rolling Stones?"

Harry laughed. "No, Rocky. She means Mozart. Beethoven."

"Really?"

"Really," Valerie said.

"Well, it's great to have you here, Val!"

"Thanks. And Rocky? Would you call me Valerie, please? I prefer that."

"Huh?" Rocky looked puzzled.

Harry cleared his throat. "Valerie, let me give you the tour. This is Rocky's desk. My office is to the right. Yours is to the left." He pointed as he spoke. "The supply closet is over there, and the powder room is behind the door next to it."

"Got it," Valerie said.

Harry gestured to Valerie to follow him into his office, a much smaller space than the reception area. A laptop was open on one side of the desk, partially obscured by papers and files that drifted over it. There were also a few personal items partially buried in the avalanche of paper: a signed baseball from some sports team, a striated rock from a vacation, and a Magic 8 Ball that someone had given him as a joke. Valerie recognized all of them from Harry's days at TransReliable, not that Harry was ever at his desk much back then.

"Your office is..." Valerie smiled, "compact."

She glanced at the wall where his framed degrees and a few personal photos hung. Harry never talked about his family, and he had never hung pictures at TransReliable, so her attention was drawn to them. One photo in particular interested her: a much younger Harry in a graduate's cap and gown, holding a diploma, shaking hands with an older man in glasses. The man beamed almost as much as Harry.

"Who's that?" she asked. "Your dad?"

"You could say that," Harry said. "It's Evan Eastlake, Professor Evan Eastlake. My mentor at Drexel, remember?"

"Of course I remember. The never-give-up-looking guy, right?" It was a line she'd often heard from Harry.

"Right. Eastlake was a big deal in the Chicago PD as a detective, but he transferred to Philadelphia in the nineties and started teaching. What he said was, 'Never give up looking for the facts, no matter how hard they might be to find, or how hard they are to accept as true.'" Harry handed Valerie two file folders and motioned to the door. "Come on. Let's take a look at your new digs."

A large bunch of yellow tulips in a vase waited for her on the desk. A three-by-five card taped to it proclaimed, "Welcome!"

"How lovely," Valerie said. "Thank you."

This was the Harry Zimmer she remembered from TransReliable, the tough guy who did thoughtful things for people, little touches that went far with the office ladies. And with her.

*Before the trouble, before he left TransReliable.*

*Before he hung out his own shingle as an investigator.*

*And now here they were, starting over, partners again.*

The smell of fresh pastry hung in the air. A pink box from a donut shop sat on Valerie's desk next to the flowers, along with two large paper cups in a cardboard carrier.

"I thought you might want to start the day with breakfast," Harry said.

Valerie opened one cup and inhaled the aroma of coffee. "This is great. Thanks," she said. She flipped open the box and saw that one donut was already missing. She looked at Harry.

"I was hungry," he said.

Rocky barged into the room. "Do I smell coffee?"

Like Harry's office, Valerie's office was too small for more than two people. As the third person, Rocky sucked all the oxygen out of the tiny room. Valerie felt dizzy and claustrophobic.

"Ooh, goodie," Rocky said, helping herself to the other cup and a donut. "Let me know if you don't eat all those, okay, Val?"

"Sure. Help yourself. And Rocky? Would you call me Valerie, please? I really do prefer that."

Rocky, donut powder on her lips, said, "Really? I thought you were kidding."

"I wasn't kidding," Valerie said.

"Well, I'll let you settle in." Harry motioned to the desktop. "I've left some files on your desk, a little recent history. Take a look at those first. Then I'd like you to go over the open cases. I'll check back with you later." As he left the room, he called over his shoulder, "Let Valerie get to work, Rocky. And if you don't call her 'Valerie' and she quits, I'm going to fire you."

"Sure you are," Rocky called back, laughing as she went to her desk.

Alone at last, Valerie closed the door to her office, hung her suit jacket on the back of her chair, and sat down. She slipped off her heels and rubbed her feet. *Maybe a driver isn't a bad idea,* she thought.

The office was not much bigger than the cubicles at TransReliable, with about as much personality. No pictures on the walls, thin carpet over the concrete floor, two small windows behind her chair with slatted shades to pull down if the light interfered with her laptop screen.

*Serviceable.*

Valerie reached for the paper cup of coffee and took a sip. She exhaled deeply, relaxed her shoulders, and took inventory of her desk.

File folders were stacked neatly in her inbox. She slid them out and saw they were cases Harry had worked over the past six months. *You've been pretty busy. No wonder you called me,* she thought. The files contained typical cases like car accidents and theft. One was a workers' compensation case. One was a dognapping, of all things. Any claim an insurance company thought was questionable and worth looking into, it was Harry Zimmer's job to find ways to prove—or disprove—the claim.

As Valerie read through the cases, she remembered Harry's preferred method of investigating: careful and thorough. Above all, he documented everything. Harry was a dedicated field investigator and a defense lawyer's dream.

Her job entailed supporting his work: research, phone calls, and later, database searches. She prepared and filed reports based on his investigative work. They were in constant contact by phone. She knew his schedule inside and out, knew what cases he was working, knew where he'd be at almost any given time. He even discussed cases with her and bounced ideas off her, using suggestions she made.

After fifteen years of working together, Valerie thought she knew Harry fairly well. But he never chose to confide in her.

His dismissal at TransReliable last year surprised everyone but her. TransReliable, understandably, thought she was protecting him. Was she? Maybe so. She knew enough to guess what was going on and could have gathered the evidence to prove it, but chose not to. So, although she had her own suspicions about Harry, she didn't know how to alert the managers without incriminating him. And in the way of long-time partners, she loved him too much to do that.

She heaved a huge sigh.

One of the cases in front of her was an elaborate, high-profile theft. Valerie used to enjoy this type of case, at least when she had the time to absorb the details of the paper file in the comfort of her office. This one involved a robbery at the home of Olivia Soutner-Rutherford. Valerie recognized the Soutner-Rutherford name. The family members supported the Philadelphia arts scene in a big way. Their pictures were regularly in the news. *Professional philanthropists.* Some of their exceedingly valuable family jewels had been stolen.

According to the case summary, Harry located the stolen jewelry and the three perpetrators pretty quickly and worked with the police to catch them, cracking a jewelry ring. She studied his notes from each stakeout and interview. It almost read like a novel. His last memo was to wait for payment and then close the file.

Valerie fell under the spell of the case. When she looked at her watch, she was shocked to see most of the morning was gone. She turned her attention to the files that Harry handed her, his current open cases.

The first case involved a man who claimed an on-the-job back injury that disabled him. Harry had pictures of him lifting a beer keg out of a truck while he was supposed to be recovering. The vehicle had been hidden behind some trees, but the photos caught him in action.

*I wonder how long Harry followed the guy around to get these pictures,* Valerie wondered. *The case goes to court next month. I'm sure the judge is going to deny the guy's claim and slap him with a hefty fine after seeing these photos.*

19

The second case, involving a vintage guitar theft, was a little more interesting to her. What caught her eye was the amount of the coverage, $250,000. *Not as much as you'd pay to cover a Strad or a Guarneri violin,* she thought. *Guess guitars don't require the same coverage. Must be a new case. No notes.*

Harry stuck his head in her door. "How's it going? Ready to break for lunch?"

"Yes, I think so," Valerie said. "I've been reading over the pending cases."

"Good. Did you see the claim about the guitar?"

"Yes," she said, holding up one sheet of paper. "Right here.

"It just came in. Some guy named Cafferty from Bryn Mawr filed the claim. The money is big."

"Violins sell for a lot more than that."

"Yeah? I gather that guitars don't, usually." Harry motioned to the folder. "The Lambert brothers asked me to look into it."

"The Lambert brothers?"

"Yes. They are the agents representing the insurance company locally. They liked how I handled the Soutner-Rutherford case—did you see that one?—and thought I could handle this, too. And I'm turning it over to you for your first investigation."

"But I don't know anything about guitars."

"Isn't a guitar a big violin?" Harry asked.

"Well, they both have strings, but...."

"What do you think?" Harry asked. "Can you handle this?"

"I guess so."

Harry's face hardened.

"That's not the answer I'm looking for," Harry said. "You said you needed a job. This is the job." He softened his tone and added, "I know your history and your strengths, Valerie. I have the idea that you are capable of a lot more than what you did for TransReliable. I wouldn't have asked you to join me otherwise."

"I know," Valerie said sheepishly.

"Look, why don't you grab lunch and talk to the Lamberts this afternoon? I took the liberty of setting up an appointment for you at three. Rocky will drive you to their office."

"All right," Valerie said.

# CHAPTER THREE

*Bryn Mawr, PA*
*June 5, 2009*
*11:45 A.M.*

**DR. REUBEN CAFFERTY, DDS,** leaned over the last patient of the day to check the work of one of his hygienists. The patient was the wife of a township commissioner. Chocolate, red wine, coffee, and cigarettes stained her teeth. As her dentist, his job was to keep the damage to a minimum. He bleached her teeth every other year.

Reuben straightened and gave the woman a broad, practiced smile. "Everything looks good. You've been taking good care of your teeth." He was stretching the truth, but they already had the discussion about how to keep her teeth white. She informed him then that her habits were not going to change. To Reuben's surprise, his work was holding up against her best efforts to undo it.

She smiled back and said, "Thank you, doctor. People ask me if I've had something done. They think I've had Botox or surgery." She flushed with what Reuben guessed was pride at the thought that whitening her teeth could be mistaken for plastic surgery.

"I'm glad you're pleased." Reuben stripped off his gloves and moved around the chair. His thick body barely fit in the tight quarters of the tiny room. He glanced at his hygienist, a lovely young blonde with full lips and fuller breasts named Tammy, who coincidentally was his current girlfriend. She stood at the ready behind his patient. "Tammy, set a six-month and we'll do bitewings then."

"Of course, Doctor," Tammy replied. She handed the patient a small mirror and, out of the woman's sightline, Tammy straightened her spine and pressed back her shoulders, displaying her breasts for Reuben. Reuben rewarded Tammy with a big grin. The woman, caught up with her own reflection, noticed nothing.

Reuben stepped out of the little examination room and headed for his office, waving a hand at the receptionist as he passed by. "Is that everyone, Gloria?"

"Yes, sir," she responded. "Are you headed out?"

"Yes, I'd better get going. I'll see you on Monday."

"Have fun at the wedding, Doctor."

Reuben stepped into his office. He stripped off his scrubs and t-shirt and dropped them into the basket he kept there for laundry. He opened his closet and checked his reflection in the mirror mounted on the inside of the door. His khaki pants still looked newly pressed, a miracle of modern fabric, so he picked a fresh white t-shirt off a shelf inside the closet.

He tucked in the shirt and glanced back at the mirror. *My pants look better than I do,* he thought. *I look tired. I need a nap, but there's no time.*

He rubbed his hands over his round face, feeling the inevitable scratch of his one o'clock shadow, then ran his fingers through his short brown hair. He slipped a dark green cashmere sweater over his tee shirt and grabbed a buttery leather jacket from the closet. *Shore nights in early June. Might be chilly.*

Closing the closet door, he glanced at the collection of eight-by-tens of rock stars decorating the wall behind his desk. A fair amount of those stars came from Great Britain. Reuben admired the dentists that transformed the notoriously bad teeth of those British stars into the smiles that graced his wall. He believed that it was good dentistry that gave them their career longevity. Absolutely. People don't want to look at stars with bad teeth or an overbite. Dentists could make someone's career. Reuben was entirely sure of that.

Reuben didn't have any famous musicians as clients. Family dentistry was his specialty, with a side involvement in sports dentistry. Philadelphia was a sports town, and it was sports dentistry that kept his practice afloat. But he knew that all of his work was important, whether it was for a woman who overate candy, drank too much coffee and red wine, and smoked, or if it was for a hockey player who needed a removable bridge or dentures. He improved the health of teeth, the position of teeth, the look of teeth. That's what being a dentist was all about.

Reuben let a lot of the basics fall to his hygienists, Jen and Tammy. They did preliminary work, updating the client's file, cleaning teeth, and bitewings. His assistants, Dawn and Bonnie, helped with the cavity fills and crowns. Reuben checked whatever needed checking, and decided whatever needed deciding. He kept up with the business, studying, networking, and maintaining a presence in the local community. Gloria oversaw the office, made the appointments, and called patients and insurance companies when necessary. Eileen helped Gloria with the paperwork and handled the filing. Most days it ran pretty smoothly and gave him time for his hobbies, his collecting. But he was the man in charge, and he liked it that way

Reuben enjoyed doing the cosmetic work the most, where a fistful of veneers or an hour with the bleaching light and carbamide peroxide paste could make a person look ten to fifteen years younger. Cosmetic work took knowledge, patience, and talent. He was good at it. It made his patients feel great. It made him feel like he was Michelangelo.

Zap! You're beautiful!

Reuben turned to look at the opposite wall, the one in front of his desk. There was a photo of him with his favorite guitar, a 1958 Gibson Les Paul Standard, sunburst finish with tiger striping. In the photo he struck a rock star pose, pointing upward at the fans in the second deck of the imaginary arena where he was performing. A photo of his band, The Rays, blown up to poster size, hung in a black frame on the same wall. A silver frame held a sprayed-silver record with their song "Elevator to the Moon" and a small plaque that labeled it "Record of the Year, 1986." Of course, that was a sort-of joke that their manager, Frank DelVecchio, played on them. Their song, "Elevator to the Moon," received some airplay on local radio stations, but never earned them much money. They did, however, develop a following around Philly. Next to the record was a framed photo of the band with Frank, along with a couple of articles about them from local newspapers.

One of their Rays t-shirts in a shadow box completed the collection. The Rays all signed and dated the t-shirt when they released their record. Reuben couldn't remember exactly how he came into possession of that t-shirt, but it probably had something to do with him being the unofficial archivist of The Rays' memorabilia. He knew that none of the other guys cared enough to keep stuff like that—critical historical markers—from their career. And Reuben certainly knew that they would never take care of things the way he did. Everything on these walls was saved in preservation-quality materials behind the innocuous-looking glass.

The t-shirt was only available at their record release party, with the last of the batch sold at subsequent gigs. *That release party was the high point of The Rays' musical career,* Reuben thought. He remembered the looks on women's faces when the band played and the way they fawned over the members during breaks. It was a favorite memory of his, one he revisited often.

Reuben was excited about seeing the guys from the band at Frank's wedding in Atlantic City. He'd gotten Frank's call three months ago, asking him to play at the wedding, and telling Reuben that he was calling all the guys in the band. Reuben had been practicing ever since. Yeah, actually practicing! Like he'd ever forgotten those songs—but he thought it might be good to refresh his memory. The band hadn't played together in a while, a long while now, not since that benefit they played in 2004. The guys had all gone their separate ways after that gig, and as usual, Reuben didn't bother to stay in touch, so there were no gigs and no rehearsals since. Reuben needed to practice, even if the other guys didn't.

Reuben had always had mixed feelings about the rest of The Rays. They knew each other well enough to have a bond, but also to generate some animosity. Reuben refused to give the guys an opportunity to mock him, although they tried with some regularity when they were all in the same room.

They loved, for example, to tease him about being a dentist. He quit the band for a while to go to dental school. Every time they got together after he graduated, the guys teased him about it. They didn't perceive the artistry involved. They didn't understand he could be a dentist and a musician, too. Plus, they had no idea how lucrative dentistry could be. If only they saw his house or his cars. Reuben snorted, thinking that, even if they saw those things, they probably wouldn't understand the value of what they were looking at.

In a way, it was too bad that Tammy wasn't going along. Reuben would have enjoyed showing her off to the guys. They would have been so jealous. *But when the guys see how young Tammy is,* Reuben thought, *well, I don't want to hear that shit.*

Of course, he knew all along that Tammy couldn't come with him. She had a family reunion to attend in Ohio, and her parents were adamant about her being there. Reuben's obligation to perform at Frank's wedding meant she would attend the reunion without him, luckily. It was a win-win. He didn't have to meet her family, and the wedding he had to participate in would be a bachelor weekend, no needy girlfriends allowed.

Tammy, of course, was not happy. She wanted him to come to the reunion, or she wanted to come to the wedding with him.

"It's a wedding gig," he told her weeks before. "It's not like a big rock show or anything. Besides, I have to do band stuff, you know, set up, rehearse with the guys. I won't have time to pay attention to you. You'll be neglected." He was so good at saying it, he almost believed it himself.

The office door clicked behind him, and he turned in time to see Tammy letting herself in as quietly as she could. He gazed at the snug t-shirt under her uniform jacket, one of the many snug t-shirts that she wore to torture him all day. Her breasts beckoned to him even now, when he knew he should be thinking about heading for Atlantic City.

Tammy paused to look at the poster of Reuben on the wall, all sunglasses, skinny polyester pants, and shiny white teeth. She heaved a long, audible sigh. "So you're leaving?"

"Yeah." He gazed at her breasts for a long moment, not sure what to say to her. She was so beautiful but so young. She had that dewy look she got before she cried. Like last night, when she repeated that she wanted to come along with him.

Tammy slipped off her uniform jacket and wiggled her way into his arms. He felt the heat of her body against his. He pulled her close and said, "I'll miss you."

He would miss her, all right, but not as much as she might wish.

"Are you sure that Alice won't be there?"

Reuben stiffened at the mention of his estranged wife's name.

"No, I told you before, she won't be there."

Tammy leaned back to look at him. She was definitely not happy, even with this verification. "Okay. I wanted to make sure."

"You don't need to make sure. Alice will not be at this wedding. Wild horses couldn't drag her to this wedding. For any reason," he told her.

"Okay. Then don't forget what we talked about. I think it's time."

"I'm still thinking it over."

"Will you give me an answer when you get back?" she asked, her voice a breathy tear-laden whisper, yet barely hiding her impatience. "It's important to me. Besides," she said, her voice softening even more, "I love your house. It's beautiful. I can't think of a better place to live." Her voice shifted subtly. "Plus, I have to let the landlady know by the end of the month if I'm renewing my lease for another year. This would be great timing."

# CHAPTER FOUR

*Overbrook Farms*
*Philadelphia, PA*
*June 15, 2009*
*2:00 P.M.*

**"ROCKY!"**

Rocky's little Ford barreled through the yellow light as Rocky threw back her head for the final note of the song, letting the full force of her enthusiasm power her voice. The tires protested as she spun the car onto Township Line Road.

She grinned at Valerie. "I love this song!"

"What was that?" asked Valerie, righting herself in the passenger's seat.

"The song or the band?"

"The light. Wasn't it red?"

"The song is 'Every Rose Has Its Thorn.' The band is Poison. I've seen these guys in concert eighteen times. I know all their songs. They are so great. I can't believe you don't know who they are." Rocky lifted her thick hair with one hand and let the layers flutter down, the strawberry streak making it look like cotton candy. "Do you like sports, Val? I do. Well, I like the guys who play sports. They are so hunky. You should hook up with a sports guy sometime. You should come with me the next time I go to Chickie's and Pete's."

"Chickie's and Pete's?"

Rocky hit the horn and swerved to avoid hitting the car in front of her that stopped suddenly for a pedestrian.

"Hey, jerk! Watch what you're doing! Asshole!" she yelled at the driver.

Valerie reached out her hand to change the station on the radio. Rocky slapped it away.

"Don't do that! That's my favorite station!" Rocky's voice took on the DJ's drone. "That's 'WTTM ninety-eight point two, To The Max. The 1980s, twenty-four-seven.'"

"But you're distracted!"

"Ooh, listen to this! I haven't heard this song in years!" Rocky turned the volume up. Her head bounced along to the beat of the song.

Valerie realized that her right hand gripped the door handle so tightly that her fingers were locked. She consciously released them and forced herself to breathe more deeply. She tried to listen to the song on the radio. "Who is this?" she asked.

"Warrant. I saw them a few times."

"Rocky? Please be more careful. Slow down. Quit tailgating. I'd like to get places in one piece."

Rocky snapped off the radio, annoyed.

"What's the big deal? This is how I always drive. I've never had an accident or even a ticket. Well, not one that I ever paid. Trust me, I'll get you where you need to go, and I'll get you there on time," Rocky said. "How come you never learned to drive?"

The question caught Valerie off-guard and she blurted out, "I don't think that's any of your business."

The silence in the car pressed down on them more than the thump of the music had. Valerie leaned over and snapped the radio back on. Rocky took that as a signal to speed up.

Rocky was so close to the car in front of them Valerie could almost smell the driver's aftershave. "If you don't slow down, I swear I'll take the bus," Valerie said.

"All right," Rocky growled.

By the time they got to the Overbrook Farms area, Rocky slowed down, unsure of where they were going. Tucked in amongst the old Georgian and Tudor homes and the more modern architecture of medium-rise apartment buildings nearby, Valerie recognized the turrets of the Lamberts' aging mansion. She pointed it out as Rocky turned onto Overbrook Avenue.

The Lamberts' home was very different from the rest of the homes in the Overbrook Farms area. It was the only one in the neighborhood built in the Victorian Gothic tradition, with three stories of green clapboard trimmed with intricate gingerbread detail, heavy wooden doors polished to a high sheen, and windows trimmed with heavy shutters.

*It's the kind of place you might avoid on a dark and stormy night in case the vampires came after you,* Valerie thought. *Or the Lambert twins.*

The driveway was u-shaped, with two entrances from the street. The u was filled with dense pink spirea bushes that offered privacy. The driveway curved in front of the house and was wide enough for two cars to pass. No sign indicated the presence of a business, but Valerie told Rocky to stop the car at the short sidewalk leading to the front door.

"Wow," Rocky said, turning off the engine. She eyed the exterior of the house. "Creepy."

Valerie shrugged. "It's not that bad. Come on."

"I'm coming with?"

"Yes."

Rocky followed her to the front porch. "What do you think, Val? Should I ring the bell?"

"Yes. And please don't call me Val. I'm Valerie."

"You got it, Boss."

"I'm not your Boss."

"Yes, you are."

Valerie was about to argue, when Rocky rang the bell. A young man, probably in his twenties, immediately opened the door. He was impeccably dressed in sharply creased black trousers and a white shirt buttoned to the neck. All that was missing was a cummerbund and cutaway jacket.

Valerie was glad she was wearing one of her suits from her days at TransReliable, the navy blue all-season wool with a white blouse tied at the neck with a loose bow. Her saddle-tan briefcase matched her heels perfectly. Rocky, on the other hand, was wearing that god-awful turquoise suit with a way-too-snug knit top under the jacket. And she had that hair and that bag. Maybe the heels were acceptable, but they looked so cheap.

The doorman's eyes darted from Valerie to Rocky and back to Valerie. "Welcome, Miss Sloan. Please watch your step." He pointed to the step up into the house. "You are expected. Right this way."

Valerie and Rocky followed him through the foyer and under the large curving staircase that led to the second floor. He opened a door at the back of the grand entrrance and the women stepped into the Lambert brothers' office.

The oblong room reminded Valerie more of a library than an office. Bookshelves filled with books lined three of the four walls. Two large windows at the far end of the room offered a bright and panoramic view of a formal garden. A pair of leather club chairs and a small coordinating sofa faced the windows. A fireplace graced the middle of the long wall to Valerie's right.

Across the room from the fireplace, an oak table with three straight-backed chairs, two on one side, one on the other, echoed the shape of the room. A delicate china tea service waited on the table, two of the three matching cups already filled.

The Lambert brothers, seated in the two chairs facing the fireplace, rose as one to motion the women into the two chairs opposite them. When they saw Rocky, their eyes widened.

The brothers were identical twins. After all these years -- at least twenty, by Valerie's reckoning -- the brothers still looked amazingly alike. She felt like she was looking at a mirror image.

The brothers were shorter and bonier than she remembered. They dressed in identical gray suits, white shirts, and black ties. Their suits looked too large, gaping at their necks and wrists and sagging over their shoulders. That was a bit of a surprise to Valerie, since she thought of them as rather dapper in their younger years.

Now their wrinkled faces had become even more wrinkled. Their white hair -- which she remembered as dirty brown, so that also had changed -- receded in the same places, like they each wore a wig sliding back from the front of their skulls, their high foreheads making them look constantly surprised. Even their hand movements and facial expressions echoed one another.

The doorman lifted a chair from the side of the room and brought it next to Valerie so that Rocky would have a place to sit. He pulled another matching cup and saucer from a cabinet and put it on the table in front of the chair.

The brothers peered at Rocky through identical thick glasses with square, dark brown frames.

"Thank you, Hanson," one of them said.

"That will be all for now," said the other.

Hanson backed out of the door, closing it quietly. The brothers turned to Valerie.

"It's so very good..." started one.

"...to see you," finished the other.

"Do you remember us, Miss Sloan? I am Darryl, and this is my brother..."

"Del. Delmar, but I've always gone by Del."

"Of course I remember you," she said, shaking hands with each of them. She regretted it immediately. Their moist, dead fingers lay in hers like damp washcloths. Valerie's stomach rolled and she attempted to dry her hands by laying them flat on her trousers as she sat down. "I believe the last time I saw you was the night my dad played the Tchaikovsky concerto."

"Yes. He played..."

"...brilliantly that night."

"This is my associate, Raquel Russo," Valerie said, waving her hand in Rocky's direction.

The brothers focused on Rocky again, and Valerie could distinctly hear at least one of the brothers adding "hmm," like an extra beat under his breath.

Rocky politely shook their hands, but Valerie could see discomfort flit across Rocky's face when she sat down.

"Would you care for tea?" Darryl asked.

"And perhaps your associate?" Del added, but he looked at Valerie rather than Rocky.

"Yes, thank you. That's very kind. We don't want to take much of your time, though." Valerie took the cup one of the brothers offered her and sipped. Earl Gray. Nice. "Harry said that you asked us to work on a case for you."

"Ah, yes. Mr. Zimmer has spoken..."

"...highly of you. We're so glad..."

"...you chose to work for him."

"I worked with him before, while I was at TransReliable Insurance in King of Prussia."

"Yes, we know," Darryl said.

Del said. "We are familiar with..."

"...your time there." Darryl finished.

Valerie was about to ask how they were familiar with her time there, but Del plowed ahead.

"Did you have a chance to look..."

"...into the case at all?" Del asked.

"I read over the case file. There's not a lot of information so far. I looked for some background on the guitar on the Internet," Valerie said.

"The policyholder says it was stolen from him..."

"...shortly after he attended a guitar show."

The brothers shuffled around the room, one pouring more tea while the other pulled a manila folder out of a drawer from a bank of matching oak cabinets on the wall opposite the windows.

When they returned to their chairs, Valerie wasn't sure if they were sitting in the same chairs they inhabited earlier, or the opposite ones. Del – or was it Darryl? – opened the folder and pushed two photos across the table to her. They were of the front and back of an electric guitar in a brown leather case with a faux fur interior a color of neon fuchsia not found in nature. *Much like the color in Rocky's hair,* Valerie thought.

Valerie didn't see anything about this particular guitar that would be valuable, except, perhaps, its age. It appeared to be in acceptable condition, but she could see it had been well used. The photo of the front showed two marks, one on the face of the guitar and one on the bottom edge, an indication it had been bumped around. The second photo, the back, showed an area of scuffing in the midsection that marred the surface.

"It was insured for a quarter of a million dollars," one of the brothers said.

Valerie nodded, but her pulse quickened slightly. Hearing the figure from Harry – even seeing it in print on the case file – hadn't seemed as impressive as it did coming from the reedy voice of one of the Lamberts. She stared at the photo, willing it to show her something she didn't already know.

"Why would this be so valuable?" she asked. "I've done research on new models and they only run about two to three thousand dollars."

"Perhaps its provenance?" Darryl suggested. "We were hoping..."

"...that you were familiar with this and could tell us."

Valerie shook her head. "My specialty is violins."

The Lamberts appeared distressed.

"We were certain..."

"...that you could help us."

Valerie scratched her head. If it was a violin, part of the value was in the construction, the glue, the wood, the finish, as well as its history. She didn't know for certain that any of those things applied to guitars. Even if they did, this guitar had nothing about it to show handmade quality or unusual beauty. The top was constructed of some pretty wood, and the striping of the back, the part that didn't show any damage, was nice, but it looked average. And possibly mishandled.

*But maybe the brothers are right. Maybe there is something in its provenance. Maybe someone famous owned or played it.*

"What kind of policy did you write for the guitar?" Valerie asked.

""We wrote a Commercial Inland Marine policy..." explained Darryl.

"...with the special risk inclusion for musical instruments, of course..." added Del.

"...providing for an instrument to be used in a location other than the owner's home," Darryl said. "It's no different than any other policy that we would write for a musician with a valuable instrument.

"In fact, we used the same policy..."

"...that we use for members of the Philadelphia Orchestra..."

"...which I'm sure you're familiar with..."

"...and Dr. Cafferty always paid the premiums on time..."

"...so there was no question that the policy was valid."

"The problem is that the policyholder, Dr. Cafferty, has been pressing for settlement," Del said.

"That's not unusual, is it?" Valerie asked. "When Stanley Orbach's Strad was stolen, the claim was settled quite quickly, wasn't it?"

"That's true. But Mr. Orbach insured his entire collection with us..." Darryl said.

"...and the police verified the theft immediately." Del said. "Dr. Cafferty's situation is more difficult."

"Difficult?"

"This is the only piece Dr. Cafferty insured with us. Or anyone. And the policy is only a few years old." Darryl added.

"But you agreed to insure it, right?" Valerie asked.

"Oh, yes. The value of the guitar was verified by a reliable appraiser..."

"...Mr. Mark Patton from Phoenixville."

"So if the appraiser certified the value and the policy was paid, why is the company questioning the claim?" Valerie tried to keep the sharpness out of her voice, but her impatience leaked through. Is this one of those times when the company makes a business of refuting the claim in order to avoid paying out the funds? *I always thought the Lamberts were better than that,* Valerie thought.

The Lamberts looked stricken. They seemed to hold their breaths, as if not wanting to divulge the reason. Del finally relented.

"They think Dr. Cafferty is not telling the truth..." Del said.

"...because of the circumstances surrounding the loss," Darryl said.

"What circumstances?" Valerie asked.

"The night of the loss, no one saw him with the instrument. And even though he was injured during the theft..."

"... Dr. Cafferty called the insurance company..."

"... before he called for an ambulance."

"The company questioned the claim..."

"...because they were suspicious."

"What do the police say?" Valerie asked.

"Other than the fact that Dr. Cafferty was assaulted..."

"...they can find no proof that the guitar was taken from him."

40

"Interesting," Valerie's brain spun into high gear. "How long did it take him to call the insurance company? And how long after that did he call for an ambulance?"

"We don't have the details. We thought that you..."

"...could look into that for us."

"I know violins," Valerie said, "but not guitars. Shouldn't you find someone who works with guitars?"

"We would rather work with an investigator we know," said Darryl.

"We know your father and we knew your mother very well," Del added. "Make them proud."

Del slid the folder to her, the one that originally held the photos.

"This is all the information..."

"...that we have."

Darryl's mouth twisted into a wheedling smile. As did Del's.

Valerie took the folder. *There really isn't a reason to turn them down,* she thought. *The case does have some curious twists.*

"Okay. I'll look into it and let you know what I find," she said, sliding the photos back inside the folder.

"There's one other thing," Del said. "It's important that you find the answers in the next five days."

"Or Dr. Cafferty says that he will sue our company," finished Darryl.

# CHAPTER FIVE

*Upper Darby, PA*
*June 15, 2009*
*4:00 P.M.*

**"HOW ARE THE LAMBERTS DOING?"** Harry asked as Valerie and Rocky came in the door of the office. He held his jacket in one hand as he swept into Valerie's orbit.

"Boy, are those guys creepy!" Rocky dumped her green faux-leather shoulder bag on her desk. She shuddered. "I am so happy to be back. I'm going for coffee. Anyone else?" She pulled an orange wallet out of her bag, spilling receipts and coupons out of the bag and over her desk like confetti. "I'll buy."

"No, thanks, I'm headed out," Harry said.

"None for me, either," Valerie said. "Thanks anyway."

Rocky shrugged. "Can't say I didn't offer," she said, letting the door swing shut behind her, blinds rattling.

"So, what happened?" Harry asked, turning around and following Valerie into her office.

"They gave me some photos. I think this is a fraud case."

"Something you dealt with at TransReliable." Harry shrugged.

"Lots. Any time money is involved, there's an opportunity for fraud." Valerie sat down at her desk and took the Cafferty folder out of her attaché. "They're suspicious of the filing timeline." Valerie slid the Lamberts' report out of the folder and pushed it to Harry. "You already know the basics. The policyholder is Dr. Reuben Cafferty, a dentist from Bryn Mawr. The home address is Brookwood Road."

"Nice area."

"Yes, but not Main Line nice or modern construction nice," Valerie pointed out.

"Yeah, that area was developed in the early nineties. I guess it's considered to be an aging neighborhood now. Go on."

"According to the Lamberts, Cafferty took his guitar, a 1958 Gibson Les Paul, with case, to the Valley Forge Guitar Show on Saturday to try to sell it. When he couldn't find a buyer, he left the guitar show and went to a bar. He was attacked in the parking lot and the guitar was stolen from him. He called the insurance company while he was still in the parking lot. Later the bartender called an ambulance and the cops showed up when the ambulance did. Dispatch sent the cops along with the ambulance."

"Huh. That's odd." Harry took the sheet and straightened up.

"911 dispatching the cops?" Valerie asked.

"No, the whole business about Cafferty at the bar," Harry said.

"Yes, it is odd," Valerie agreed. "I mean, what made him decide to go to a bar after the show? Why did he go to that particular bar? That address isn't exactly on his way home from the hotel hosting the guitar show."

"Right."

"I wonder if he made sure the guitar was in the case before he went into the bar? Maybe it was stolen at the show. When did he last check on it? Was he checking on it the whole time he was at the bar? Did he see anyone? Talk to anyone? Did he mention the guitar to anyone? How did the attacker know the guitar was in the car?"

"You're missing a couple really important questions," Harry said.

"Oh, like why did Cafferty call the insurance company before the bartender called for the ambulance? I suspect that's what the underwriters want to know. And what I'd like to know is, if Cafferty was aware enough to call the insurance company, why did the bartender have to call for the ambulance? Why didn't Cafferty call for it himself?"

"Yeah, those would be the ones." Harry handed the sheet back to her. "So I guess you'll be talking to Cafferty in the near future."

"Yes, I will." She turned to the original policy. "The insurance policy is, according to the Lamberts, standard issue for an instrument. I've seen a few of these, including the policy on my dad's instruments, and they're all written pretty much the same as this one. It protects the guitar from theft, accident, and fire, with a special risk clause covering usage of the instrument outside the home. The guitar was insured for $250,000, as you already know."

"You've got to admit, that's a nice piece of change," Harry said.

Valerie pulled out the appraisal and laid it on top of the other papers. "The appraiser is Mark Patton, working out of an address on Bridge Street in Phoenixville."

She pointed to various spots on the appraisal as she spoke and Harry leaned closer.

"I believe this is the serial number of the guitar and these describe details about it. 'Gibson' is the maker. I recognize that. I'm guessing that 'Les Paul' is the model and 'Sunburst' refers to the finish."

"Sounds right, but I know even less about guitars than you do. I recognize the name 'Les Paul.' He was a guitar player, right?"

"I think so, but I'll make sure," Valerie said. "That's only one of the things I need to verify. 'No Bigsby' must be a guitar term. Same thing with 'Not Grovered'."

Harry tapped his index finger on the appraisal. "You should call this guy," he said, pointing to Patton's name, scrawled at the bottom of the sheet. "Maybe he can give you more details."

"I can check online for most of this, but I should probably talk to Patton anyway to verify the appraisal. Assuming he's still in business. How far away is Phoenixville?"

"Not far." Harry straightened up. "Maybe 20, 30 miles."

Valerie had never been to Phoenixville and wondered if they had bus service there. It sounded like a world away. It must have shown on her face.

"Get Rocky to make an appointment and take you there," Harry said, putting on his jacket. "I have a stakeout over in Fishtown. I don't expect to be back in the office today."

"Should I close up?" Valerie asked, stuffing her disappointment down deep. The last few minutes were like old times. She would have liked to talk more with Harry.

"Rocky has a key. She'll lock up and give you a ride home. I'll make sure she gets a copy of the key made for you, too."

"Okay."

"See you tomorrow?"

Valerie nodded. "Of course."

"Good." Harry nodded as he headed for the door.

Valerie watched him go, then straightened the papers and pulled out her laptop. She stared at the photos of the guitar and then started tapping on the keyboard.

The first thing she looked for was information on the guitar itself. A simple search for "1958 Gibson guitar" gave her enough hits to be daunting. Scanning over the results, she noted several articles by collectors and dealers. Eventually she settled on one article by a dealer that not only described in detail the type of guitar she was looking for, it also delved into some Gibson history and defined the terms that she didn't understand. 'Not Grovered' meant that the tuners had not been replaced by a more modern tuning peg; 'No Bigsby' indicated that there was no additional vibrato added. The guitar she was looking for was the original piece, unaltered from when it was produced.

Valerie made some notes in a small notebook that she carried with her, deciding that she could refer to the information when she talked to Mark Patton.

Valerie flipped though the sheets on her desk again. This time she chose the copy of Cafferty's statement.

*What really happened that night?* she wondered. *And where is the guitar now? Who has it? Another musician? A collector? So often in cases at TransReliable, motive was everything. What is the motive here?*

Valerie's cell phone buzzed and she accepted the call when she saw her dad's picture on the screen. "Hi, Dad, what's for dinner?" she asked.

"A surprise," he said, "but I'm sure you'll like it."

Her heart sank a little. She wasn't as sure as he was.

"I wanted to check what time you'll be home."

"I'll try to leave here in an hour or so."

"Okay," her dad said. "That'll work. By the way, Walter Nakamura called. I wasn't here at the time, so he left a message on the machine for you to call him."

"He has my cell phone number, Dad. Why doesn't he call that?" Valerie could hear how peevish she sounded.

"I don't know. You'll have to ask him."

"Okay." She sighed deeply. "It probably isn't critical, so I'll call him when I get home. Thanks, Dad."

"Sure. See you soon, honey."

They said their goodbyes. Valerie heard the rustle of the front door blinds and then Rocky stuck her head in Valerie's office, coffee cup in hand. "How's it going?" she said, taking a sip.

"I've been going over paperwork. There are a few things to check on. Do you know much about guitars?"

"I like to listen to bands that use them," she grinned.

"Have you ever seen any like this one?"

Rocky shrugged. "Sure. It looks like a guitar lots of guys in bands would play."

"Why do you think this one is worth so much?"

"Maybe it belonged to Slash."

"Who's Slash?" asked Valerie.

"You don't know who Slash is? Everyone knows who Slash is." Rocky squinted at her. "How can you not know who Slash is? Wait, I can play you some of his stuff. I'm sure I have some Guns N' Roses here." Rocky turned to go to her desk to find her iPod.

"No, Rocky, wait. Don't do that," Valerie called after her. "I don't want to hear any music right now. I want you to track down this guitar expert. Mark Patton, in Phoenixville. His phone number is on the report." Valerie handed the sheet to Rocky. "See if you can get us an appointment with him, okay?"

"Sure. But I bet this guitar belonged to someone famous, that's why it's worth so much. Maybe the guitar player from Cinderella, Tom Keifer." Rocky's eyes glazed. "Yeah, I'll bet that's who used to own it. Tom Keifer."

"Please, Rocky, will you call Patton and set up an appointment for me?" Valerie repeated. "I need to do some research. Then we ought to wrap this up. I want to get home."

While Rocky called the appraiser, Valerie did a quick Internet search for information on Reuben Cafferty. His dental practice website came up, with Cafferty's smiling round face and shiny, white teeth prominent on the front page. There were some other, smaller photos of satisfied customers and some quotes from them. A few, she gathered, were local sports stars.

The next few articles dealt with some of Cafferty's community work. Participation in the local dental association, including a year as president. Charity work for a local shelter was mentioned in one article, but that was from eight years ago. The newer articles referenced his work with players from the National Football League and the National Hockey League.

Further down the list were older entries with his name attached. She almost passed them by because they didn't seem related, almost like they were about some other person, but then she saw they were about a rock band called The Rays. A local favorite in the eighties, the band was referred to as a 'one hit wonder' due to the popularity of their song "Elevator to the Moon." She looked at the grainy photos that went with the articles, the fuzzy group pictures and the stage shots. Zooming in on them made them fuzzier, but she could see the round outline of Cafferty's jaw above the skinny tie and jacket.

One of the items in the list of links was for a fan site for The Rays that compiled information on the band and linked to articles about them. The fan banter in the comments section hooked Valerie. The dates of the entries were current, so she read quickly through comments about how much people missed seeing the band.

A few fans talked about what the band members were doing now. Reuben Cafferty, the keyboard player, was a dentist. The front man was a real estate agent with his own business, Pat McMullen. The bass player, Dennis Hammond, sold kitchen appliances. The drummer, Larry Flinchbaugh, worked for a construction company. Austin Barclay, the guitarist, was the only full-time professional musician. Some entries mentioned their agent, Frank DelVecchio. The chatter included the band members' families, names of wives, which of them had kids, which never married (the musician, Valerie noted) and a mention of a pending divorce. For Cafferty.

*Divorce. Now, there's a possible motive for needing money.*

Valerie sat back and propped her chin in the palm of her hand. *I wonder if the ex-wife knew how much that guitar was worth,* she thought, and started typing.

Alice Owens-Cafferty. Articles about the hospital where she was a pediatric surgeon. A couple awards, mentions of local charity work, including several articles on her work in Haiti. Earlier articles mentioned her marriage, and some of the really early articles mentioned her engagement and, even earlier, her coming out party when she was eighteen.

*Her coming out party?* thought Valerie. *Not unusual in this area, but that means she comes from money. And as a surgeon, she makes money. So where's the motive?*

Valerie stared at the picture of Alice in her wedding gown. She was a beautiful bride, with dark serious eyes and a tentative smile. *She looks unsure, as almost all brides must be,* thought Valerie. *But it's almost fifteen years later and there is no official mention of a divorce showing up in my search. If they are still married, why does he need money? Why would she need money? I don't see a clear motive.*

Valerie heard Rocky finish setting up their appointment. She shut down her laptop and packed it into her attaché with the case file. *I'm missing something,* she thought, *but I'll look at this later. If I give it a break, maybe something will jump out at me next time.*

# CHAPTER SIX

*Bryn Mawr, PA*
*June 5, 2009*
*1:05 P.M.*

**REUBEN HEADED OUT THE BACK DOOR** of his dental office where his gray Lincoln MKX waited in its parking space, already packed with his keyboard, guitar and amp, his duffel, and his suit for the gig. It was after one o'clock, the time he usually closed the office on Fridays. Barring emergencies, Fridays were never the office's busiest day. He knew that the girls in the office loved the schedule, even if they had to work a couple evenings to make up for it.

Reuben slid onto the leather seat, turned the ignition, and tuned in the eighties satellite radio station. The first chords of "In the Air Tonight" by Phil Collins poured out of the sound system. Reuben touched the button that slid back the cover of the sunroof and began the drive to the Seaside Hotel in Atlantic City.

The sun was warm on his head and he liked the slight brush of the air against his face from the air conditioning. He felt good. He was getting away for a couple days, for some R&R with the guys. *Now, is that rock 'n' roll or rest 'n' recreation?* he thought. *Take your pick.* He liked being a dentist, but he liked to get away, too. Even if it was to play a gig with a bunch of guys that didn't want to play together much anymore.

Reuben would have preferred to drive his red BMW Z4, the low-slung convertible, but he had too much equipment to take for the gig. *Almost like back in the eighties, when I had to pack up the PA system and lights,* he thought. *Good thing I had that van back then. I was the only one who could handle all that equipment, not that the rest of the band ever thanked me for it. They acted like that was the only reason they let me in the band.*

He thought about taking the 1958 Gibson Les Paul for this gig but packed the 2003 Epiphone instead. Even though the Gibson was insured, it still worried him to take it out to gigs.

The guys would have gone crazy over the Les Paul because it was so valuable. Austin Barclay, The Rays' guitarist, would have been especially jealous. *Even now, he'd be jealous,* Reuben thought with a satisfied smile. *He'll never get over it, not really.*

Reuben's thoughts drifted back to 1986 when The Rays played steadily and packed clubs with their fans. At one club on South Street, they opened for a band whose guitarist brought several guitars for the gig, including the 1958 Gibson Les Paul.

Austin obsessed about guitars. He studied whatever guitars his favorite players were using and talked about them incessantly. He knew that the Gibson Les Paul models from the fifties were sought out for their tone and beauty.

And here was a vintage 1958 Gibson Les Paul in near mint condition, right in front of Austin.

Of course, Austin noticed the guitar right away. When the band took a break, Reuben tagged along while Austin talked to the guitar's owner. The guy was looking to sell it. He needed some money and was willing to let it go very reasonably.

Austin went a little crazy, he wanted that guitar so badly. But Austin didn't have a day job like the rest of the guys in the band. He was living from gig to gig, sleeping on friends' couches and scrounging food off whoever would buy him a meal or give him change for fast food. No matter how reasonable the price of the guitar might have been, Austin simply didn't have the money.

Reuben did. But initially he wasn't interested. He was a keyboard player, after all, not a guitarist, at least that's what the rest of the band told him. He knew how to play guitar, but they kept telling him he wasn't very good.

Austin brought up the guitar all week, every time The Rays rehearsed. Reuben listened to Austin say things like, "No one else has one," and "They're really hard to find." He actually heard Austin use the phrase, "special appeal." The guitar was all Austin talked about. It was almost like he thought one of The Rays was going to buy it for him.

The collector in Reuben listened carefully to everything Austin said, and after a few days the idea of buying the guitar seemed natural and right. Like the guitar was something Reuben should have, especially because Austin couldn't.

Reuben sought out the guitar's owner the following weekend. He hung around after his band's last set to talk to him about the Les Paul. "If you have cash," the guy said, "I'll sell it to you right now." He took a long look at Reuben, then added, "I'm asking a thousand."

Reuben didn't flinch. "Let me take a look at it," he said.

The guy handed him the guitar and Reuben played a few riffs. The guitar was sweet, all right. It fit Reuben's hands just so. He strummed a chord, then noodled a bit. *That sound!* Even unamplified, it rang loud and clear. The waitress clearing tables turned to look his way and smiled. Reuben puffed out his chest above the guitar he was holding and nodded in her direction. *Yeah,* Reuben thought, *I have to have this.*

Reuben rummaged in his hip pocket and found his silver money clip. He carefully unfolded ten crisp hundreds and bought the guitar. He remembered the pleasure, the sheer joy, of counting off the bills, first for himself, and then for the surprised guitarist.

He felt a sudden warmth in buying the guitar, of paying the money, of owning it. The soothing cloak of collection settled over him. *Mine,* he thought as he took the guitar to his car that night. *Mine, and no one else's.* He didn't think about Austin then. He only thought about owning, possessing another special thing, something unlike what anyone else had.

The pleasure of crushing Austin came later.

Reuben took the guitar to the next Rays practice. *The look on Austin's face was worth every cent I paid,* Reuben thought.

Over the years, Reuben never stopped reminding Austin that he bought the guitar when Austin couldn't afford to. Reminding him always felt great, always brought back the rush of the buy.

Eventually, Austin's anguish over the guitar faded into silent bitterness and he stopped responding to Reuben's taunts. Without a flammable target, Reuben lost interest in the nasty game between them, although he never lost pleasure in remembering.

But Reuben's place in the band was to play keyboards, not guitar. Reuben was a reasonably good keyboard player, but he always wanted to be a guitar player. No, he wanted to be *the* guitar player. To Reuben's way of thinking, guitar players got all the attention. That's what he wanted.

*Jimi Hendrix. Eric Clapton. Carlos Santana. Eddie Van Halen. Jimmy Page. Those guys are household names, Reuben thought. Keith Emerson, Rick Wakeman, Ray Manzarek, Billy Preston, Nicky Hopkins? Nobody talks about them except other keyboard players.*

Reuben fumed silently during every Rays gig as he listened to Austin play his old Teisco, a junky guitar, but about the only thing Austin could afford. Austin was a good guitarist, maybe even great. He had natural talent that he honed over the years with incessant practice and constant gigging. But his equipment was always crap. And Reuben, on the other hand, had to fight the rest of The Rays to let him play guitar on one or two songs with his much better guitar. The guys told Reuben he should loan it to Austin to play.

*No way that was gonna happen. Not after I spent a thousand bucks on it,* Reuben thought.

The guys said they needed Reuben to play keyboards. That's why he was in the band. The keyboard was part of their sound. Deep down Reuben knew they didn't want him to play guitar because they thought he wasn't a very good guitarist. So Reuben played his keyboard. Over time, he argued to play guitar less and less. The beautiful 1958 Gibson Les Paul Standard guitar sat in its case in a closet, unused.

As the nineties rolled on, The Rays' manager, Frank DelVecchio, started to have trouble booking the band. "Elevator to the Moon" faded into history. The Rays weren't able to come up with another hit and other local bands stole their followers. Times changed, music changed, but The Rays stayed in their niche until the niche closed.

In 2006, The Rays got together to play their class reunion. At their first rehearsal, Austin mentioned the Les Paul, prodding Reuben to see if he still had it.

"You play it every day, I'll bet," Austin sneered, his long yellow canines visible. "It's your whole life."

"No, I... I hardly even think about it. I should get it out and play it."

"You're an idiot," Austin said. "You've got pure gold there, and you let it rot.

"It's not rotting," Reuben said. "It's stored away, in the case. I'm taking care of it."

"Well, don't let it get around that you still have that thing. Every thief in your neighborhood will be looking for it. Hope your insurance is paid up."

That night Reuben dug the Les Paul out of the closet and hung it on the wall of his studio. After a few days, the seed Austin planted about thieves took hold and Reuben took the guitar to Mark Patton in Phoenixville to have it evaluated. When Mark told him how much the guitar was worth, Reuben tried to look casual. He had no idea how much this particular model had skyrocketed in value.

Reuben called the Lambert Brothers the next day. They were happy to help him insure the instrument. With Mark's evaluation in hand, they didn't question the value placed on it. The deal was done.

The Les Paul went up on the wall of Reuben's home studio. Reuben took it down and played it occasionally, but it was mostly decoration. Even though it was insured, Reuben still didn't trust taking it to a gig. *Too chancy*, he thought. *Last thing I need is for something to happen to my Les Paul. If anything happens to my Epiphone, it's no big loss.* So the Epiphone was in the trunk for the wedding gig.

"Dancing With Myself" came on the radio and reminded Reuben of Tammy. She had been crazy about the song ever since she heard Green Day sing it, and Reuben didn't have the heart to tell her it was a remake of this song from the eighties by Billy Idol. He wished these little things didn't remind him of their age difference. He thought how great it was to drive to Atlantic City by himself instead of to Tammy's family reunion in Ohio. It was so much better than their stares and whispers, or their snickers, or worse yet, hearing them tell her straight out that he was too old for her.

It was definitely better than listening to her yammering about living together.

Traffic thickened as Reuben got closer to Atlantic City. He focused on his driving, struggling through traffic as quickly as he could. His cell phone woke up and played the "You Give Love a Bad Name" ringtone. Against his better judgement, he picked it up.

"Alice, what do you want?" He couldn't seem to keep the edge out of his voice when he talked to his estranged wife.

"Well, happy to talk to you, too, Reuben. I guess I'm bothering you, aren't I?"

"I'm in Atlantic City and I'm driving, so make it quick."

"Ah, the wedding. I forgot. Sorry, I've been a little preoccupied."

"That's been the story of your life, Alice. You were preoccupied and forgot we were married."

*Doctors make lousy spouses,* Reuben thought. Several people had pointed that out to him before they married, but he didn't listen. Sadly, they were right.

Alice sighed. "Look, Reuben, I have some business to discuss with you. Can you hold the vitriol until I'm finished?"

"Go ahead." Reuben tried to concentrate on traffic, downplaying the interruption.

"Do you remember me talking about the town in Haiti that I visited?"

"Of course. You spent weeks and weeks there. You talked about nothing else when you came home. Even if I tried to forget, I'm sure you wouldn't let me." Reuben flipped on his left indicator, making the turn toward the hotel.

"I know, I know. I can't apologize, Reuben. That trip was too important to me. It changed my life, my worldview. Being a doctor in the United States is a challenge, but nothing like what Haiti's people face every day. I was horrified at first, but after spending time there... now I... I want to help all I can."

"Old news, Alice. What's your point?" He pulled into the parking lot and slid into the first available spot, letting the car idle.

"I'm moving to Haiti, Reuben. I'm not planning on coming back."

"Are you out of your mind?" Reuben exploded. He couldn't believe it. This was his wife talking, even though she hadn't lived under the same roof with him for the past eight months. *My wife? Moving to Haiti? Leaving the country for good? Leaving me for good?* He turned off the engine. "That's crazy!"

"Thanks for your support," she said, ice dripping in her tone.

"What did you think I'd say? 'Go, with my blessing?'"

"That would have been nice."

"You've got to be kidding!"

"I should have realized you wouldn't want me to be happy."

"That's not it. It's... it's not safe for you there."

"Safer than it is for the people living there. I'm a doctor, Reuben. It's what I'm supposed to do—help people."

"Are you sure you want to do this?"

"Of course I'm sure. It's all I've thought about since I came back from my last trip there."

Reuben let the prospect of her living thousands of miles away sink in.

"Maybe you should just go for a few months."

"No," Alice said. "I've made up my mind. Now is the time."

The air between them was dead. Reuben honestly didn't know what to say to her. Their marriage was over, he knew that, but for her to leave him forever? Anger coursed through him.

"I've got to get going," Alice said.

"Well, thanks for letting me know," he sneered. Then, as an after-thought, "Will I get a forwarding address?" He heard the neediness in his voice under the sarcasm. Angry as he was with Alice, she was still his wife. She was still part of his collection. Maybe he even still loved her.

"Of course. But there are a few things we should take care of."

"Such as?"

"We need to finish those divorce papers we started."

"You started."

"You need to sign them, Reuben. I may not ever come back to the States, and even if I do..."

"I get it."

"I reviewed the accounts, and I think everything can be split very simply, as it's laid out in the papers. But we never decided about the house. I thought we could sell it and split the money. I could really use the cash to help me get things rolling at the hospital there."

"I'm not so sure I want to sell the house," Reuben said, thinking of how disappointed Tammy would be if he did.

"Well, then, buy out my half."

Reuben thought this over. "For how much?"

"Half a million would be fair. The house is easily worth a million."

Reuben made a choking sound into the phone. "No way. I don't care how much you think the house is worth, you are not getting five hundred thousand dollars from me for any reason. How about one fifty?"

"You know, Reuben, with a quick phone call I could make this very ugly. I could have my attorney make your life hell, but I'd rather go to Haiti and work without the distraction. Four hundred."

"Two hundred," he countered.

"Three fifty."

Reuben was starting to sweat. He really didn't have that kind of cash laying around the house. He hoped she knew it would take weeks, maybe months, for him to pull together that kind of cash. That was assuming that he wanted to do it. "No."

"Three hundred thousand. That's my best offer," she said.

Reuben gritted his teeth. "Two fifty. That's two hundred forty thousand more than I should give you."

"I really need the money," she said. There was silence, then she said, "Done."

"Alright. I'll start getting the cash together. It's gonna take awhile."

"How long?"

"Awhile. How soon do you need it?"

"I'm leaving in two weeks."

"Two weeks? You really are nuts! There's no way I can have all that money for you in two weeks."

"Then I guess we'll have to sell the house."

"We won't be able to sell the house in two weeks, either."

"No, but at least my lawyer will make sure that I get half the money. Which, I should point out, is the least I'm entitled to."

"Is half what you're entitled to when you walk out on your husband after fifteen years of marriage?"

Reuben heard her deep sigh.

"In this state, it is." Alice paused, then said, "If you can come up with two hundred and fifty thousand in two weeks, great, I'll drop negotiations for the house out of the divorce papers. If not, my attorney will handle everything. And that's gonna cost you more. A lot more."

Reuben wanted to say that the money didn't matter to him, that he still loved her and would give her anything she wanted, but, of course, it did matter and he wouldn't give her anything. And loving her? That was a complicated question.

"I'll see what I can do," he said.

She clicked off the line. He stared at the phone in his hand and said aloud, "How am I gonna come up with that kind of money in two weeks?"

# CHAPTER SEVEN

*Chestnut Hill,*
*Philadelphia, PA*
*6:15 P.M.*

**VALERIE LET HERSELF IN THE FRONT DOOR** of the Chestnut Hill house she shared with her father. She heard Rocky squeal the tires as the car pulled away from the house. *It's good to be home,* Valerie thought, *and away from that crazy woman.*

She looked to her left, into the music room, and saw the familiar hardwood floor, the baby grand, and the yellow Queen Anne side chair. A violin was positioned neatly on the chair, a metal music stand nearby holding multiple sheets of music with a bow hanging to one side. *Dad must have been practicing,* she thought. *What was it today? Hadyn? Schubert? Maybe some Beethoven?* Since retiring as concertmaster of the Philadelphia Orchestra, he liked to practice regularly. *You would think he'd be tired of practicing, but I guess it's ingrained in him.*

Valerie got a whiff of dinner. *Dad is cooking international again. I wonder what he's made this time? Cinnamon, ginger, with an undercurrent of what? Onion? And something else, something I don't know.* Her dad's

65

cooking classes often resulted in unfamiliar dinners made from combinations she never knew existed. Tonight's smell was spicy-sweet in a way that Valerie couldn't quite place.

*Why couldn't Dad grill a steak or, if he was feeling experimental, make a nice meatloaf?* She almost missed the fast food and takeout dinners that they used to share. She stuck her head in the kitchen and the scent redoubled, but her father was nowhere in sight. She pulled a bottle of spring water from the refrigerator. "Dad?" she called.

"Out here, Valerie."

Valerie opened the screen door to the patio behind the house. Liam Sloan sat on the wrought iron settee there, balding head glistening in the late June sun, holding a hurricane glass with a dark liquid in one hand and binoculars in the other. He offered the binoculars to her and said, "Look, the nuthatch is out. Over there, on the maple."

Standing behind her father, Valerie tucked the water bottle under her arm. She took the binoculars and adjusted them to her vision. The gray and white nuthatch made its way head-down on the tree, pecking at the odd piece of bark. A round-bellied chickadee was on one of the lower limbs, bouncing from the limb to the ground and back, over and over.

"Drinking dinner, Dad?" She tried to be gentle, but concern edged into her voice. Her dad was pretty good about his drinking these days, keeping it under control, but she remembered times that were not so disciplined, especially in the years after her mother's death.

"No. It's just a little appetite enhancer, that's all. Iced tea. Want one?"

He sounded clear, so Valerie relaxed. She handed the binoculars back to him and showed him the water bottle.

"No, thanks. How soon is dinner – and what is it?"

He looked through the binoculars. "We're having jerk chicken with mango chutney and grilled bananas. The chicken needs to simmer some more. I should give it another thirty minutes, I think. I was going to try to fry some plantains, but I thought you'd like the sweetness of the bananas better."

"Okay." Valerie was unsure how she felt about dinner. Caribbean food was not her favorite, but she tried to keep an open mind for her dad.

"So, tell me about your job. What's it like? How was the first day?"

"It's different than what I expected. I thought I'd be in an office most of the time, but it looks like I'll be driving around more."

"Driving? You?" He took the binoculars away from his eyes and laughed his surprise.

"No, no. Harry got a driver for me. Rocky."

"Sounds more like a bodyguard. Is he handsome?"

"Rocky's a woman. Her real name is Raquel, Raquel Russo. She's very... hard to take. Loud. Noisy. And the way she dresses! Skirt up to here, high heels, bleached blonde with pink streaks in her hair. She's a sight, let me tell you." Valerie sighed. "I'm not sure it'll work out."

Liam put the binoculars on the small round table next to the settee. He picked up his tea and took a sip. "Don't be so critical, Valerie. She's your driver, after all. Maybe she has other skills. Besides driving, I mean."

"I can't imagine what."

Liam put the glass down on the little table. "So what kind of work will you be doing?"

"Track down details on claims, like at TransReliable, but do you remember how I worked on corporate research? These cases are a lot smaller, more personal. Most involve only the claimant." She came around and sat next to him on the settee. "Might not be fascinating, but I'll give it a try." She sipped from the bottle. "And guess who I met with today? The Lamberts."

"Really? Those old codgers? How are they?"

"Okay, I guess. They're still old."

"I think they were born old," her dad said.

Valerie and her dad both laughed.

"They were friendly, like I remember them, but I think they were a bit put off by Rocky. And believe me, I understand why," Valerie said. "Rocky thought they were strange and creepy. They probably thought the same of her but were too polite to mention it. It was a culture clash, for sure. Did you know they have a servant?"

Liam nodded. "Yes. They've always had one, I think. Is it some ancient man in a tux? Gunther?"

"No. A young guy in a tux. In his twenties, maybe. Hanson. I keep wondering how he got hired. He seems like he's really tuned in to them."

"Hmm. Gunther was not so sharp. He was hard of hearing and got things wrong a lot. I haven't talked to the Lamberts for years, so I guess it's no surprise that they have a replacement. Are you getting hungry?"

"Yes, I am."

"Okay. Go change clothes and I'll finish dinner."

She had already turned to go when her father said, "And don't forget to call Walter. I left the message on the answering machine so you could listen to it."

"What did he want?" Valerie could hear the testiness in her own voice.

"To talk to you."

"What if I don't want to talk to him?"

Her father smiled his sad, tolerant smile, but Valerie could see fire in his bright blue eyes. "He's trying to be friendly, Valerie."

She sighed. "He wants me to join the Alliance, Dad. He thinks I have 'something to contribute'." She mimed air quotes.

"Maybe he's right."

"I don't want to be involved with the Japanese American Cultural Alliance, Dad. I don't care much about Japanese culture. I'm American, through and through. This is not up for discussion, with him or anyone." Valerie started to walk away.

"I do wonder what your mother would think, to hear you say that," her dad said.

Valerie pivoted. Her dad didn't often mention her mother unless he was desperate for Valerie's cooperation. "She'd say I was doing the right thing," Valerie shot back. "It's what I learned from her. Be American." She could feel the stubborn set of her own jaw and saw her father raise his hands, conceding defeat.

"All right, then." Her dad turned back to the birds and lifted the binoculars. "Dinner in half an hour, okay?"

"Okay."

---

Valerie opened the door to her bedroom and felt a rush of relief. The generously-sized room, with its pale pink walls, white ceiling, and mahogany furniture, had been her personal space since her birth. Large windows opened onto the side of the house, where through the sheers she could see both the garden in the back yard and the street in front of the house.

Her parents had never been into overly precious decorating for children, so there had never been any murals or stencils on the walls and no glow-in-the-dark stars on the ceiling. She still loved the pale peony pink color contrasting with the dark, dark wood. The room contained a bed, a single dresser, a vanity table with mirror and bench, and a small bookshelf. A desk with a straight-backed chair was an addition in her grade-school years, when schoolwork became more central to her life.

Before her world exploded.

Before her mother died.

After her mother died, she spent long hours at that desk, trying to forget about the accident and focus on schoolwork. If her room was her oasis, her desk was her disciplinary center, where thinking about the personal was set aside for the logical.

The pink and burgundy floral curtains and matching bedspread were a much later choice, made when she was in her thirties. She even found a large oval rug that coordinated. Flowers reminded her of her mother. They were feminine and made her feel connected. At times, she could almost forget that her mother was gone.

Friends, the very few that Valerie had, were astonished to learn that she had never moved away from home. Even her choice to go to Temple University for a degree in business allowed her to commute – and to keep an eye on her dad, who was still having issues of his own at that point. But this room was hers and hers alone. It was the place she went to center herself. She never wanted to find an apartment or a house for herself. Not as long as she had this room.

Valerie began her old, familiar routine, honed during her many years with TransReliable. She leaned her briefcase against the desk. She slipped off her heels, took off her suit and blouse, hung them carefully on hangers, and stepped into the bathroom. There she washed the day's makeup off her face, along with her work problems. She pulled on a pair of dark-wash jeans over her long legs, added a thin light-blue long-sleeved t-shirt, and brushed her hair back into a pony-tail. She felt better. For the first time in the months since TransReliable let her go, she felt almost normal.

*Almost good enough to talk to Walter Nakamura.*

Walter was the son of old family friends of her mother's, folks that her dad liked. Valerie and Walter were the same age and shared classes in school. When she was a kid, she remembered overhearing Walter's parents say how cute it would be if the two dated and maybe married. In a steely voice, her mom replied how that sounded too much like an arranged marriage. Everyone laughed uncomfortably and changed the subject.

That overheard conversation, the very conversation that made Valerie withdraw from Walter, seemed to encourage him. During college and all through his job-hopping years, Walter stayed in frequent, annoying contact with Valerie. Even now, when he was the Director of Activities at the Japanese American Cultural Alliance, he was determined to date her even though she wasn't interested. She attempted to treat him as a friend, but she thought of him more as a thorn in her side.

After he went to work for JACA, Walter wanted her to get involved in the organization, although she was even less interested in that than in him. He was always inviting her to one of JACA's meetings or events or classes, and she always refused. *Just because my mother was of Japanese descent was no reason for me to get involved.*

Like her mother, Valerie had been born in America, but she looked Asian. People immediately thought of her as Asian. She had the face, the eyes, and the hair of an Asian. Her tall, lanky build reflected her dad's Irish heritage. But Walter insisted that it was important for

Valerie to understand her Asian heritage, to encourage her Japanese roots. Nevertheless, she wasn't about to get sucked into some group that sought to protect a culture that she was never part of. Why Walter kept harping about it mystified her. *He works there, yes, but he is as American as I am, born and raised in Philadelphia, for heaven's sake.*

Still, she found it curiously flattering that he would pursue her after she turned him down so many times.

Valerie checked the machine from the upstairs phone. Walter's message was brief. "Valerie, give me a call. There's something I want to discuss with you."

*Innocuous, but left on the home line, not her cell phone. A definite ploy to involve her dad in the transaction. Ugh. Another invitation to yet another Alliance event, I'll bet.*

She punched his number into her cell phone and almost immediately heard him answer.

"Walter?"

"Valerie! I'm really glad you returned my call. Remember Akio Tanaka? He opens his restaurant, Twist, this week. I got an invitation from him. Will you go with me to check it out?"

If Walter was looking for a way to get on Valerie's good side, it was smart to use Akio Tanaka. She liked Akio, thought he was cute in a way, even if a bit overbearing. Okay, he could be an ass. He was full of himself and his rank of sous chef because he worked at the Rittenhouse Hotel downtown. Opening his own restaurant was a huge step.

"I'd like that very much. I want to see what Akio's done."

"The invitation is for tomorrow night. How does that sound?"

"That sounds fine."

"Great. I'll pick you up at seven."

"Seven, it is." Valerie hung up and went downstairs to find her dad and tell him. He was in the kitchen, stirring a large pan of chicken in a dark brown sauce.

Valerie still couldn't quite get used to the kitchen, partly because it was the most recent of the house's renovations and partly because its rust color had such a masculine feel. It was attractive, but it wasn't pretty or familiar. Even though the changes were mostly cosmetic, she had to remind herself that this was her family's kitchen. It was so... different.

Then there was the cost. She couldn't deny that the money her dad sank into the kitchen renovation still made her angry.

Of course her dad loved the kitchen and spent many hours there, practicing his recently-learned cooking skills. Tonight he hovered over the cooktop, fussing with the steaming pots.

Valerie sat on one of the high stools at the kitchen's island and watched her dad dish up dinner. She noticed that he wore a crisp, new rust-colored apron that matched the walls. *I wonder when he got that?* she thought, and mentally kicked herself for thinking it. *After all, how much does an apron cost? Should I begrudge him that?*

Aloud she said, "I called Walter."

Her dad said, "Good."

"And guess what? He didn't ask me to go to a JACA event."

"Is that good?"

"Yes. It's a relief."

"So what did he want?"

"He asked me to have dinner with him tomorrow night, at Akio's new place. Do you remember Akio?"

"Of course. He's at the Rittenhouse, isn't he?"

"Not since he decided to open the new place. Walter got an invitation. He wants me to go along."

"You have a date." Her dad looked pleased.

Valerie made a face at him. "I'm not sure I'd put it that way. We're checking out a new restaurant."

Her dad served dinner on the kitchen island. It was handier to eat here than to take plates over to the table. They rarely used the table except to spread out the Sunday *Inquirer* to read.

"Does Walter know that it's not a date?"

Valerie looked at the brown chicken circled by banana pieces swimming in the sauce on her dish, her father's attempt at decorative plating.

"Probably not."

"You might want to discuss that with him."

She shook her head. "I don't think so."

"Well, I'm glad you're going. You should go out more. You hid in the house the whole time you were laid off. Your mother would not have liked that."

*Ouch. Mentioning Mom again? That hurts.*

"And work is not the only important thing in life, remember?"

"So you keep telling me," she sighed. "And I guess you like Walter, right?"

"As I also keep telling you." He gestured to her plate. "Taste?"

She tested the texture of the chicken with her fork. It fell apart easily with minimal prodding. Steeling herself, she took an experimental bite. One chew, then another. Her eyes met her father's.

"Wow. It's delicious, Dad," she said, genuinely impressed.

"Thanks," he said, sitting down next to her at the island. "Honey, I know you think Walter's stodgy, but remember that he's made something of himself. His family didn't have much, and yet he was able to get an education and a good job. He is a very focused and dutiful son. He helps to pay his family's bills. Think of all the people he helps at the Alliance, too."

Valerie had heard it all before. "I know."

"Your mother would have liked him."

Valerie cringed again. *Three mentions of Mom in one night? Way too much.*

"Do you think she would have wanted me to join the Alliance?" Although Valerie suspected she knew the answer to that, she was curious what her dad would say.

His eyes grew misty. "I'm not sure I can answer that. I know she wasn't interested when we first met. When we were young, we thought the rest of the world didn't matter much. That didn't change until later."

"Later? Why? What happened?"

"I don't know, Valerie. She changed. I changed. We had responsibilities. It happens, especially after years pass. JACA might have helped us... adjust."

Valerie stared at him. *The Cultural Alliance, help them? How?*

"There's no point in wondering." Her father pulled himself out of his reverie. "Your mother is gone, and you and I go on without her. You have to decide these things for yourself. What matters is that you have a date tomorrow night. Go. Have fun."

"Okay." Valerie tried to lighten her tone. "I just wanted you to know I won't be here for dinner tomorrow night."

"Noted."

"And it's not a date."

"So you keep telling me." Her dad grinned.

"You're okay with me not being here?"

"I have friends, too, you know. I might have dinner with them." His laughter bordered on devilish.

"Oh. I didn't know I was keeping you from them." Valerie's lips curved, but her heart wasn't in it.

"You're not. But I have cooking class tomorrow night, so maybe I could have coffee with one of the other students after."

"Any one in particular?"

Her father looked startled. His mouth worked silently for a moment, but then he said, "Well, no, I was thinking out loud."

Valerie enjoyed teasing her father the same way he did her. "Well, let me know if you're out past curfew."

"I will. Now, eat. I don't want you starving before your big date tomorrow."

"Dad! Enough with the date thing already."

Her father's laughter echoed in the kitchen as he filled his own plate.

# CHAPTER EIGHT

*Atlantic City, NJ*
*June 5, 2009*
*3:30 P.M.*

**THE SEASIDE HOTEL, ONCE AN EXAMPLE** of the best that Atlantic City had to offer, was no longer a grand hotel. Doomed by its location at the far end of the boardwalk, it simply couldn't compete with the casinos. Tourists chose to stay where there was easier access to the action, nearer the center of the boardwalk. All of the other motels at the Seaside's end of the boardwalk had closed years before. Many were demolished, leaving bare concrete slabs where they once stood. Only the Seaside remained, alone and struggling, run by a string of inexperienced managers, with little money from its owners to keep it up to date.

The Seaside was where Frank DelVecchio, ex-manager of The Rays and prospective groom, chose to get married.

Reuben parked as close to the entrance as he could and got out of the car, greeted by the sharp smell of sea salt and decay and the sight of pink early-evening clouds. *It's going to be a perfect June sunset,* he thought, *even if my wife is leaving the country and I'm stuck in this dump.* The harsh squawk of gulls caught his attention and he followed their takeoff and flight from the parking lot.

"Hey, Cafferty! Welcome to Atlantic City, buddy."

"Frank, how are you?" Reuben said, his feet crunching sand. "Congrats on the upcoming nuptials," he added, offering his hand.

Frank shook it enthusiastically. "Hard to believe, isn't it?" Frank said, talking around a fat cigar, and shaking his head so that the ponytail of gray hair at the base of his skull tossed. Held between the thick moustache and beard where Frank's mouth was hidden, the cigar sparked orange fire at the tip. The dentist in Reuben could only imagine the tarry yellow discoloration of the teeth hidden by that moustache. He thanked God that he couldn't actually see it. Frank added, "As a married guy yourself, I imagine you have lots of advice for me."

Reuben laughed. All he could think of was Alice and the money he didn't have to pay her off. *Advice? You don't want to hear from me.*

"I think I'll keep my advice to myself. They say that wise men don't need it and fools don't heed it," Reuben said.

"And which category do I fall into?" Frank asked, the outer edges of his moustache lifting into a furry smile.

Reuben laughed again, louder this time, but answered the question with one of his own. "I've gotta ask, why are you having the wedding here, of all places?"

"All the banquet rooms at the casinos were taken. Who would have guessed that you had to call before May to book a wedding in June? Besides, this is a cozy little place, plus it didn't cost me a fortune."

"Same old Frank, always trying to save a buck."

"Yeah, I tried. But when I told Judy where I booked us, well, let's say she was not too happy. I had to spend a small fortune at her favorite jewelry store to calm her down. Diamonds help a woman forgive almost anything."

"This sounds like the same last-minute approach you used when you booked the band. Guess some things never change. Although I don't remember any jewelry being involved."

"Screw you, Cafferty. You always got paid and I kept you guys busy.

"Yeah, you did. Well, I'd better go check in. See you later, Frank."

"Right. You know where to find me."

"Of course. The bar."

Frank's laugh drifted over his shoulder as he sauntered back to the patio next to the hotel's entrance, leisurely puffing the cigar.

Carrying his bags to the elevator, Reuben ran into Larry Flinchbaugh, the drummer of The Rays. Larry's hair was cut a bit shorter than Reuben remembered, but Reuben would have recognized Larry's square jaw and tiny teeth anywhere. Reuben reached out to shake his hand, but Larry burrowed in for a hug. "Whoa, dude," Reuben said and backed away as quickly as he could. "Did you load in already?"

"Not yet."

"Have you seen Dennis or Pat?" Reuben asked.

"No, but Dennis called me about an hour ago. He's on the way."

"I talked to Pat earlier in the week. He said he expected to get here around six. It sounds like he has everything set up. He said that the happy couple is expecting us to play around eight, to kick off the weekend."

Larry nodded. "I know this is a special occasion for Frank, but I'm here for the buffet. I hear Frank arranged to bring in prime rib for the reception," he said.

"Who on earth told you that?" Reuben asked.

"Frank. He said I'd love it."

"Did it occur to you that he might have been joking?"

Larry looked flummoxed. The guy didn't have a suspicious bone in his body. Reuben realized he ruined Larry's day.

"No worries, Larry. I'm sure we'll be well-fed," Reuben said. "Where did you put your gear?"

"It's still in the van. I wanted to check in first, then I'll move everything to the ballroom."

"Do you need any help?"

"Like you plan to help me? That would be a first."

"Well, no. But I'm sure that the hotel has someone around to give you a hand.

Larry laughed. "I knew it. I'll always be loading my own gear in and out. I'm gonna go set up."

"Okay." Reuben watched Larry go, and realized he hadn't even asked Larry about his family. Which was fine, since Reuben really didn't care about Larry's family. He had more important problems. Like where to get $250,000.

The Rays gathered at seven o'clock in the Rose Ballroom, where the deep red walls featured roses embossed right into the wallpaper. The garishness of the room had struck Reuben earlier when he brought in his gear. Now, because he was nursing a headache from thinking about Alice, all that red made him feel like the whole world was bleeding. *Including my bank account,* he thought. *Where the hell am I going to find $250,000 for that self-centered do-gooder?*

To add to his headache, Reuben heard Dennis on bass, playing the same warm-up he played back in the eighties.

Dah dah dah DAH dah, dah dah dah DAH dah.

*Led Zeppelin. Immigrant Song.* Reuben wanted to poke his own eardrums out. *Couldn't Dennis pick something else after all these years?*

Surprised to see everyone gathered there—The Rays were never known to be punctual—Reuben shifted himself into high gear and quickly set up his keyboard and placed his Epiphone on a stand within reach.

"Yeah, I live in this hell-hole of an apartment building," Austin, their lead guitarist, said, his guttural voice carrying over Dennis's bass, "and somebody broke in and took my TV and some other stuff."

Austin didn't look very upset. In fact, he was all smiles.

"I got the insurance company to replace my stuff. It was great. The insurance company paid for everything. I actually got a bigger TV than the one that was stolen."

"I'm surprised you even had insurance," Pat said, and Dennis and Larry laughed.

Austin glared at him.

Reuben scratched his head. "So, you're saying that you got a better TV for the one you had? No questions asked?"

"Yep. I asked and they replaced it."

"That's fraud, Austin." Pat frowned.

"People do it all the time," Austin shrugged. "Nobody questioned it. Besides, I paid my insurance bills all those years. They got their money. I deserved a new TV."

Pat shook his head. "I oughta report you."

"Go ahead. It's my word against yours."

Reuben watched Austin's anger struggle with his pride. That was Austin, always trying to show off and then becoming angry when nobody oohed and ahhed.

Austin caught Reuben staring. "What, are you gonna report me, too?"

"No."

"Then what are you lookin' at?"

"Nothing."

Pat took charge, like he always did. "Here, guys, if you have so much time, try taking a look at the set list." He handed them around and gave instructions about how he wanted things performed on stage. Pat ran his fingers through his shaggy blond hair, subtly preening. He pinned each person he talked to with his sharp blue eyes, but it was his perfect smile that Reuben always noticed. Pat had strong, wide teeth, straight and balanced, with the gum line hidden by his lips. They were blue-white, with no evidence of metal fillings or caps to distract one from them. Fine, fine work, whoever his dentist was, and Pat was as successful maintaining them as he was in his real estate ventures.

In his "real" life, Pat McMullen owned Rock Steady Real Estate, the leading independent realtor in the Philadelphia area. He ran a tight business. Even in these tough times he was able to make a profit, or so Reuben had heard.

Pat had an innate ability to make most people feel they were his best friends, even if they were simply passing acquaintances. With Reuben he had to work a little harder, but even Reuben was swayed in the end. After all, Pat always closed his deals.

Pat was doing that same thing tonight, being all warm and fuzzy, working on each of them individually to get what he, Pat, wanted. Reuben sat at the keyboard, looking down at the keys and playing scales, warming up, while he watched Pat out of the corner of one eye.

After a few minutes, Reuben picked up his Epiphone. He fiddled with the tuning, then heard Austin say, "Need help tuning, Rube?"

Austin laughed, a harsh, sarcastic laugh. "Hey, Pat, Reuben needs to tune up. Again." Austin smiled in Reuben's direction, his long, pointy, gray-tinged teeth exposed.

*That smile. That grotesque, vampire-like smile,* thought Reuben.

"No, thanks," Reuben said, remembering all the times Austin and Pat gave him grief for stopping to tune during shows. He couldn't help it if he wanted his guitar to sound perfect. But constant tuning was another reason the band didn't want him to play guitar. "I got it. Look. New tuner." He attached the new tuner to the head stock and added, "Works fine."

"Maybe you should stick to the keyboard," suggested Austin.

*Fuck you, Austin,* Reuben thought. *I don't need your approval.* He did a slow sizzle that must have showed on his face.

Pat's eyes were on Reuben, and he didn't look happy. Reuben could almost feel heat being generated. He knew that Pat liked things to go according to plan. Crabbing at each other was not part of that plan. Pat turned his gaze to Austin, and some silent interchange took place between them. Turning back to Reuben, Pat said, "I think you could do a lead or two. But keep it short, Rube. Don't drag it out."

In the next moment, Pat's smile was back along with the sparkle in his eyes. "Okay, guys. Let's run through a few tunes and see how we sound."

# CHAPTER NINE

*Chestnut Hill*
*Philadelphia, PA*
*June 16, 2009*
*8:30 A.M.*

**LONG BEFORE ROCKY TURNED THE CORNER** onto Millman Street, Valerie heard rock music thumping inside Rocky's car. Valerie pictured the birds in Pastorius Park dropping out of trees with paralyzing heart attacks, their tiny little earholes hemorrhaging. *Rocky must be hearing impaired,* she thought. *No, just inconsiderate.*

Rocky screeched to a halt in front of Valerie's house. Valerie wasn't sure she wanted to get in the car, but figured she had no choice.

Rocky turned the music down as Valerie folded her long legs into the small car. "Mornin' Boss," Rocky said, smiling as bright as the June sun outside.

"I'm not your boss," Valerie grumbled. She settled into the passenger seat, staring at her driver. Today Rocky wore jeans with torn sections slashed across each leg. A snug red jacket that clashed with the fuchsia in her hair covered a tight white button-down shirt. She topped the whole look off with a generous heap of eye makeup and a newsboy cap. Valerie wasn't sure what sort of statement Rocky wanted to make with this outfit, but it was quite different from her own tailored gray suit, white blouse, and black heels with matching black attaché.

"Is there a reason you are dressed this way?" Valerie said, trying hard not to sneer.

"What's wrong with what I'm wearing?"

"It's pretty casual for work," Valerie said.

"Well, in case you didn't notice, you're way overdressed," Rocky shot back. "We don't work downtown."

"Oh, I noticed, alright." Valerie kicked some White Castle fast food papers away from her with distaste. "Do you live in this car?"

"No. I have an apartment in Manayunk. That's from last night. Throw it in the back with the others." Rocky adjusted the volume on the music and stepped on the gas. The car lurched away from the curb, the tires squealing enough to wake Valerie's entire neighborhood if they weren't already up.

Valerie gritted her teeth, tossing the wrapper into the back seat with the tips of two fingers. She checked her seat belt one more time to make sure she was buckled in as tightly as possible. "Are you sure you know where we're going?"

"Of course I do. I used to date a guy who lived in Phoenixville. You relax and leave the driving to me."

"Relax?" Valerie could feel herself stiffen as Rocky pulled up tight to the bumper of the Mercedes in front of them.

"Yeah, it's going to take us about forty-five minutes to get there. Phoenixville isn't exactly next door to Philly, you know."

"It didn't look that far away on the map," Valerie said.

"Well, it is. Did you know that they call it 'Blobville'?" Rocky asked, turning the music down a little.

"No, I didn't."

"The movie house in Phoenixville, the Colonial, was used in the movie 'The Blob' in the fifties. They have a festival celebrating the movie every year. My boyfriend was really into sci-fi and old movies, so we went to it. It was fun, watching everyone run out of the theater screaming when they recreated the scene."

"You're kidding, right?" She had no idea what movie Rocky was talking about. Though Valerie once attended a lecture by Camille Paglia at the University of the Arts, she had little interest in popular culture.

"No, I'm not kidding. Anyway, it's a bit of a ride," Rocky said, still managing to stay within inches of the Mercedes. "I brought plenty of tapes along to play for you."

"Tapes?" Valerie asked.

"Yeah, I brought tapes of some of my favorite bands from the eighties. Since you're not very familiar and all."

"Oh, goodie," Valerie said.

"Let's start with Pat Benatar. She rocks."

They drove by strip malls, housing developments, and farms to get to Phoenixville. Valerie was grateful when the car slowed to what she guessed was the posted speed limit, but Rocky still managed to tailgate every car they followed. Valerie concentrated on the scenery to help her block out the rock blasting from the car's speakers while Rocky sang along. Eventually, even that became background music and her mind wandered.

As always when she had too much time to think, Valerie ruminated about her mother and what must have happened on the night of her accident. Even after all these years, not knowing the details frustrated her. This road set Valerie off. Was her mother driving on a road like this, straight for awhile, then making a sharp angle, then straight again? Valerie imagined the darkness and the rain. No lines to help her mother see where she was on the pavement. The sliding, the sense of flying as the car lost control. Would she have seen the turn? At night? In the rain? Vertigo overtook Valerie and she jerked herself back to reality.

*I hate riding in cars,* Valerie thought.

Now she saw signs indicating that they were coming to Phoenixville. As they crossed the bridge into town, she saw a large factory that had been converted into apartments. A few blocks more and she saw that they were on Bridge Street, the street she was looking for. They passed a large music store with a grand piano visible through an expanse of plate glass.

"Is that it?" she asked Rocky, straining to be heard above the music.

"No, the address is farther down the street," Rocky said, turning the music off.

"I've never been here before. It looks like a pretty nice town," Valerie said. "I read about the iron and steel mills here. We just crossed the Schuylkill River, right?"

"Yep. Still looks the same, to me." Rocky slowed the car, looking around the town. "I'd better take it easy. The cops are funny about their speed limit. They think it actually applies."

Valerie ignored her. "Wow, look at the shops. A lot artsier than I expected."

Rocky pulled into a vacant parking place. "My boyfriend lived in that building, above the gallery," she said, waving her hand toward a building across the street with large glass windows and scrollwork letters above. "And here's the guitar shop."

They got out of the car. A sign hanging above their heads read, 'Patton's Vintage Guitars. Buy, Sell, Trade.'

The display windows contained some instruments for sale. Two electric guitars, a mandolin, and three acoustic guitars were positioned in the window. Each one had a piece of paper next to it with a description of the instrument and the year it was made, along with the price and some facts about it.

Rocky was more excited that Valerie was. "I wonder who owned these before?" Rocky tugged Valerie's jacket sleeve. "I bet famous people owned these. I bet they belonged to bands I've seen."

Valerie pulled her sleeve out of Rocky's grip. "Is that good?"

"It's better than good. It's cool," said Rocky, drawing out the "oo."

Valerie stepped into the entryway, which was set back from the street. She paused to pull a folder out of her case, and let Rocky open the door for her.

A clean-shaven, heavily tattooed man in a wife-beater tee, black leather vest, and black jeans stood behind the counter inside the shop. His shiny black hair was smoothed back from his forehead in a style that Valerie thought of as a low pompadour. He looked up from his cell phone. His dark eyes widened as the women walked up to the counter. "Hey, ladies, what's up?" he asked.

Although he looked young from a distance, as they got closer to him, Valerie could see he was older, probably in his fifties. "I'm looking for..." Valerie paused to look at the papers in her folder and verify the name again. "Mark Patton. Would that be you?"

"Uh, no, I'm Bic." He smiled, but his smile was directed at Rocky. Rocky shot a blinding smile back at him.

"Would it be possible to talk to Mr. Patton?" Valerie asked, fighting the urge to snap her fingers to get his attention.

Bic nodded in Rocky's direction and pointed at a staircase on the left side of the room. "He's upstairs, working on a repair. I'll get him." Bic started up the steps, then turned and said, "You're not cops or anything, are you?"

"Mr. Patton is expecting me. My name is Valerie Sloan and I'm following up on an appraisal that Mr. Patton wrote some time ago."

"Oh, right, cool, he told me about that. Wait a minute." Bic disappeared into the upper level of the building.

Valerie looked around the store. It had the smell of a workshop, all dust and oil. Slim glass cases were lined up in front of them in a bar formation, with a small opening between two of them for people to go through to get to a second room in the back. Guitars hung side-by-side on the back wall of the storefront and along the walls of the room behind the storefront.

From what Valerie could see, the back room also contained a few stools, a small wooden table with several mismatched chairs, and some larger boxes sitting on the floor. Amplifiers, she noted. A few instruments hung from the ceiling, and they included some other instruments besides guitars: mandolins and banjos, but no violins. *Patton invested a good bit of money in all this stock,* she thought. *Costly operation, especially with a large music store down the street competing with him. Can't be easy.*

Bic's voice preceded him down the steps a few minutes later. "He's coming down."

"Thank you."

Bic stationed himself at the counter, keeping his eyes on Rocky. "Investigators, huh? Cops without the uniform?"

"Yeah, uniforms are way too stuffy," Rocky said. "We try not to wear them as often as we can." She glanced at Valerie, then back at Bic.

Bic chuckled and said, "I bet you do your best work without them."

Valerie heard the odd staccato of Patton's feet on the steps before she saw him. Black boots, well-worn. Slim jeans, tight at the knee, remaining tight up through the hips. Loose black t-shirt, faded to near-gray, with a logo on it that she recognized. "D'Addario," as in strings. *They make strings for violins. Guitars, too, I guess.*

Patton had good shoulders, broad and solid. His arms were muscled in the way of a man who worked often with his hands, like a carpenter or a plumber. You could actually see the muscles move in his forearms when he gripped the railing. His short, dark brown hair was misted with gray at the temples and he sported a salt-and-pepper stubble. He had trouble navigating the steps. He kept a firm hold on the railing until he was solidly on the floor, then transferred his hold to the closest glass case.

"Hello," he said, leaning heavily on the top. "I'm Mark Patton." His brown eyes seemed to swallow everything at once, pulling it into some dark place inside. Valerie felt the sweep of his glance, immediately judging her as a person either to trust or not. Whether to take any time for her. Or not.

"Valerie Sloan, Mr. Patton. I believe you talked to my associate, Rocky, on the phone. I'm investigating the theft of a guitar."

"So Rocky said. And call me Mark."

"Mark. I'm sorry to make you come down the stairs."

"No need to apologize. I twisted my back moving a Twin Reverb. I'm trying to get it back to normal." He gave her a small, pained smile. "My back, and the amp," he added. "I'll be better in a day or two. I'm not so sure about the amp."

"All right, then," she said and pulled the appraisal out of the folder and turned it so that Mark could read the sheets. She juggled a legal pad to the countertop for notes. "I believe you put together this appraisal. Is that correct?"

Mark glanced over the front sheet. "Looks like one of mine." He studied the attached photo and used his finger to outline the edges of the guitar. "Someone snatched that Burst?"

"Burst?"

Mark stabbed a forefinger at the picture. "That guitar. Sunburst finish." Now his finger traced the lines of the stripes that crossed the guitar's body. "With tiger flame."

"Oh. Yes."

"Sad. What happened?"

"The owner was attacked by two people in the parking lot of a bar."

"He took the Burst out to a gig?" There was a note of outrage in Mark's voice. He shifted his weight. "Why on earth was he playing this out?"

"He wasn't playing it," Valerie said. "He was trying to sell it. If you would take a moment to look that over, I'd like to verify the information on the appraisal."

Mark pored over the report and said, "Yes, I remember this."

"And this is your signature?"

"Yes."

Valerie took the sheets back from him. "Do you remember Dr. Cafferty at all?"

He pointed at the date written next to his signature, July 28, 2006. "It was a long time ago. I didn't really get to know him, but I knew who he was, because of the band he was in during the eighties, The Rays."

Bic said, "I used to work for the radio station WMMR. We latched onto one of their songs and it became a minor hit. 'Elevator to the Moon.' You remember it, right?"

Valerie shook her head, but Rocky said, "Yeah, that was a great song!" and she and Bic shared another smile.

Mark said, "I remember Cafferty had a collection of guitars, or at least he said he did. As I recall, most of the guitars he mentioned were not what I would consider collectible. They'll hold their value, most of them, but the Les Paul Standard that he had was worth much more than the rest."

"What made that one so valuable?"

"Gibson produced a small number of them beginning in 1957," Mark said. "They only produced them for a few years because they didn't sell well. Then Eric Clapton started playing one and saved the Standard from disappearing completely from the market. He picked it up in 1965 and used it when he was with John Mayall's Blues Breakers. That inspired a comeback of the model in 1968. Gibson still makes the Standard model today. They aren't quite as collectible as that initial run, but they're still in demand. Bic, can you reach that Standard over there?"

Bic pulled a guitar off the wall and handed it to Mark.

"This is the reissue." Mark played a quick riff, giving them an idea of the sound.

Rocky nudged Valerie. "Do you even know who Eric Clapton is?"

Valerie hesitated. "I think so. He was mentioned in a couple articles I read."

Rocky laughed and said to Mark, "If he didn't play classical music, she wouldn't know who you're talking about. He's the 'I Shot the Sheriff' guy, right?"

"Well, yeah, Clapton did a really popular cover of that. It was originally a Bob Marley song," Mark told Rocky, but then he turned to Valerie and said, "You never heard of Clapton? Never heard him play?"

"My parents were classical musicians. That's the music I grew up with," Valerie explained. She felt warmth crawl up her neck and into her cheeks. "Violins are more my area."

Mark handed off the guitar to Bic, but his eyes were still on Valerie. "Sloan. Sloan's Violins?" he said. "You're that Sloan?"

"Yes, that would be me."

"I've heard of you."

"You have?" Valerie asked, perking up. "Do you play violin?"

"No. My sister, Sylvia, does, though."

"Sylvia? Sylvia Hearst? She bought a violin from me a couple years ago. She was at my workshop the other day."

"That's her. She was married for awhile, but her husband couldn't compete with the orchestra. At least, that's her story," Mark chuckled. "You know, that was me driving her around in my truck. I'll tell her you were here. She'll get a kick out of that."

"You know what's weird?" Bic interrupted. "Another one of The Rays was in here a couple weeks ago. You were out of the store, Mark. But Austin Barclay was here."

"Really? What did he want?" Valerie asked.

"He brought in a Fender Strat to have it set up for a gig he had."

"Oh, right, I remember setting it up," Mark said.

"He told me he was thinking about buying something new," Bic said. "He tried out a few things but didn't buy anything. He liked that reissue but said he couldn't afford it. He mentioned that he could have bought an original back in the day, but another guy in the band had the cash and he didn't."

"He probably meant the one Cafferty has," Mark said.

"Interesting. Do you know where I can get in touch with him?" Valerie asked.

"I have his cell number. I called him when the repair was ready," Bic said, rummaging through papers near the cash register. "Yeah, here it is."

"Thanks," Valerie said, jotting down his name and number in her notebook.

"Hey, Bic, do we have a copy of that John Mayall disk around? I was playing it the other day."

"I'll get it for you. I took it downstairs." Bic said, and disappeared through a door to the basement.

"Thanks." Mark turned back to Valerie and Rocky. "Between the two of us, Bic and I have a lot of music around. I've collected music all my life and, like he mentioned, Bic worked in radio. Vinyl, tapes, CDs, we've got it all."

Bic returned with the disk in hand. He gave it to Mark, who slipped it into a CD player behind the counter. "Listen to this and you'll hear what's special about the Burst. It has a distinctive sound. Clapton made it sing. This is the album that inspired people to use the phrase, 'Clapton is God'."

"God, huh?" Valerie listened to the track he played. "Interesting," she said as it finished. "I've been around violins all my life so I understand how a handmade instrument from the 1700s can have great value, but I still don't understand how a manufactured guitar from the fifties is worth so much."

"Well, like any collectable item, it's supply-and-demand. Today they're not making guitars like this even though they try," Mark said. "The major guitar makers went through a rough period in the seventies, and quality suffered. That caused players to look for guitars made in the fifties and sixties. Back then they were called 'used' guitars and you could buy them for a few hundred dollars. As the demand went up so did the prices."

Valerie nodded and said, "Okay, I understand that. I guess the fact that it wasn't Grovered or had a Bigsby vibrato added to it made it more collectible. Is that right?"

"Right. Those are what would be called 'aftermarket modifications.' Before people realized how valuable the guitars from the fifties and sixties would become, they often replaced parts to improve or customize the guitar. They didn't know that they were hurting the value." Mark tapped the copy of the appraisal. "The fact that this guitar has not been modified means that it would be worth top dollar."

"How would they turn such a rare guitar into cash?"

"Most criminals already have ways to turn stolen goods into cash. They probably wouldn't put it on eBay. You might check into some of the pawn shops in Philly, though."

"Okay, thanks. What about guitar dealers?"

"You know, we really don't like to be involved with stolen goods."

Valerie felt her cheeks getting hot again. "That's good to hear."

"Info travels fast with dealers like me. I'll spread the word to the ones I know in this area. Maybe that'll uncover something." Mark looked at the appraisal again. "You know, it could be on its way out of the country. There's always been a big interest in vintage American guitars from collectors in Japan."

"Really?"

"Yes. There's quite a market there for them."

"Okay. I'll look into that, too." Valerie tucked her files and notepad into her case. "Thanks for the information, Mark. Would you mind if I called you again if I have more questions?"

His smile warmed her. "Not at all. I'd be happy to talk with you."

"And tell your sister I said 'hello'."

"I will."

As they moved toward the door, Rocky pointed at the guitars in the window and asked, "Do you have any guitars like the ones that Eddie Van Halen or Poison play?"

"Uh, no," Mark said. "You'll have to go to Guitar Center to see those."

Rocky's face fell. "Oh."

"Come on." Valerie tugged Rocky out of the shop and the two of them headed to the car. "We should get back to the office."

At the car, Rocky said, "Where to next?"

"I'd really like to talk to Dr. Cafferty," she said. "When is our appointment with him?"

"Not until Thursday," Rocky said.

"Okay. Maybe we should take a look at the scene of the crime." Valerie rifled through the papers from the case file. "The Dutchman Motel. Where on earth is that?"

"Boy, you have led a sheltered life," Rocky muttered. "The Dutchman is this dive off the Old Main Line. I don't know what it's like during the day, but it's a real hangout at night. C'mon, I know where it is."

# CHAPTER TEN

*Atlantic City, NJ*
*June 5, 2009*
*10:30 P.M.*

FRIDAY NIGHT, THE ICEBREAKER DANCE set went pretty well, by Reuben's standards. He even forgot about Alice. The set list was made up of songs from the eighties that the bride had selected: Duran Duran's "Hungry Like the Wolf," Tommy Tutone's "Jenny (867-5309)," and the Cars' "What I Needed" to start off the set. All the members of the band had worked on the list of songs separately since they heard from Pat that they were hired, so even though The Rays' only in-person rehearsal was a couple hours earlier, they were fairly smooth. Reuben got to play guitar on two songs, one in each set. Austin didn't make fun of him or get pissed off, and Pat actually smiled at him after he played a solo. Larry and Dennis were solid, as always. They finished the set with Loverboy's "Workin' For the Weekend," followed by The Rays' own hit, "Elevator to the Moon," which drew a satisfying amount of applause from the crowd.

Afterwards, a few guests came up to talk to a few members of the band. Reuben started to pack up his gear, listening to the conversation. One pretty young woman gushed to Pat, "You guys are great!" which sounded terrific until she added, "My mom was such a big fan of yours. I've been listening to your music since grade school."

Reuben felt, rather than saw, Paul Norman approach the stage. Reuben had recognized him in the crowd, even after all these years. His pockmarked face and double chin, his ever-present glasses, and his snooty expression gave him away. Paul was the former bass player for Charisma, another band Frank managed years ago. Reuben remembered how critical Paul had been of The Rays, especially after "Elevator to the Moon" became a local hit.

*Jealous? Oh, yeah, you bet.*

Paul dropped rock and roll for a career as a high school music teacher. Reuben always thought it was so Paul would have a captive audience, lording it over wood-shedding musicians he could best with his own less-than-stellar work.

*That's the only way I'd listen to that jerk,* Reuben thought. *You'd have to force me.*

Paul appeared to want to talk to Austin, but Austin pointedly avoided him. Paul caught Reuben looking at him, so he made a beeline for Reuben. Reuben leaned over his mic stand, grabbing some cords to wrap, making himself busy. That didn't stop Paul.

After a few minimal pleasantries, Paul said, "Y'know, Rube, Austin stole that song. You know, your big hit?" Paul removed his glasses and polished them with his handkerchief. "It was my idea."

This was news to Reuben. His mouth flapped open for a couple seconds, then snapped shut. He turned away, looking for someone else, anyone else, to talk to. The only other person left on the stage was Larry, who was busy tearing down his kit.

"What are you talking about?" Reuben asked irritably.

"Austin and I used to hang out and jam," he said. "I kept playing that riff that he liked and we were trying to come up with lyrics." He finished wiping his glasses and settled them on his nose. "I'd been listening to Robert Hazard's song 'Escalator of Life' and 'Elevator' popped into my head." Paul smiled triumphantly. "Then I added, 'To the Moon.' My idea."

"I've never heard this," Reuben said. "Why didn't you say something before?"

"Austin gave me a beat-up Hondo electric guitar and a case of beer for that song. I figured you guys would never make anything out of it, anyhow." Paul jiggled his glasses from side to side.

"And you're bringing this up now? How do I know you're even telling the truth?" Reuben asked.

"Ask Austin. He'll tell you."

"No, he won't. He wrote that song." But even as he spoke the words, Reuben knew it rang true: Austin stole the song from Paul, but he would never confess to it. "So what do you want?"

"I wanted you to know," Paul said. "Besides, you already know what Austin'll say. 'That's the way the world works, right? The only way to get ahead is to lie, cheat, and steal.'" Paul gave his glasses a final nudge up his nose with his middle finger. "Go ahead, Rube. Ask him."

Reuben shot Paul a disgusted look.

"Hey, Paul, sorry to cut you short, man, but I've gotta pack up here." Reuben bent to gather his equipment, turning his back on Paul, the rest of the stage, and the few admirers left in front of it.

"Later, Dude," Paul said as he walked away.

*This can't be true,* Reuben thought. *We wrote that song. Austin did. That's what he told us, anyway. It was the best thing this band ever did. We got famous because of that song. It can't be because of Pimply Paul Norman.*

Reuben piled his equipment onto the cart supplied by the hotel and rolled it away from the small stage. Pat sauntered over.

"Hey, Rube, Frank says he wants us to book a tour of the tri-state area."

"Yeah, right." He knew Pat was trying to make a joke, but Reuben didn't laugh.

"Saw you talking to Paul Norman," Pat said. "You okay, Rube?"

"Yeah." Reuben fiddled with the cart, avoiding looking Pat in the face. "Did you hear what he said?"

"Enough. Ignore him." Pat flapped a dismissive wave toward the diminishing crowd. "He'd rather be playing with us than watching."

"Yeah, I guess." Reuben stretched his back. "I'm going to take my guitar to the room."

"I'll take the cart off your hands, then. I can put a few more little things on it. I'll put it in storage for the night," Pat said. "Are you coming down to the bar to celebrate? Frank says he's buying. He says this is the bachelor party we 'forgot' to have for him." Pat made air quotes with his fingers.

Although Reuben was in no mood to celebrate, he thought maybe a drink might sweeten the night a little.

"Okay."

"Good," Pat said, pulling the cart away from Reuben.

# CHAPTER ELEVEN

*Paoli Pike*
*East Goshen Township, PA*
*June 16, 2009*
*2:00 P.M.*

FROM PHOENIXVILLE, THE DUTCHMAN MOTEL was located on
the southwestern side of Route 30, about twenty minutes farther than
anything Valerie was familiar with and forty minutes farther than her
ears could tolerate Rocky's music. Though they passed some developments and the occasional house, the area was mostly fields and farms.

How a motel came to be here was a mystery to Valerie. *Maybe it was*
*one of those taverns that had sprung up for travelers on their way from one*
*town to another,* she thought. Her eyes skimmed the flat fields again.
*Or maybe it was someone's bad idea of a business investment.*

Valerie and Rocky arrived at the Dutchman around 2:00. The
parking lot didn't look ominous. There wasn't anywhere for someone to hide. No bushes, no trees, just a couple telephone poles surrounded by the loose stones of the parking lot. There was a strip of
crumbling asphalt closer to the motel. A few cars, older American

makes, were lined up on that strip in front of the place. A fading, weather-damaged sign that hung on the side of the building read, "Dutchman Motel." A smaller, fresher sign next to it said, "Bar," and had an arrow painted on the bottom part of an "L" so that you knew it was pointing around the corner

"This way," Rocky said, holding the entry door open for her. There was no one at the motel reservation desk, but Rocky led Valerie through the swinging doors to the left of the lobby. A cloud of cigarette smoke rolled over the top of the doors and enveloped them as they entered.

As Valerie's eyes adjusted to the dimmer light, she saw that a few guys were lined up along the bar, enjoying their afternoon beer. Two grizzled drinkers sat at a table playing checkers, a bottle of whiskey between them. They looked like they had been waiting for their next turn since the fifties. The hightops around the billiard table were empty. No one was playing pool today.

Music warbled from a dusty jukebox. In Valerie's ear, Rocky whispered, "Eddy Money. 'Baby, Hold On.' Great song." Valerie nodded to let Rocky know she heard her.

A shaggy bartender wiped the bar with a stained, gray towel as the two women approached. His brown hair was as disheveled as his shirt, and he needed a shave. Valerie took him for mid-forties, but the deep grooves under his washed-out blue eyes made him look older than that.

"What can I get you?" the bartender asked.

Valerie slid onto a stool. Rocky pulled herself up on the stool next to her. Valerie said, "A club soda. My associate will have the same."

Rocky protested, but Valerie silenced her with a sharp look and hissed under her breath, "We're working."

He brought them the drinks and waited. Valerie laid a five on the sticky bar and pushed it to him. He snapped it up and headed for the register.

"Keep the change," she said to his back.

He pocketed the whole bill in his jeans but didn't thank her.

"Hey, Kenny. How are ya?" a new customer called to the bartender as he hopped on a stool at the other end of the bar. "You look like shit."

"Thanks."

"Anytime. The old lady keeping you up all night?"

"If only." Kenny put a draft in front of the guy. "I had to work a double yesterday, lock up last night, and open again this morning. That's the same thing Roberts did to me last Saturday. That bastard gives me the worst schedule of anyone here. I think he hates my guts."

"Like your old lady, huh?"

The regulars at the bar laughed. *Crows in a row*, Valerie thought. She sipped her club soda and watched Kenny polish beer glasses with another less-than-clean towel and put them on a shelf above his head, one by one. He moved in a way that suggested he was in no hurry. Finally, she spoke.

"So, Kenny, I was wondering if I could ask you a few questions?"

"Well, that depends." He continued to polish the glasses, looking bored.

"Did I hear you say that you closed up Saturday night?"

"Yeah. Yeah, I guess I did. So?"

A new song started up on the jukebox. A different warble.

"Bruce," Rocky said. "Springsteen. 'Glory Days.' I think I like their juke."

Valerie held up one finger to Rocky. "Not now," she said. Valerie turned back to Kenny and said, "I heard there was some excitement here Saturday night."

"Yeah. I guess there was." There was a long pause before he realized Valerie was going to wait him out. "A guy got robbed in the parking lot."

"Did you see the guy who was robbed?"

Interest flickered briefly in Kenny's eyes, the tiniest of flashes. He stopped polishing. "The guy who came in here with his head split open? Yeah, I saw him. I called the ambulance for him."

"Do you know him?"

"No. But he seemed pretty upset compared to when he was in here earlier"

"Earlier?" she asked.

"Yeah, he was here in the afternoon. He met some guy here."

"Do you know the other guy?"

The flicker was gone. Kenny went back to polishing the glass. "Nah."

"Do you remember what the other guy looked like?"

Kenny stopped again. He cocked his head, squinted his eyes and looked at Valerie more closely. "Who wants to know?"

"I do."

"Why? You a cop?"

"No. I'm an insurance investigator."

She flashed her old insurance company ID so quickly she knew he wouldn't be able to verify anything but that the picture on it was her. *I have to remember to ask Harry for some sort of official credentials,* she thought.

Kenny pulled a cigarette pack out of his shirt pocket and tapped one out. "Same thing."

106

"Not really. Did you already tell the police your story?"

He lit up and took a deep inhale. As he let the smoke puff out of his mouth and nose, he said, "They came in here all huffy and asked a couple questions, but they didn't ask me if I ever saw the guy before." The words seemed to mix with the smoke and disperse into the rafters.

"And you didn't mention it?"

Kenny laughed and put the cigarette in the corner of his mouth. He talked around it, the cigarette bouncing up and down, the tip flickering. "Nah. They weren't much interested in what I had to say. They wanted to get the guy's car closed up and him to a hospital."

Valerie scratched a few words in her notebook. She took a twenty-dollar bill out of her jacket pocket and laid it on the bar between her glass and the bartender, two fingers holding it in place on the bar lightly. From the corner of her eye, she saw surprise register on Rocky's face. "I'm interested. Tell me about this other guy." She lifted her fingers off the bill.

Kenny looked at the twenty, then at her, then at Rocky, then back at the twenty. He slipped it off the counter and into his pocket. "He was tall, thin, a white guy. Longish brown hair, sort of dirty, greasy. About a three-day beard, I'd guess. Didn't look like he had much of anything in common with the guy who got hurt." He paused. "But they had a conversation."

"Did you hear any of it?"

Kenny went back to polishing the glass. "I might have. But maybe not. I'm pretty busy. Maybe I forgot."

Valerie slipped another twenty out of her pocket and put it on the bar. "How's your memory now?" she asked.

The twenty hardly hit the bar before it disappeared. *Kenny's getting good at this,* Valerie thought. *Like a magician.*

"They were talking about making a deal. I wouldn't have paid any attention, but the guy who got hurt..."

"His name is Cafferty."

"Yeah, okay, Cafferty. Cafferty said he tried to sell this expensive guitar he had. I play guitar, I used to be in a band, so I was curious. He was real proud of his expensive guitar, but he said he had to sell it. He said he needed the money. Something about his wife and his girlfriend."

Kenny paused to tap ashes off the cigarette into a small metal ashtray already heaped high. He put the dry glass on the shelf and fetched another from the tiny sink and set to polishing it. "He said he tried to sell it at a guitar show and couldn't find anyone that would buy it."

As the next song loaded on the jukebox, Kenny took another deep drag on his cigarette. When the music blared, smoke spurted from his nostrils. *Oh, my god, it's choreographed,* thought Valerie. *I bet he does that all the time.*

"They had their heads together, real close, to try to keep me from hearing, but that made me listen closer. I'm used to the way sound bounces around in here, and I know where you can hear best, so I stood where I could hear. Greasy was asking what time he should come back and Cafferty said around ten. Greasy asked where the money was, and Cafferty said it was in the car. He said the rest was in the guitar case and that he'd get it when he got the case. Then they left."

Valerie added more words to her notebook, then said, "And about what time was this conversation?"

"Like I said, during the afternoon. Maybe four-thirty or so."

Valerie made a few more notes, then said, "Kenny, you've been a big help to me. If I need to ask you more questions later, where can I get in touch with you?" She slid her notebook across the bar to him.

Kenny shot a look at the other end of the bar. None of the customers were looking in his direction, not at him, not even at the women. Kenny scribbled a phone number on the page and slid the notebook back to her.

———————

"Good grief, if I didn't know we were outside, I'd think we were still in the bar. All I smell is cigarette smoke," muttered Valerie. She sniffed her sleeve. "I'm gonna have to send this suit to the dry cleaners."

"So, are we authorized to bribe witnesses?" Rocky asked.

"No, only to encourage them."

"Can't wait to see your expense report. 'Witness encouragement.' That's a new category, I think." They got into the car and Rocky added, "I didn't know Cafferty had a girlfriend."

"How about that. Cafferty's a busy guy," Valerie said, looking at the phone number Kenny scribbled.

"And what about that business about money in the guitar case? What the hell is that about?"

"Good question. Let's see if we can find out."

# CHAPTER TWELVE

*Atlantic City, NJ*
*June 5, 2009*
*11:30 P.M.*

**IN HIS HOTEL ROOM, REUBEN WAS KEYED UP.** He recounted his entire day to Tammy over the phone, from the drive to Atlantic City to playing the icebreaker to talking to Paul Norman. He was judicious in the facts he shared and the way in which he shared them. He didn't tell her about talking to Alice. It would make her crazy jealous and frantic that the house was in jeopardy.

It was too early to turn in, so Reuben found Pat, Frank, Austin, and some woman at the bar. Reuben took the stool next to Austin, since Pat's head was bent low to listen to the brunette sitting close to him. Reuben couldn't see her face because she was so close to Pat. Reuben jerked his thumb in their direction and asked Austin, "Who's she?"

Austin took a sip of beer, then said, "Ah, you know how this goes. He's still a chick magnet. From what I gather, she's not one of the wedding people. Frank says he doesn't know her." Austin took another sip, and then leaned over to keep his voice down. "I didn't get a real good look at her, but I think she's about sixteen."

Larry, along with Dennis, the bass player, sat down on the other side of Reuben. Dennis's eyes were wide and searching the room as though he didn't want to miss a thing. He kept pressing his lips together, a nervous habit that he carried with him from high school. He ground his teeth, too, a fact Reuben remembered from Boy Scout camp. The sound had kept Reuben awake for all seven nights they spent there and even now Reuben thought that may have been where his obsession with teeth and becoming a dentist started. Reuben was glad not to room with Dennis—or anyone—for this event.

Frank interrupted Pat's conversation with the brunette and she walked away. Frank bought a round of beers for all the guys except Reuben, who preferred scotch. When they all had their drinks, Frank raised his glass and said, "A toast to the best band on the east coast! To The Rays!"

Glass clinked against glass. Pat graciously added, "To Frank and the lovely Judy! May you be very happy for the rest of your lives!"

The glasses clinked a second time.

"So, who was the brunette, Pat?" Larry was the one who got the question out first.

Pat smiled. "A fan."

"Did you get her room number?"

He held out a folded piece of paper that, presumably, had a room number on it. "What do you think?"

"Isn't she a little, uh, young?" Reuben asked.

"Wasn't checking ID."

"You might want to think about checking it when you get to her room," Reuben said, then took a sip of his scotch.

"Wow, what's up with you?" asked Pat. "Paul Norman really got to you, didn't he?"

"Maybe. We should check with Austin about that." Reuben slammed his whiskey glass on the counter. "When were you going to mention that Paul Norman wrote 'Elevator To The Moon?'"

"That's horseshit." Austin did his best to look innocent. "We settled over that song long ago."

"A guitar and a case of beer? Really?" Reuben downed the last of the whiskey and gestured for another.

"It was a long time ago, Rube. What's done is done. Let it go."

"You lying, cheating shit."

"Wow. Like you've never done anything less than honest? It's the way of the world, Rube. You gotta take to get." Austin stood. "I'll be back."

"That's pretty much what Paul said Austin would say." Reuben watched him head to the restroom. "What a jerk."

"Sounds like you could blow off a little steam. You should've brought Alice along."

"No, it's better that I didn't," Reuben said. "She's off doing her own stuff. She doesn't care what I do."

"Really? I thought..."

"She filed for divorce."

"Sorry, man, I didn't know. That sucks. I really thought you guys were good together." Pat looked genuinely concerned. *Part of his act,* Reuben guessed.

"I thought we were, too. Then she went to Haiti for work and came home a different woman. She's obsessed with this orphanage that she visited while she was there. I thought she was a bit low when she came back, but I also thought that the whole thing would blow over once she re-acclimated. Instead, after a couple months she moved out and filed for divorce."

"Just like that?" Frank asked.

"No, of course not. We had a fight." Reuben thought for a few seconds. "Maybe two fights."

"What, did she get involved with one of the other doctors?" asked Frank.

Reuben shook his head. "Cheat on me? No way. She just spent more and more time at the hospital working. I stopped by to see her, and she'd be working. Every time. No matter what time. She hardly came home anymore. I got mad and said things." Reuben paused. "I pushed her once. That's when she left. But I never hit her or anything. I'd never hit her. I just wanted her to come home."

"Did you agree to the divorce?" Pat asked.

"No. I've had the papers for a few months, but I haven't signed anything. Today she told me she's going back to Haiti. She made it sound like she's not coming back. At all."

"Wow.

"She wants money. The bad news is that I have almost all my cash tied up in the business."

"Uh-oh." Pat scrunched up his face.

"Yeah."

"But I guess you've got to cough it up, huh?" said Frank.

"Alice wants me to sell the house," Reuben sighed. "But there's a complication."

"A complication?"

"My girlfriend."

"You dog!" Pat grinned widely and patted Reuben's shoulder. "I'm proud of you, my boy! Is she hot?"

Reuben nodded. "Best sex I've ever had. She works for me, so she comes into my office when we have a few minutes, while the bitewings process or when the luma light is doing its work. She is so into it. Man, it's hard to concentrate some days. Her tits scream my name every time she walks by. She gives a whole new meaning to oral hygiene." Reuben was gratified by the laughter that followed.

"Jeez. Doesn't sound like much of a problem to me." Pat scratched his head. "I mean, if Alice wants a divorce, and you have a new woman in your life, what's the problem? Sell the house, give Alice the money, and consider it a wash. What do you think, Austin?"

Austin nodded. "Sounds good to me. What's the big problem?"

"The problem is that Tammy likes my house. I mean, she *really* likes my house. She's been after me to move in."

"Tammy's the girlfriend?" Austin asked.

"Yeah."

"You could buy her another house," Pat suggested. "I could help you with that."

*Of course you could,* Reuben thought. He could almost see the dollar signs reflect in Pat's eyes. And naturally Pat would steal Tammy away from him. There was no way Reuben would ever consult with Pat on this. "Even if I could sell my house tomorrow, I'd only have half the money because Alice would get half and that won't be enough to buy the kind of house that will keep Tammy happy"

"So, the house is kind of a big deal," Frank stated it as fact, not a question.

"Yeah." Reuben shook his head. "I don't want to lose Tammy. I can't give up sex this good. It's worth it to me to keep the house."

"So how much does Alice want?"

"A quarter of a mil."

"Ouch."

"That's way less than what half of the house is worth. I'd come out ahead, if I could find the money."

"What are you going to do?" asked Pat.

"I don't know."

"What else do you have that has any value? I mean, there's always eBay," Pat said.

"Yeah, right."

"Don't you have some coins or baseball cards or comic books?"

"You want me to liquidate one of my collections? I don't think so. It all takes time to sell." Reuben said.

"Come on, Rube," Austin said. "You've got a bunch of guitars. Why don't you take some of your stock to the guitar show coming up next weekend?"

"Guitar show?"

"Yeah. It's at the Marriott in King of Prussia." Austin thought for a moment, then said, "Why don't you take the Burst?"

"I don't know," Reuben said. "I'm not crazy about taking the Burst anywhere."

"You still have it insured, right?" Austin asked.

"Well, yeah."

"Then you've got nothing to worry about. Look how I made out when the TV got stolen. If anything happened to it at the show, the guitar would be covered. Completely. Nothing to worry about."

Reuben hesitated. "Well..."

"Take it to the show and see if you can sell it. That would be a quick way to get the money."

Reuben rubbed his face with his hands. "Let's face it. I'm going to lose my wife, my house, and my girlfriend."

"No, you're not," Austin said. "I'll help you. I'll go to the show with you."

# CHAPTER THIRTEEN

*Paoli Pike*
*East Goshen Township, PA*
*June 16, 2009*

**AS ROCKY DROVE FROM THE DUTCHMAN** back to the office, Valerie snapped off the radio. Rocky complained, but Valerie pulled out her cell phone and waved it at her.

"I need to make a call," she said, and set the speaker so that Rocky could hear the conversation.

"Hey, Valerie, it's good to hear from you." Mark Patton's voice was warm and friendly.

Valerie liked that.

"I have a question for you," she said, "if someone wanted to sell a guitar, where would they go?"

"You can usually find buyers online. Ebay. Craigslist. Dealers have websites, but dealers will generally only pay about half what the instrument is worth. You can also find buy-sell-trade listings in guitar magazines. *Guitar Player, Vintage Guitar, Guitar World,* that kind of thing. The dealers take out ads."

"What about guitar shows?"

"Yeah, that's another option. There was a big one this past weekend in King of Prussia. The promoters call it the All American Guitar Show. It's the biggest one on the east coast. I was all set to go, but this damned back was painful enough that I didn't want to carry my stock into the hotel. I guess I could have gotten Bic to do it."

Valerie could hear Bic in the background, yelling "There's no way I'm gonna lug all your shit all over a hotel. You don't pay me that well, dude."

"So you didn't go?" Valerie asked, disappointed. She would have liked his opinion of the show.

"No. Lost my deposit and everything. They sent me all this information, and I couldn't do a thing with it."

"Sucks to be you, dude," Bic said from the background.

"How would I go about finding out which dealers attended the guitar show?" Valerie asked.

"Well, you could contact the people that set it up, Roll On Productions. But I have a better suggestion."

"And that is?"

"I've got the list in my hand. They included it in the stuff they sent me."

"Ooh, nice," she said.

"Shall we head back to Phoenixville?" asked Rocky. She was all smiles.

"Yes, I think we should," Valerie said to her. To Mark, she said, "We'll be there by..."

"Four-fifteen," Rocky finished for her.

"Great!" Mark said.

Valerie clicked off the line and was about to say something to Rocky when her cellphone rang again. Walter. Not now, she thought and sent the call to voicemail.

Rocky snapped the radio back on and loud rock blasted out. Over the din, Rocky said, pointing to the radio, "Motorhead."

"Wonderful," Valerie said sarcastically, sure that Rocky couldn't hear her. "Just wonderful." Feeling the vibration of her cell phone in her hand, she looked at its screen and saw Walter's name again. *What on earth could he want that's so important?* she wondered.

"Should I turn it down?" Rocky said.

"What? No. Yes. But not for the phone."

Rocky turned down the sound. "I thought maybe it was your dad."

"No, it's this guy I know, Walter."

"Asking for a date?"

Rocky laughed when Valerie glared at her.

"No, it's not important. I don't want to talk to him," Valerie said.

"Why not?" Rocky turned off the radio, giving Valerie her nearly-full attention.

Valerie didn't want to discuss this with Rocky, but the silence was worse than the music. "I've known Walter a long time. Everything he does is everything I'm not interested in, everything I don't believe in. And every time I talk to him, he brings up all this stuff, tries to make me see things his way. He doesn't want to hear what I think or why. And he's not going to change."

"So, he's as stubborn as you are."

"I'm not stubborn."

"Okay, Val, whatever you say."

"Don't call me Val. My name is Valerie."

"My point, exactly."

———————•••———————

Bic took coffee orders all around and went to retrieve them from the coffee shop down the street while Mark settled the women at a small table in the back room of the store. Valerie looked through the list of dealers, Rocky reading over her shoulder.

"If I wanted to get top dollar for a guitar, who should I talk to?" Valerie asked Mark.

"If it was my guitar? Considering what it's worth, there are only a few big dealers on this list who have the cash to make that kind of deal. They know the tastes of their buyers, or they know someone that might be looking for a specific make or model. Those are the ones that would be worth talking to."

"Such as?"

"Baker's Top Guitars is a dealer that likes unique pieces. This model is something they would be attracted to. Larrabee's deals in Gibsons exclusively, so you should definitely talk to Art Larrabee. And Ben MacKay. I don't know him well, but he deals strictly in Bursts. You will probably get some insight from him about the guitar, even if your guy didn't talk to him."

Mark scanned the pages quickly. He marked dealers with a yellow marker, but after five of them, he paused.

"Too many?"

"No, keep going," Valerie encouraged him. "At this point, I can't afford to skip anyone."

"Besides, she's probably going to make me do the calls," Rocky said, rolling her eyes.

"A fellow lackey," Bic said, distributing cups of coffee. "I knew we had a lot in common."

"Oriental Exchange is a big dealer, you should check with them. So is Quentin's. You'll hear dealers call it 'Q'."

Mark spent a few more minutes going through the list, highlighting and making notes. When he got to the end of the list, he sat back.

"I think that's about it. You've probably got nine or ten calls to make. This is where I'd start."

"I really appreciate you taking the time to do this."

"No problem. I hope at least a few of these guys will help you. Sometimes dealers aren't very forthcoming about their customers."

"Protecting the customer's privacy?"

"Yes, but also their own. They don't like to discuss transactions. The big dealers all know each other and buy and sell among themselves all the time. They know the value of every guitar ever made and they know how to buy low and sell high. That's how they stay in business."

"And maybe, when they are offered a guitar like this, they don't care if it's been stolen."

"It's not that they don't care. They do," Mark said. "They may not know."

"What about you?"

"Most of my transactions are pretty small in comparison to what some of these guys do. I've never been approached with anything at this price point. But some sellers don't want to be asked a lot of questions when they sell their stuff. When I get a seller like that, it discourages me from dealing."

"You think the guitar is, um, borrowed?" Valerie suggested.

"Let's say, of possibly questionable lineage. I try to get the story on the pieces I carry, so my customers know what they are getting."

Mark gathered the papers from Valerie and slipped them into their original envelope. "Here you go. You can take these with you."

"You're sure you don't need them?"

"No. Take them."

They all stood. Valerie took the envelope from him and her hand brushed his. His hand was warm, alive. Her own hand tingled from the contact. She glanced up into his eyes, flustered.

"It was nice seeing you again," Mark said.

"And you." Valerie's face burned and she knew she was blushing. Sometimes she hated her Irish half.

"If you have trouble getting information from these guys, let me know. Maybe I can talk to them, get them to cooperate."

"Gee, Boss, maybe he should go with you," Rocky suggested.

"Well, I... I don't know. Maybe we should call first and see how it goes."

Rocky elbowed her sharply but in such a way that, to anyone watching, it looked like she bumped into Valerie. "It would be better to have an expert along," Rocky insisted.

Valerie almost laughed aloud but caught herself. "I guess it would be a good idea. That is, if you would like to," she said to Mark. "If you have the time. I'm thinking we could go to a few of these places tomorrow afternoon."

"I'll make the time. I'd be glad to help. Besides, I've got business with Jim Larrabee. Bic can handle things here."

"Sure, boss," he said and winked at Rocky. "It's always up to us, right?"

# CHAPTER FOURTEEN

*Atlantic City, NJ*
*June 6, 2009*
*2:00 P.M.*

FRANK AND JUDY'S WEDDING TOOK PLACE in the hotel's atrium, a huge room built of faux fieldstone and decorated to look like paper roses and plastic ivy grew naturally in pockets in the walls. One corner of the atrium had folding chairs and a little archway wrapped in tulle and flowers, ostensibly the site of the service, where the guests gravitated first. Another corner held a small, low stage where the band would play. The third corner held a temporary bar staffed by two bartenders. The wall between the band and the bar was lined with a buffet of hors d'oeuvres.

Pat eyed the bar. "Wish we had time for a drink," he said, herding the guys toward the chairs. "We'll have to hit that later."

The room filled and the officiant—a judge who was a friend of Frank's—took her place under the archway. Frank and Judy came in together and stood in front of her.

By most standards, Frank and Judy's twenty-minute wedding service was considered short. For Reuben, the service stretched into infinity. He had to be there, all of The Rays did, because Frank wanted them there. But for Reuben, the service was a reminder of his own marriage and its ultimate crumbling. The agony felt interminable.

Reuben remembered how happy he and Alice had been. Back then, everyone said they were right for each other, both of them young and ambitious. She still had med school to finish, of course, but he already had his own dental practice.

When a local high school called him to do dental work for some students on their sports teams, he jumped at it. It meant extra income and, to his surprise, a boost in his community standing. The kids loved him. So did their parents. He got recommendations from the school that brought him more work in other schools, more money, and eventually the opportunity to work with the National Hockey League.

Meanwhile, Alice became a pediatric surgeon, a good one, judging by the increase in her income and demands on her time. Reuben was proud of her, but he also thought she chose the wrong specialty. He thought she should have chosen plastic surgery, because it was more lucrative and she could set her own hours. She insisted she could do more good in pediatrics.

That was Alice. She always wanted to "do some good." All Reuben saw were people taking advantage of her.

Alice persisted in spite of Reuben's attitude. But then some unpaid medical missions ultimately took her to Haiti in the aftermath of Hurricane Jeanne in 2004. That was the beginning of the end, from Reuben's perspective. By the time a quartet of similar storms hit in 2008, Alice was deeply involved with a hospital there. She insisted on going back again and again, in spite of the political unrest and the physical danger. Never mind that she didn't get paid a cent for the difficult duty.

Reuben didn't understand her affinity for the hospital or her need to keep going back. He thought perhaps it was something to do with him. Perhaps Alice thought he didn't make enough money. He would never command the money she could as a surgeon, NHL or no. But she didn't seem to mind working for nothing in some godforsaken country thousands of miles away.

Reuben could understand if she had an affair with some guy who made her happier than Reuben. Another doctor, perhaps. Reuben would hate it, of course, but he could at least understand it.

But Haiti? How could he compete with a country that was bankrupt? How could he compete with something so small and inconsequential and yet so big and needy? For Alice, it was a perfect outlet for her need to help. For him, it made no sense.

In the brief flash it takes for any bad decision, Frank and Judy's wedding was over. The flash in this case came from their wedding photographer, a portly man with an ill-fitting toupée named Donovan. While he arranged the bride and groom for photos, the guests moved on to the buffet and the bar.

Donovan posed The Rays for photos with Frank and Judy, then with just Frank, but when he called out for family members, Pat shepherded the band away. They muscled their way to the bar, got drinks, then stepped onto the stage. From their vantage point, they could see almost everyone.

And everyone could see them, Reuben realized. Last night's little icebreaker went well, but it was only a portion of the crowd. This was more people than Reuben had played in front of for years. In the eighties, at the height of their popularity, stage fright never bothered him, no matter what size the crowd. Never bothered any of the other guys, either. Or if it did, no one mentioned it. But now Reuben felt a funny quivering in his gut, and when he reached for the keyboard, he saw his hands shake. *Snap out of it,* he growled to himself. *You've got a job to do.*

The reception went south fast. Pat announced Frank and Judy's first dance and the band played a couple verses of Eric Clapton's "Wonderful Tonight," when Frank's Uncle Edgar grabbed the mic from Pat. "A toast to the happy couple!" Edgar bellowed. "May they forever be entwined!" With a leer, he added, "At least longer than Frank's last three brides!" Edgar toasted the bride and groom multiple times, clinking his glass with a fork so they would kiss while the rest of their family and friends took a drink. With each toast, Edgar gulped deeply from a tall glass full of an amber liquid that Reuben was certain wasn't soda. Turning toward Pat to watch for his next cue, Reuben caught Austin rolling his eyes.

"Bottoms up!" Edgar hollered, over and over. "Everybody! Take a drink! Frank's gonna need your support!" Several of Judy's cousins had to pull Edgar off the stage to end the insults.

As they escorted him away, Reuben glanced back at Austin again. "Classy, huh?" Austin called to him. All Reuben could do was laugh and shake his head.

As Reuben scanned the room, he realized that every questionable friend and relative that Frank had was there. *Nice clothes and expensive jewelry only go so far in establishing a person's class,* Reuben thought. *The rest is told in behavior and this crowd is low-low-low.*

Off to his left, Reuben watched as Frank's Cousin Stan, an aging, sleazy, pretty boy, told off-color jokes to every woman he could get his hands on. Literally. He would grab an arm or shoulder and lean into her face to tell his joke. You could see the women pull back from him and, depending on the woman's sensitivity, simply laugh uncomfortably or look horrified and turn away. Word spread quickly, and Reuben could see a wide gulf develop between Stan and the rest of the room.

When the band took a break, they headed for the bar. Reuben stood next to Austin while they waited for the bartender to draw their beers and Reuben his whiskey.

"Did you see that guy with the camera?" Austin asked.

"Donovan?" Reuben said.

"No," Austin pointed. "Over there."

Every table was equipped with a small camera for people to take candid shots for the bride and groom. Earlier, Reuben watched while several tables took photos of each other to show Frank and Judy how much fun they were having, even if they weren't. The tall guy that Larry pointed out commandeered the camera at one table and took photos down his dress pants while the rest of the table hollered things like "Frame not big enough for ya,' Tony?" During the second set, Reuben saw Tony sidle up to various women without their knowing and take shots of their breasts or backsides. Reuben could imagine what Frank and Judy would think of these photos when they developed the film later.

"Wow," Reuben said. "I'm glad I don't do this for a living."

"What do you mean?" Austin said, and Reuben could see he was insulted. "You think you're too good for the wedding circuit?"

"That's not what I meant, I..."

"Yeah, you always thought you were too good to play with anyone. I remember. You thought you were so special, so talented, you spent all your money for the best equipment. I thought you might have changed, but I guess not."

"And you're as thin-skinned as you were back then, too."

"Thin-skinned? When you go behind my back and steal that Les Paul away from me? Because you thought I couldn't afford it? And then rub my nose in it?"

"Good god, Austin, that was twenty-five years ago!"

Austin's eyes glinted. "Feels like yesterday, asshole."

"Well, it's for sale now," Reuben said. "If you've got the cash."

"You jerk," Austin said. "You were a jerk then and you're a jerk now. Go sell your own damn guitar."

Pat stepped between them and said, "Guys, back off. We've got another set to do."

Fueled by Austin and Reuben's anger, the second set flew by. Near the end, Frank's Uncle Louie took the stage in an attempt to belt out "New York, New York." The Rays played it with style, but Louie couldn't quite make it through the entire song. At the last "gonna make a brand new start of it," Louie slid down the microphone stand and Pat, singing that Louie couldn't "make it there, or maybe anywhere," finished the vocals with Louie clutching one of his legs, moaning the last lines with him.

Meanwhile, Edgar, bitter at being pulled from the stage earlier, hit the bar several times during the afternoon to refresh his glass. He took a seat at a table near the stage and whined to himself through both sets. He got louder in the second set, particularly as the band got to the end of Louie's song. Reuben tensed, expecting Edgar to confront Louie at the end of the song. Instead, Edgar's head hit the table as he passed out.

Frank hadn't gotten far past his roots. Yes, he helped The Rays, back in the day. He was a Jersey boy who used his abrasive personality and a few questionable business tricks to get ahead. But Reuben could see now that Frank must have learned those tricks from some of the geezers in this room. Reuben couldn't believe that Frank found a woman who would put up with him or his family. It took four tries, if you could believe Edgar. *Thank God all I have to do is play this last set, avoid Austin, and then get the hell out of here.*

A gunshot cracked. Shouts and screams layered the air. People scrambled in all directions, jackets flailing and high heels scuffling on the tile floor, acting as though movement, any movement, would save them from a bullet.

The band scattered. Reuben had his share of liquor, but not enough to dull his brain. He simply stepped down off the stage, slid under a table and looked around the edge to see who the shooter was and where he was headed.

To Reuben's surprise, the shooter was a wiry woman with short, gray hair, dressed in a stylish red sleeveless dress and matching pumps. He vaguely remembered being introduced to her as yet another of Frank's cousins. Her smile emphasized deep frown lines on either side of her nose. She had almost broken his hand when she shook it. She had visible muscles on her well-tanned upper arms that made him wonder what she did for a living.

Although his bride was nowhere to be seen, Frank remained at the head table. He stood up and yelled, "Nadine, what the hell are you doing? Put that gun down! Now!"

Nadine was in no mood for being told what to do. "Shut up, Frank." She fired another shot into the ceiling and another round of scrambling and screams followed. Nadine smiled at the chaos she created. "This party was way too dull," she yelled at Frank.

Hotel security guards—rentals, Reuben guessed from their girth—hustled in Nadine's direction. They were all motion and no progress, like those cartoons where the characters' feet go in circles and raise dust, but the characters themselves never move. Nadine turned the gun in the direction of the security guards, and they ducked behind any piece of furniture that they thought would protect them, although parts of their bodies were still clearly visible. If she was serious about hurting them, they would be easy pickings.

Frank charged across the atrium and, after a brief tussle, wrestled the gun out of Nadine's hands. Reuben heard her screech, "I was just trying to liven things up, Frank! Tell Judy I was trying to liven things up," as the guards scurried out from their hiding places to lead Nadine away.

Frank sank into the folding chair nearest him. He put the gun down on a neighboring chair and put his head in his hands.

Reuben crawled out of his hiding place and went over to Frank. He patted Frank on the shoulder. "It'll be alright," he said. When Frank looked up at Reuben and shook his head wordlessly, Reuben added, "Looks like the show's over."

It took him a moment to register Reuben's comment, but finally Frank stood up and said, "Thanks for coming, buddy. It was good to see you again," as though nothing had happened.

The two of them shook hands and Reuben went back to the stage to pack up his gear.

<hr />

Reuben was happy to leave the Seaside Hotel. On the way out he ran into Pat.

"It was good to see you, man," Reuben said. "I'm goin' home."

"Here's a little something to take with you," Pat said, pulling a wad of bills out of his tuxedo jacket. "Frank paid us in cash. Just like the old days."

Reuben grinned and pocketed his share of the cash. "Tell the other guys I said goodbye. Maybe we'll get together again somewhere down the road, but I don't think I want to hang around and run into Austin."

"That's probably best. You know in a day or two he'll cool down."

"Yeah, maybe," Reuben said. *But I doubt it. Twenty-five years is a long time to hold a grudge.*

Alone in the car Reuben realized that he wasn't going to have an easy time at home, either. Decisions had to be made. Tammy's ultimatum played in his head. The specter of selling off his collections hovered over him. The cash in his pocket for playing the wedding didn't help enough. Blasting Billy Idol from his iPod didn't soothe him. The what-ifs of choosing drove him crazy. His brain ping-ponged from thought to thought the entire way home. Pulling into his driveway, he considered again simply selling the house.

*In twelve days? Not a chance.*

What was that other sound inside his head? That annoying little tick, tick sound? Oh, yeah, the invisible clock reminding him that he was that much closer to losing everything. He had to make a choice, and fast.

His collection of baseball cards? Too painful. The coins? It would be like throwing away all the time he spent searching for and finding them. What about the stamps? They were part of him, part of his childhood, each one an indelible memory. And the comic books? No way. Not only were they a part of him, they would be complex to sell. It would be too hard to find a quick buyer. Same with the cars. They would take too much time to liquidate. And none of them would bring enough money, certainly not quickly.

Reuben opened the door that led from the garage to the kitchen. He dropped his duffel on the floor.

*Home at last.*

The relief of being on his own turf diminished as he thought about losing the house. As he unpacked the car and worked on putting equipment back where it belonged, Reuben paced, looking for items that might sell quickly. For every item that was worth selling, he had reasons not to. Exasperated, he took his guitar, amp, and keyboard to his music studio.

He loved this room, the open look of it, the hardwood floors he had installed, the thick rugs that softened the sound. He loved the cables that snaked across the floor and the small mixing board and the microphones and stands sprinkled around the room. He sat on his favorite high stool, took one of his guitars off the wall—one of the Fender Ultras—and noodled on the strings. That simple act made him feel better, feel more in control of himself. *How can I even think about selling any of my guitars?* he thought.

Then he spotted the Gibson Les Paul Standard hanging on the wall away from the others, in an area reserved for the guitars he didn't play very much but liked to look at. The guitar he had beaten Austin to. It was a beautiful guitar, but not in the sense that it was pristine, straight from the factory. It had a couple dents, but it was beautiful in its age, in its sound, and in its place in guitar history. Reuben had bought it when it was still available cheap and not considered collectible. Back in those days, it was considered expensive as electric guitars went. Later, after Austin needled him about it, Reuben took it to that appraiser and found out he had a serious investment. So he insured it. For $250,000.

The idea clicked into place in his head again. *Insurance. The Les Paul Standard. $250,000.* He immediately rejected it. *No. I'm not like Austin, I don't need to stoop to his level. No. Maybe I can sell it.*

His heart clutched at the thought of selling it, but he knew, the logical side of him, the business side of him, knew that it was perfect for this situation. It was definitely worth the money. The right buyer would fork over the money easily. Maybe even more than what he insured it for. *I'd be able to pay off Alice and still have some lunch money,* he thought. *And the guitar show, the one Austin mentioned, is a big one, guaranteed to attract the right sort of person to be the buyer. Yeah.* It meant waiting a couple days. But it was a sure thing.

Reuben picked up the Les Paul and held it for a few moments, stroking the tiger striping that matched so beautifully under the strings. He strummed it, picked it, let the sound roll around the room unamplified. *It sounds so good. Oh my, yes.* But in his heart Reuben knew that, out of necessity, he and the Les Paul had come to a parting of ways.

He held the guitar a few moments longer, then went looking for its case.

# CHAPTER FIFTEEN

*Upper Darby, PA*
*June 16, 2009*
*5:30 P.M.*

**WHEN VALERIE AND ROCKY GOT BACK** to the office Tuesday afternoon, Harry was at his desk doing paperwork. He called out to them as they arrived.

"Are you just getting back from Phoenixville? I didn't think it would take so long."

"It didn't," Rocky said. "We went to look at the Dutchman, too. Valerie's never been there before."

"I'm sure that was a treat," Harry said sarcastically.

"Oh, it was," Valerie said. "Then we went back to talk to Mark Patton again. He gave us some leads, some other dealers that were at a big guitar show, to talk to. We think Dr. Cafferty may have tried to sell the guitar at the show, so I'm trying to find out what happened there. Maybe he met someone or someone saw him and that triggered the theft."

"I'm going to see if I can talk to any of the dealers tonight," Rocky said and sat down at her desk.

Valerie leaned against the doorjamb of Harry's office. "I also chatted with the bartender where the guitar was stolen. Cafferty met someone at the bar for a drink, so I want to find out who that was."

"Sounds good. How's your driver working out for you?"

Valerie swallowed hard, then said, "Fine. Everything's fine."

Harry nodded again, missing her hesitation. "Great. I'm glad." He dropped his voice so that Rocky couldn't hear him. "I did some checking on Rocky before I hired her. She's valuable. What you see is definitely not what you get, in her case. She has some hidden talents. Martial arts skills, in particular, but I also hear she's pretty handy on the shooting range, as well. She's quite the bodyguard."

"I... I guess I got lucky. I really needed a driver."

"You probably won't need her extra skills on this case, but it's nice to know she's got them. Right?"

"Sure."

"Can I make a suggestion?" Harry asked, leaning forward over his desk.

"Of course." Valerie leaned in to hear him.

His voice dropped to a whisper. "You probably don't need to wear suits and heels for this job."

"What do you mean?"

"You look good in them, but you look like you're still working for TransReliable," he said. "Lose the suits. It'll put people off."

"Oh. Okay. I didn't think of that."

"Great. Well, then, back to it. Let me know if you need anything."

"There is one thing."

"What's that?"

"Do we get some sort of official company ID or something? And shouldn't I apply for a license? I used my TransReliable ID and..."

"Good thought. I haven't adjusted to having associates working with me. I'll have Rocky work on it."

"Thanks."

"Well, I'm about finished here, then I'm headed home." Harry said. "Don't stay too late."

"I won't," Valerie said. "I'm going to check out a new restaurant tonight."

"Which one?"

"Twist. Downtown."

"I heard about that place. Supposed to be impressive."

"I hope so. The chef that's opening it is someone I know."

"Wow," Harry teased. "Friends in high places?"

Valerie laughed. "No, a friend who's been working his way up."

"Let me know what you think of the restaurant," Harry said. "Might be somewhere to take clients I want to impress."

"I'll let you know," she said.

# CHAPTER SIXTEEN

*Marriott Hotel*
*King of Prussia, PA*
*June 13, 2009*
*10:45 A.M.*

**THE ENTRANCE TO THE ALL-AMERICAN GUITAR SHOW** and Exchange was down an escalator and two short stairways. At the first table, Reuben juggled his guitar case in order to pay his fifteen-dollar entry fee and put his color-coded wristband on. He moved to the next table where a grossly overweight man with red hair clipped close to his scalp sat. The man was armed with a clipboard, a bored expression, and a nametag that said "Chet."

"Hey, Chet," Reuben said.

Chet didn't look like he wanted to chat. He gestured impatiently to the case. "Open it up," he said. "I need to see what you've got."

"Were you named for Chet Atkins?" Reuben asked while he swung the case onto the table.

Chet heaved a long-suffering sigh. He'd heard that line before. "Yeah. My mom's idea of a joke. I'm more a Slayer kind of guy."

Reuben jiggled the catches and opened the case. Chet's piggish eyes went wide. "A Standard? What year?"

"Fifty-eight."

"You got a buyer here?" Chet's eyes drilled into Reuben's.

Reuben cocked his head. "That's what I came here for, to find a buyer."

"But you don't already have a deal?"

"No."

Chet's expression bordered on disgust. "You're taking quite a chance, bringing it here. Most of our dealers don't bring the kind of money this should get. Trade-in?"

"I need cash, not guitars."

Chet shook his head and pulled out a tag from a pile on the table next to him. He scrawled Reuben's name and the serial number of the guitar, then tore off the numbered bottom of the tag and tied it to the handle of the guitar case. "Don't lose this. You'll need it to get the guitar out of the building."

"Thanks."

Chet leaned forward as much as he could with his stomach pressing against the table. The table shifted toward Reuben slightly. In a lowered voice, Chet said, "You might want to check with the Asian guys in the back corner. Maybe they'd be interested."

"In the corner? How will I know which corner?" Reuben asked.

"You'll know when you see them. Trust me."

Reuben nodded. "Thanks for the tip." He walked around the table, through some temporary curtains, and found himself staring into a huge room with a couple thousand guitars lined up on tables, their cases piled on the floor next to or under the tables. He paused, dazed by the sheer number and variety of offerings, the bright colors of the guitars, the glare of high-gloss finishes, and the number of people shuffling like zombies along the walkways. It was an ocean of blue denim, black leather, and glittering instruments.

He took a moment to get his bearings, then moved into the stream of gawkers. As soon as possible, he left the main pathway and stood next to a table that held several amplifiers. He sat the guitar case on its end next to him on the floor, balancing it carefully with one hand on the top. He took a moment to assess the room.

Dealers had arranged their areas in such a way that customers could see the instruments that were for sale but couldn't take any items for a stroll. Tables were labeled with the dealers' shop names and many of them held a prominent sign that suggested serious buyers ask for assistance.

There was a small show of security, with two uniformed police officers moving through the crowd. Then Reuben noticed a guy, dressed in casual pants and an open–necked shirt with the sleeves rolled up, standing in a small nook created by the room's irregular layout of tables. His sharp eyes were trained on the people moving by, giving them a quick glance down, then up. He had a "which one is not like the others" look that made him stand out. Reuben suspected he was either private or hotel security and wondered how many more like him were around.

Reuben studied the dealers as he went by their tables, checking the quality of their offerings in order to decide which dealer to approach. He finally saw a dealer who displayed pieces with more care than many of the other dealers. The name "Burstin' at the Seams" hung on one of the tables. Reuben had heard of them. They specialized in sunburst guitars like his.

"Looking for anything special?" The dealer wore the obligatory blue denim jeans, a corduroy jean jacket fraying slightly at the sleeves, and a t-shirt that said "Fender Fine Electric Instruments. Since 1946." The front of his brown hair hung almost into his eyes, but the back was shaved short.

"I'm thinking of selling this guitar," Reuben said and opened the case to let the dealer see.

"Les Paul. Standard. Fifty-eight, fifty-nine?"

"Fifty-eight."

"Nice condition, but not pristine. There's some wear. I see you have the original tuners. What are you looking to get?"

"Well, it's rare." Reuben was embarrassed to say such a simplistic thing to a dealer who worked with nothing but rarities, but he was out of his element, rattled. He took a deep breath and said, "I checked the *Vintage Guitar Price Guide* and I saw what people were asking on the web. I'd like to get three hundred thousand." Reuben did not look at the dealer but ran his hands over the guitar.

"Three hundred?"

"Thousand. It's worth at least that."

The dealer laughed. "You've come to the wrong place, buddy. I might be able to come up with something like thirty thousand and maybe a few guitars in trade. I'd let you pick three off the ten thousand-dollar table. How does that sound?"

Two guys walking by stopped to gawk at the guitar. They both had ruddy complexions and shiny black hair. They wore gold neckchains and heavy gold rings. They could have been related, brothers, Reuben guessed. They started talking to each other with gunfire rapidity in a blurred language that took Reuben a few seconds to translate.

"Hey, Deano, lookathat. Looks like my birthday present. Whaddyasay?"

"Geddahdaheer. Noggonnahappen."

Ah, Reuben thought. New Jersey. When he was in The Rays he played all up and down the shore but never really got the hang of listening to the dialect.

Reuben turned his attention back to the dealer and shook his head. "Can't do it. I need the cash."

The two guys moved on, still yammering about the guitar to each other. Their noise caused a few people to turn and stare at the guitar, then at Reuben. Then more people craned to see what guitar the two Jersey guys were talking about, and the walkway gradually jammed with people ogling the guitar.

The dealer frowned. "Sorry. I can't help you. If the situation changes, let me know."

Reuben packed the guitar back in its case. "Okay. Thanks. You got a card?"

The dealer pulled one from a cardholder on the table and handed it to him.

"Thanks," Reuben said again, and pocketed the card.

The crowd dispersed and Reuben moved further along the line of dealers. The next one he picked, Sunrise Audio, had much more merchandise displayed, including some acoustic guitars and a few vintage amplifiers. Reuben put his case on the floor and opened it. Again the walkway slowed with rubberneckers looking at the guitar. The dealer shook his head immediately when he saw what Reuben had in the case.

"Can't use it. Too rich for us."

"But I didn't even tell you..."

"I know what you've got there. Those bursts are like gold. Worth a lot, but only a few can afford them. You're a lucky guy to have it. I'm telling you, I can't even make you an offer."

"Right. Okay." Reuben closed the case and moved away, when the dealer called him back. Reuben could see the guy was fighting his better instincts.

"Hey, let me make a call." The dealer looked at his cell phone for a few moments, scrolling for a number. "A friend of mine might be interested. Don't know how high he can go, but it's worth a shot. What're you asking?"

Reuben propped the case against his foot and told him. The dealer nodded. "Okay." He waited while the dealer listened, talked in a low voice, then listened again. He shook his head at Reuben.

"He says no, he's already got two of these."

"Fifty-eight Standards?"

"One fifty-nine and one fifty-eight. He's looking for a fifty-seven."

"Okay. Thanks for trying."

Reuben moved to the next row of dealers. This time he chose Larrabee's, one with an all-electric guitar display. The dealer was wearing shades, a black leather jacket that had seen better days, and an unnecessary wool cap.

Even though the room was large, it was stuffy and warm. Reuben wondered why the guy dressed for cold weather. Maybe he was expecting snow. In June? *Well, not my concern*, Reuben thought, and approached the dealer. He pulled his case up on a table and opened it. The dealer whistled and pushed his shades up onto his cap.

"Wow. I haven't seen one of these for sale in a few years."

"Are you interested?"

"Whatcha askin'?"

Reuben paused. Maybe he shouldn't be so greedy. "Two hundred sixty thousand."

"Dude, you're fuckin' nuts. No one in this room is gonna give you that kind of cash. Get the fuck outta here."

Reuben closed the case. "Look, Dude," he said, emphasizing the word "dude," letting sarcasm drip all over it, "I'm sure I can find the right buyer. You don't happen to be him. You or your cheap-shit shop."

He pulled the case off the table and walked away, muttering "Damn dealers. They've blackballed me already. Not gonna give me the time of day, no matter what."

Behind him, the dealer said, "Good luck, asshole."

Reuben stopped, turned, and glared at the dealer. *Focus,* he thought. *This is not the time to pick a fight. I need money, not a black eye.*

"Hey, I remember you," a voice to his left said. It was one of the Jersey boys. "Sell it yet?"

"No," Reuben said. "No one's got the money I want."

"Hey, I might be able to hook you up with some cash."

"You know someone who will buy my guitar?"

"Yeah, sure." He ran his fingers through his glossy hair.

"Who?"

"Well, I'd have to take you to him. He'll wanna see the guitar before he says for sure. But if you need money, we'll have a little chat with him. He'll think of a way to get you the cash."

"Ah, no thanks," Reuben said, a vision of someone being hit with a baseball bat materializing in his head. "I've got some other people to talk to here."

The Jersey boy shrugged. "Too bad. Come lookin' for me if you can't find a buyer. I'll be around."

Reuben started moving with the crowd again. He saw a couple women there—they stood out because there were so few—and he noted that most trailed behind husbands or boyfriends who were doing the actual shopping. One woman was tattooed and heavily made up. She wasn't trailing anyone. In fact, she looked like she had an entourage. Lead singer, he supposed, fronting some heavy metal band.

He stopped by several other dealers who all said essentially the same thing he had heard before: No. Reuben was getting tired. The guitar was getting heavy.

Then he came to the last aisle and saw the table in the back. The table was empty except for a small wooden box. Guitar cases were lined up behind the table. There was no indication of a shop name, and no inventory displayed, just the cases lined up against the back wall.

Three young Asian men stood near the table. They all wore dark pants and white t-shirts, as though it was a uniform. A fourth man, older, wearing what looked like a silk jacket, was seated behind the table. There was something off-kilter about his eyes. One of them looked wrong.

*Odd,* thought Reuben.

Reuben watched as a young man with long brown curly hair approached them with a guitar case much like his. The young man was invited to put his case on the table, which he did. The seated man, acting as the dealer, opened the case and examined the guitar. He asked the young man a couple questions. The dealer replaced the guitar into the case and said something Reuben couldn't hear to the young man. Reuben guessed he was making an offer for the instrument. The young man nodded, his curls moving with his head. The dealer opened the wooden box and pulled out a stack of bills. He counted off several hundred-dollar bills and gave them to the young man, who thanked him and moved away from the table. The dealer waved a hand at the young men behind him and one of them snapped into action, closing and locking the case, lifting it, and placing it next to the ones behind the table.

*Wow, my guitar is much better than that one,* Reuben thought. *This'll be a piece of cake.* He watched as another transaction took place in much the same way. Then he remembered Chet's words. "You'll know them when you see them."

Reuben stepped up to the table. The dealer was much older than Reuben had first thought, with tiny lines around his eyes and mouth. His left eye was filmy, as if he had thick cataracts. He didn't have much hair, but what he did have was dark, shot-through with gray. The other three men were definitely younger and more muscular than the seated man. *His minions,* Reuben thought.

"Place the guitar on the table, please," the dealer said. His voice was soft yet emphatic enough that Reuben had no trouble hearing him. He placed the case on the table with the opening towards the dealer who deftly clicked it open and held up the lid. He pulled the Les Paul out of the case, turned it once, and put it back in place.

"How long have you owned this?" the dealer asked Reuben.

"Twenty-two years."

The dealer nodded, pressing his hands together.

"How much would you like for it?"

Reuben steeled himself and said, "Three hundred thousand." *Never hurts to ask for more than you need,* he thought.

The old man's good eye stared deep into Reuben's. "I cannot be so generous. The market will not bear the price you want. I am prepared to offer you seventy-five thousand dollars."

"That's not enough."

"As you wish." The old man waved his hand and one of the gentle-men behind him stepped forward to close and lock the case and slide it toward Reuben. Reuben picked it up from the table and for some reason it felt even heavier to him now.

As he turned to go, Reuben heard the dealer say, "You are being foolish. No one will pay what you think this is worth. The market has collapsed and you will not find a single person that will pay so much, let alone a dealer."

As he made his way out of the show and back to the car, the deal-er's words weighed on Reuben as much as the guitar. *I guess he's right,* Reuben thought, *but I need more money than that. A lot more.* Reuben sighed and thought again about Austin and his TV. *Great,* he thought. *The only way I can get that much money for the guitar is if someone steals it from me and I file an insurance claim.*

That seemed so wrong.

But it was starting to seem so right.

# CHAPTER SEVENTEEN

*Philadelphia, PA*
*June 16, 2009*
*8:15 P.M.*

**WHEN THEY CAME UPON THE CHATTERING CROWD** lined up to enter Akio Tanaka's new restaurant, Twist, Valerie moved closer to Walter, taking his arm.

"Wow," Walter said. "I never guessed it would be so crowded on a Tuesday night." They moved up to the doors, past the line, despite some disgusted looks and an occasional "Hey!" from the people waiting.

A beefy Asian bouncer blocked the heavy black door at the entrance, arms crossed over his chest, scanning the crowd through narrowed eyes. His voice alone stopped Walter and Valerie. "Invited guests only," he said in a deep basso rumble.

Walter leaned into the bouncer and spoke to him in low tones while showing him a gold-embossed card edged in red. The bouncer unfolded his arms and looked more closely at the card. His eyes met Walter's, then Valerie's, and he moved to one side to allow enough space for them to enter. Walter nodded to him as they passed. Only as they went through the door did Valerie realize she had been holding her breath.

A large blue-green Buddha bedecked with gold ornamentation gazed down at them inside the entrance, his expression not unlike the bouncer's. The Buddha's position prevented onlookers on the sidewalk from seeing inside the smaller black-curtained entrance behind it.

Through that door, the room was spectacular. The interior was pale shimmering gold: walls, ceiling, tables, and chairs. The table settings were ivory and gold, accented by red linens with a small black-and-red pattern woven into one corner of the fabric. Waiters in black silk hurried from table to kitchen and back again. Soft down-lighting edged the walls and spotlighted the tables. Although the tables were all in one big room, the lighting gave each table a sense of intimacy.

*Oh, so tasteful,* Valerie thought.

A hostess in a tight red sheath dress greeted them. "Your table is ready, Mr. Nakamura," she said, and motioned for one of the waiters to seat them. He took them to a table located in a corner of the room.

In spite of the muted lighting, Valerie appreciated that she could see almost everything going on in the room except the table directly behind her. She was especially interested in the activity emanating from behind additional black curtains, which covered the entrance to the kitchen. Waiters scurried in and out with trays of steaming foods arranged attractively on little plates, or trays of empty dishes.

Walter ordered a vodka martini for himself and a tonic water for Valerie. They talked about the restaurant, about how impressive it was. Valerie unfolded her napkin, collapsing the expertly formed flying crane. Their drinks arrived and the conversation lagged.

Walter slid his black-framed glasses up his nose for what seemed like the fortieth time since they arrived. "You look very pretty," Walter said. He had already told her that. Twice.

"Thanks." They had already discussed the health of his parents, her dad, his grandparents, and his three sisters on the way to the restaurant. "It's really lovely here. Thank you for inviting me."

Valerie could feel a tension in the air, the tension of mismatched expectations. How had Walter talked her into this? She was usually so careful not to encourage his advances. What she had taken as a chance for friends to check out a new restaurant, he assumed was a formal date. *Just like Dad said,* she thought.

"You're welcome. I'm glad you could come. Your dad is always telling me how busy you are. I guess between the violin biz and the insurance biz, you don't have a lot of time for other things."

*He means the romance biz,* Valerie thought. She felt even more warmth for her father, lying to Walter for her. A behavior he developed, she supposed, from years of Valerie telling him she wasn't interested in dating the son of old family friends. At least, not this one.

"Yes, I've been a little busy, but my new job is very interesting. Involving."

"Your dad said you changed jobs. Tell me about it."

She tried to think of a single activity she could tell him about without breaking any confidentiality rules and couldn't. She relied instead on the same sorts of vague things she told her dad. "Well, I'm working for Harry Zimmer, a guy I worked with when I was at TransReliable. We were both considered investigators, but he was the guy who went out and actually visited the companies I researched. He did the contacts. I just did the background checks."

*Putting it that way sounds lame, she thought. I thought I was so important there. I worked my way up through the ranks and made a name for myself. Or at least that's what I told myself. I really wasn't anybody special, was I?*

"Harry was a terrific investigator and closed a lot of cases for the company. They were sorry to lose him when he decided to open his own agency. I'm happy to work with him again."

Lies, lies, lies.

"So, what do you do for him?" Walter asked.

"I follow up on insurance claims, mostly. I understand Harry also takes other investigations as they come up, so it won't always be about insurance."

"It still sounds pretty much like what you did before," Walter said.

"It's a matter of scale," Valerie told him. "These are small claims, not the big money stuff that TransReliable handled." She hesitated, then out of desperation said, "How are things at the Alliance?"

Walter slid his glasses up his nose. Again. "Things are going well. We have some terrific programs coming up. You might be interested in some of them. Perhaps not the geisha discussion or the Nihon Buyo series."

"I'm not a fan of traditional dance," Valerie said. At least she had heard of Nihon Buyo and knew what it was. Sort of. *I wonder if Walter is testing me?* she thought.

"I didn't think you would, but maybe you'd like to hear the speaker who is going to talk about the ramifications of the Tohoku earthquake and what's happening there now."

"Maybe. When is it?" she asked.

"July. I'll be sure to get a flyer to you."

"Thanks."

The curtains at the kitchen parted and Valerie saw Akio Tanaka himself, moving around the tables, greeting guests and smiling. He was a graceful man, she noted, slender, with well-muscled shoulders under his chef's whites.

Akio approached their table. His glossy black hair was woven into a small braid that cleared his collar. His dark, almond-shaped eyes glittered in the muted light. He bowed slightly and spoke softly to them in heavily accented English. "Nakamura-san, welcome. It is good of you to come."

"You remember Valerie, of course," Walter said.

"Of course." Akio made a much deeper bow in her direction.

Valerie smiled at him, keeping her cool. "We're thrilled to be here. I am so looking forward to dinner."

Walter added, "Valerie is right. We have been excited to try your dishes. What do you recommend?"

Akio smiled. "My kitchen creates but a humble reflection of your desires. Perhaps you would honor me by allowing a tasting platter to be prepared especially for the two of you."

Walter hesitated one second, the space of an inhalation, but it was long enough for Valerie to blurt, "Oh, yes. Please."

Akio held out his hand to her. She took it and felt warmth rush down her back. "For you, something very special." He looked directly into her eyes and squeezed her fingertips. "Please, excuse me."

Akio, bowing, backed away, then turned on his heel and headed for the kitchen. Valerie stared after him, and realized her hand was still in the air only when Walter placed his gently on top of it, pushing it down to the table.

"I'm so sorry, Walter. I spoke out of turn."

"We aren't in Japan, Valerie, and you've made it very clear to me that you care little for the old traditions. You do not need to apologize."

Valerie stared at the table, shamed by her own actions. She cast about for a way to praise him, to make up for taking over the conversation with Akio. Finally she said, "You know, my father speaks highly of you. He says you honor your family."

"Thank you for telling me," Walter said, but he was not smiling. "I'm sure that means little to you. I still don't understand. Why are you so critical of the old ways?"

Valerie sighed. *It's not like I haven't told you this before,* she thought. *I can't help it if you won't listen.*

"The old ways ignored women or, worse, made us into prisoners. I listened to my grandmother's stories. I heard my mother's anger when she questioned her place in the family. How can I accept becoming someone I wasn't born to be? I was born in the United States. I've never seen Japan. I don't speak Japanese. My mother never taught me. She raised me to be American, not some sort of hybrid flower that is lovely to look at but mangled inside."

"But isn't that what you've become?" Walter asked. "A twisted hybrid?"

Valerie felt heat rise to her face.

"Besides, it is our history," he added, the note of certainty unmistakable in his voice.

"Your history, not mine, and only because you have chosen it! And you do choose it—you are as American as I am. Our history has to do with freedom and opportunity, with leaving the old ways behind. Why do you keep running back to them?"

Walter held his drink and rolled the glass back and forth between his fingers before he answered. "The old ways are important to me.

They are a touchstone, a way of learning to appreciate the life I have, a life built by those in my family who came before me. Can't you see the value in that, at least?"

"Of course I can, but..."

"The women who come to the Alliance want to share their knowledge of the old arts, of dance and music, of the ways they dressed. They want to be accepted and appreciated in a way that they haven't since they came to this country. The men come to socialize, to speak of the old times, yes, but to feel a part of a larger group, one that understands and has evolved from the same source. They have been scattered in this country, but now have come together to create a place where they can share their heritage."

"But don't you see that the Alliance extends the reach of those old forces that held us back in so many ways over the years?"

"No, I don't."

One of the waiters placed a platter of bonito tataki in the center of the table. The flattened tuna was seared to perfection and garnished with finely diced spring onions and fresh ginger paste that was formed into spectacular tiny flowers.

"I'm sorry, Valerie," Walter said. "I promised myself that we would not discuss the Alliance tonight. Perhaps we should try the food."

"That sounds like a good idea." Valerie was grateful for the arrival of the food. *Anything to end this discussion. Was it even a discussion? Or an argument?* With Walter, she was never sure. Even now, when she looked at him, all she saw was the flat, unchanging mask that she'd seen on so many Japanese people, a mask that made it difficult to read intention.

She took an experimental forkful and closed her eyes. The tuna melted on her tongue, the barest hint of ginger and onion swirled into it. She was aware of a whiff of smokiness to the fish that surprised her. The flavors and textures overwhelmed the bitter aftertaste of their discussion. She took another bite and relaxed.

"This was a great idea," Valerie said.

Walter seemed more relaxed, too, now that they were eating.

"I think Akio is trying to impress you," he teased. Valerie hoped so.

Salads followed, artfully arranged baby greens with the lightest of sesame-soy dressing. A high-quality shabu-shabu came next, the broth delicate and not overpowering the vegetables or the sweet lobster meat. Onigiri rice triangles wrapped in black seaweed accompanied the dish.

Valerie was overwhelmed by the attention to flavor combinations and the presentation of the meal. Everything was light and balanced in some mysterious way. When dessert arrived, two tiny sweet kabocha manju cakes with hot green tea, she said, "Did you know that Dad is taking a cooking class?"

"He is? What kind of cooking?"

Valerie sniffed her tea, detecting an added flowery scent. "Some kind of international exploration, I think. We had jerk chicken last night. Last week he made his own pasta in some kind of press with pesto sauce using fresh basil. The week before that he made quiche. From scratch. Even the crust."

"Wow."

"I can't quite understand why anyone would want to go to all that work when you can buy the same stuff at the grocery store already made. Or visit a good restaurant. We have so many good restaurants in this town to choose from." She sipped her tea.

"He's probably enjoying the chemistry. I'm not a cook, myself, but food chemistry is the big thing now, isn't it?" Walter said.

"I guess. I know that every time a new dish comes out of Akio's kitchen, I want to call my dad and say, 'You should come here and taste this food. You won't believe it.'"

"Maybe I should have invited your dad."

Valerie could see the faint lines of a frown on Walter's face.

"No, no, nothing like that. I wanted to have dinner with you."

"But you will never see things the same way I do, will you?"

Valerie put down her cup. "No. But that doesn't mean we can't be friends, does it?"

Walter stared at her for a few moments, then stabbed his cakes apart with his chopsticks.

"I suppose so."

There was defeat in his face, Valerie noticed. *My fault,* she thought. *But I just can't encourage him.*

"Nephew? Nephew, how are you?"

Walter looked up, startled by a man standing next to their table. "Uncle?" Walter scrambled to his feet and bowed to his uncle. To Valerie, he said, "Valerie, this is my Uncle Minaru Nakamura. Uncle, this is Valerie Sloan."

Minaru was a powerfully built older man, probably in his sixties. His dark hair was lightly frosted with white. His face was lined and scarred on the left side. *I bet that hurt,* she thought.

Minaru bowed to Valerie, but because she was not sure of the etiquette expected, she extended her hand to shake his. He straightened up and when he reached out to take her hand, she noticed that most of the little finger on his right hand was missing.

"It's a pleasure to meet you," Valerie murmured.

Min's grip was firm, and his smile friendly. "And you, Valerie Sloan. You look so... familiar." He was still gazing at her. It was disturbing. "Are you pleased with the food?"

"Very," Valerie replied.

"Uncle, are you having dinner here, too?" Walter asked.

"No, no. I'm here on business."

"What is it that you do?" Valerie asked.

Uncle Min smiled and the scar disappeared into the folds on his face. "Customer liaison for the restaurant," he said. "Do you mind if I ask you a question?"

"Uncle Min..." Walter intervened.

"No, it's okay," said Valerie.

"Do you know Mai-Ling Yoshida?"

The question was like a little electric shock to Valerie's system. She looked more closely at Uncle Min. "Yes. She was my mother. Did you know her?"

"Yes, I did. She was a beautiful woman, your mother. You look very much like her."

Valerie blushed at the compliment. "Thank you. How did you know her?"

A brief flash of pain flitted over Uncle Min's face, but it quickly disappeared into a neutral expression. "We were friends when we were children."

"Really? I didn't know that," said Walter.

"How do you know Walter?" Min asked.

"My parents were friends with Walter's parents," Valerie said. "We sort of grew up together. Would you like to join us? I'd love to talk to you about her. I've always wondered what she was like as a child."

"Ah, no, I'm sorry. I can't." Min's voice turned flat. "Perhaps, since you know my nephew, we may be able to arrange something at a later time."

"I'm so glad we met." She offered her hand to Min again.

"It was very nice to meet you." Uncle Min shook her hand and this time it seemed as though he didn't want to let go. Valerie flashed back to the way Rocky had first shaken her hand.

When Min finally did let go of her hand, he turned and seemed to melt into the restaurant.

"How did he do that?" she asked Walter.

"What?"

"I didn't see where he went."

Walter shook his head, laughing at her. "He's not a magician. He went over there, behind the curtains."

Then Valerie noticed the oblong white card lying on the table. She turned it over, thinking perhaps the waiter had brought them the bill. When she flipped it, all she saw was a glyph. She slid the card to Walter.

"What's this?" she asked.

Walter picked up the card, his face paling. "Where did you get this?" he asked.

"It was on the table," she said. "What is it?"

Walter placed the card face down on the table. "You never learned to read kanji, did you?" he said.

"No. I know it's the pictograph alphabet, but I never learned."

"Based on the Chinese system. Another argument for learning something of the old ways," Walter muttered. His hand pressed on the card as though trying to hold it down. "You should have taken our class."

Valerie gestured to the card. "So, this is a picture of a word."

"Yes."

"And the word is?"

"Danger. It's a warning." Walter's eyes met hers. He looked so serious, she almost laughed.

"Right," she said, shrugging.

"I wonder..." He looked off in the direction Uncle Min had gone.

"Your uncle left it? Why would he do that? Why didn't he tell you?"

Walter swiveled to look at her. "What makes you think the warning is for me?"

"Japanese character, delivered to this table, you work for the Alliance, he's your uncle. It seems like a natural progression, to me."

"But nothing major is going on at the Alliance right now. I'm planning some events, but nothing even remotely controversial. I'm not sure why I would be in danger. That leaves you. You're the one investigating people. Sounds like someone might not want you to do that."

"Maybe it was a general warning. You know, like those signs that warn you about wet floors. Or like fortune cookies."

"You're not taking this very seriously," Walter said.

"Oh, please. A warning? Maybe about my dad's cooking." Valerie laughed. It felt good to laugh. *I don't laugh enough,* she thought. *Especially around Walter.* "Why are you taking it so seriously?"

A crash, followed by a curse and a shout caught their attention. Akio stood by a table in the part of the dining room farthest from the street. One server cleared plates from the table. Two others picked up pieces of smashed pottery, food, and cutlery from the floor. They worked quickly, heads down, averted from the argument that Akio was having with a man in a dark suit standing next to the table.

Seated at the table was an obese man with a balding head, round belly cinched inside a large jacket that looked almost like a robe. The material of the jacket looked silky from a distance. Expensive. It was cut to his body well, had a lovely drape, even though he was very large at the waist. His eyes were flat lines, as though he was asleep. His mouth was turned down on his hairless face. He looked ancient, ageless. If he had been sitting cross-legged, Valerie would have taken him to be an incarnation of the Buddha in the lobby.

Akio and the dark-suited man were both spitting Japanese in harsh tones at each other and Valerie, shocked, leaned over to Walter to ask, "What are they saying?"

"Akio says that he has had enough meddling. He is fed up with the constant demands. He says the old man will get his money later."

"And the guy in the suit?"

"He says that so long as Akio can't pay him, the boss owns Akio's restaurant and he'd better be prepared to do whatever is asked of him."

"The boss? Is that the guy sitting at the table?"

"Probably."

Two younger men appeared from out of nowhere to restrain Akio, who had reached out to grab the old man's arm. Valerie looked at their suits and thought immediately of Walter's uncle. What was it? What reminded her of Minaru? *Of course,* she thought, *the sheen of the suits. They all look like they've been cut from the same bolt of cloth.*

"Who are they?" she whispered to Walter.

"Don't know, but maybe now is a good time to leave." Walter flagged a server. "Could we get our check, please?"

"Sir, Chef left instructions that you were his guests. The bill is paid."

Walter made a small o with his mouth, then said, "Thank you. And please thank Chef Tanaka. We must go."

The server nodded and moved quickly in the direction of the kitchen, avoiding the table where Akio and the men in shiny suits scuffled. Walter and Valerie headed for the door. Valerie looked back one last time, and saw Akio, face contorted in anger, glaring at the large man. Behind him, partially enveloped by the dark drapes, was Walter's uncle.

# CHAPTER EIGHTEEN

*Marriott Hotel*
*King of Prussia, PA*
*June 13, 2009*
*2:45 P.M.*

**REUBEN SAT IN HIS CAR OUTSIDE THE MARRIOTT,** staring into space. *If I can't sell the damn guitar,* he thought, *I'll get someone to steal it. If only I knew how you go about finding someone to steal something from you.* He closed his eyes. He could feel how tired and sore they were. *Too much staring at guitars. No, too much staring at people. Trying too hard.*

Reuben could hear Austin's voice in the back of his head, nagging.

"The insurance company paid for everything."

"I declared it and they wrote me a check."

"You got your guitars insured? Maybe you oughta get someone to steal 'em."

*So, how do you find a thief? Is there a number to call? Thieves R Us, no job too big, no job too small. Do they have office hours?* Reuben laughed out loud at how crazy he sounded. The ringtone for the song "Brick House" played on his cellphone.

Tammy.

"Hey, sweetie, when are you coming home?" Her voice was like honey, sweet and soothing after all the disappointment.

"Not for awhile."

"Too much to see at the show?"

Reuben sighed. He had studiously avoided telling Tammy why he made this trip, but her questions made his head hurt.

"No, it's not that. I was trying to sell one of my guitars."

The pause that followed was longer than Reuben expected.

"Why are you selling a guitar?" Tammy asked. "I thought you loved your guitars."

Reuben wanted to bite his tongue. He thought she would pass by the idea, not think about it.

"I wanted a little spending money," he said, hoping that would be the end of it.

"Are you buying me a present?" she said, her voice taking on a fizzy note of excitement.

"Maybe," he lied, and hated himself for doing it, but he realized now that he needed to get her off the phone. *No more questions, please!* "Here's the thing, Baby. Austin—you remember me talking about him?—he told me it would be easy. I should have guessed that jerk would steer me wrong. That guy hasn't liked me for a long time, and he has ways to let me know it." Reuben gritted his teeth, still hearing Austin's voice in his head. "This is just one more."

"What are you going to do?"

"I don't know. The only thing I can do is..." He stopped short. He really didn't want to tell Tammy about the only thing left, to let her know how desperate he was to get the money. Criminally desperate.

"Well, I don't know. The problem is that I'd really like to keep the guitar. It's vintage. It's collectible. It's unique. And it's mine."

"Oh." Her disappointment seeped through the phone. It took Reuben a moment to realize her disappointment had to do with the gift he couldn't give her without getting the money. The nonexistent gift. Even though Tammy couldn't see him, he shrugged it off. "I've got to go, Tammy. I have to figure out what to do."

They said their goodbyes, and Reuben looked up Austin in his phone's directory. He hated this. He really, really hated this. He pressed in the number anyway.

"What do you want?" Austin's voice snapped.

"I was wondering if you'd like to meet me for a drink," Reuben said.

"What on earth for?"

"I'd like to bounce an idea off you. About selling the guitar."

"What about the guitar show? I figured you sold it already."

"No one's interested," Reuben said. "I need another way to do this."

"So? I gave you all my ideas."

Reuben choked down his pride and said, "I remembered what you said about your TV, and I thought..."

Austin laughed, a short, harsh sound that was more spiteful than happy. "And you thought I'd be the right guy for the job."

"Well, no, I... I thought you'd know someone who could help me."

"Same difference."

Reuben was already annoyed that Austin was making him grovel, making him feel and sound like a pussy for calling. "Okay, look, I'm sorry I bothered you about this. I just thought maybe..."

"Hang on," Austin said, and exhaled loudly into the phone. "Yeah, well, okay. I'll help you. I know a guy who might be able to do it."

"What's his number?"

"Doesn't work that way. Where are you right now?"

"At the King of Prussia Marriott, in the parking lot."

"You remember the old Dutchman Motel?"

Of course Reuben remembered. Back in the eighties, The Rays actually played there a few times. It was an old dive back then, guaranteed to be an older dive now, he was sure. He wondered if they still rented their rooms by the hour.

"The guy will meet you there. Around four-thirty."

"Okay. Thanks, Aus-"

But he had already hung up.

---

The Dutchman Motel was twenty minutes off the Old Main Line. Reuben drove the road with a familiarity that astonished him, considering he hadn't been here in nearly twenty years. He recognized the rolling hills, heading west in horse country. He recognized the turns. When he arrived at the Dutchman, he recognized the empty fields, the deserted two-story house to the right, and the single-story motel and its bar on the left.

Some things never changed.

Reuben pulled into the parking lot, surprised to see five cars parked there. That seemed like a lot, considering the time of day. This was not a dinner destination and it was a little too early to be checking in for the night. He parked and headed into the motel. A small patio on his left was littered with several small round metal tables, a few chairs at each, some on their backs or sides. A large birdbath-shaped concrete flowerpot in the center was, he presumed, filled with sand. All he could see was a heap of cigarette butts.

The light that filtered inside the entrance was barely enough to outline the desk where the motel's rooms could be booked. No one was waiting for customers there. The bar entrance was to his left, through some swinging doors that reminded Reuben of the Old West. He swung the doors open, sat at one of the stools at the bar, and waved his fingers to get the attention of the bartender, who seemed in no hurry to get to him.

Reuben ordered a rum and Coke, and when it came, he stirred his drink slowly, listening to the ice clink. The drink was mostly watered-down Coke with a touch of bitter rum. All that mattered to Reuben was that it was something cold and wet to sit with.

"Are you Reuben?"

Reuben looked up. The speaker was a lanky guy with stringy brown hair, but what Reuben noticed most were his crooked teeth. The guy's upper left cuspid jutted slightly over the upper left lateral. The twisted tooth gave the guy a permanent snarly look, even when he smiled. It was all Reuben could do not to ask why his parents didn't get him braces as a kid. He suspected he knew. "Yes, I'm Reuben."

"Jeremy." He stuck out his hand and Reuben shook it. Jeremy's hand was slick with grease. Reuben wiped his hand on his pants.

"Sorry. I came right from work. I washed my hands, but the grease don't always wash off," Jeremy said.

"What do you do?"

"Mechanic, over in Paoli." Jeremy took a long pull on his beer. "Austin says you gotta job for me."

"Right," Reuben said. He paused to phrase his next comment carefully. "I am working on a project that could use an extra pair of hands."

"Okay, good." Jeremy pulled himself onto the stool next to Reuben and ordered a draft from the bartender. "You know, I was real surprised to hear from him." Jeremy said, his pale brown eyes lighting up as his beer arrived and Reuben slid money to the bartender to pay for it. "It's been a year or so. I thought he was gonna move outta town, but when nothin' happened after I did Austin's job, I guess he didn't need to."

The furrows on either side of Jeremy's nose deepened with his smile and Reuben realized his nose was almost as crooked as his teeth.

"So, you have a bit of history with, um, borrowing others' property?"

Jeremy laughed, pink lips baring the twisted tooth. His teeth hadn't been brushed for awhile, either, Reuben noticed. A heavy coating of plaque gave them a soft, darkish look. Reuben wanted to look away but couldn't. *How can people let their teeth get to that point?* he thought.

"Yeah, I've 'borrowed' a few things. Only got caught once, though. Did my time, no big deal." Jeremy took a large swig of his beer. "The trick is to be quick and invisible. I only got caught 'cause someone ratted me out." Jeremy frowned, remembering. "It won't happen again. You have to be real careful who you partner with in my line of work."

They pondered this philosophy in silence, then Jeremy said, "You want me to borrow something from you." A statement, not a question.

Reuben nodded. "A guitar. A valuable one."

"How valuable?"

Reuben puffed up a bit and said, "The right buyer will pay three hundred thousand for this guitar, maybe more. I've got it insured for a quarter of a million."

Jeremy whistled low. "That's pretty fuckin' valuable."

"I'd like you to borrow it from me."

Jeremy's eyebrows drew together. "Can't you sell it?"

"I tried. I went to that big guitar show in King of Prussia, but none of the dealers there would give me enough money." Reuben heaved a large sigh. He didn't appreciate Jeremy asking questions. He wasn't hiring him to be the brains of this operation. "I want you to borrow the guitar. Then I'll tell the insurance company that someone took it and they will give me the money for the theft. We'll wait a week or two and then you give me the guitar back."

Jeremy nodded, thinking. "I guess that could work."

"Of course it will. Here's how we'll do it: I'll be in the parking lot putting the guitar in my car. That way you'll know which car it's in. Then you come up behind me in your car. I go back into the bar. You break into my car and take the guitar and drive away."

"I'll crack open the trunk." Jeremy spoke with authority.

Reuben didn't relish damaging one of his cars. "What about the car? Are you sure you want to break into the trunk? Maybe I should leave the guitar on the back seat. Glass is easy to break..."

"It's not nearly as easy as picking the trunk lock," Jeremy said. "Plus, breaking glass is noisy."

"Okay, that sounds like a better idea, then." *Maybe Jeremy will be good at this,* Reuben thought. *No matter how he looks.*

"Sounds simple enough. Will there be witnesses? I don't want them calling the cops right away."

"I may not be able to control that."

Jeremy seemed to mull this over. "I might bring a lookout, then. And we should do this at night. How about tonight? Around ten?"

Reuben nodded, pleased. "The sooner the better. I need to file for the insurance ASAP." He paused, noticing the bartender hovering nearby. Reuben leaned forward and lowered his voice. "So, you think you can help me with this, uh, project?"

The bartender stopped by to check on their drinks. Reuben waved him off.

"Austin said you were paying to do this. Is that right?"

"Fifteen hundred now and another fifteen hundred when I get the guitar back from you."

Jeremy's eyes flashed when he heard that the money was almost in his hands. "I believe we have a deal." He drained his glass.

"Great. Let's go. Your first installment is in my car."

The two of them slid off their stools to head to the parking lot. The bartender called after them, "Stop back again, fellas."

"Will do," said Reuben. *Sooner than you think.*

When they got to the car, Reuben pulled a manila envelope out of the trunk and handed it over to Jeremy. "Your money is in there. Fifteen hundred dollars. Small denominations."

Jeremy opened the envelope and slid the bills into his hand. He did a quick calculation and stuffed the wad of bills in his pocket. He handed the envelope back to Reuben. "Yeah, okay." He said "What time tonight?

"I'll be in the parking lot around ten fifteen, okay?"

"I'll be here."

---

A few miles away from the bar, Jeremy pulled over onto the shoulder of the road and pulled the cash out of his pocket. He counted the money three times, then shoved the bills back in his hip pocket. He pulled out his cell phone and dialed. The buzzing at the other end of the line stopped and a high-pitched male voice said, "Jeremy? What's up?"

"I've got a job. I could use your help. It's good money."

"Really? How much?"

"Five hundred."

"Each?"

"Yeah."

"When?"

"Tonight. Are you at home?"

"Yeah."

"I'm coming over."

"Bring the money."

Jeremy laughed as he hung up.

# CHAPTER NINETEEN

*King of Prussia, PA*
*June 17, 2009*
*11:30 A.M.*

**VALERIE WATCHED AS STRIP MALL** after strip mall slid by. To her right, Rocky was blathering on about some eighties band. To her left, Mark punctuated Rocky's chatter with "Uh, huh," or "Right," or the occasional comment. Between them, for these few moments at least, she was happy right where she was.

She was happy that, because they were in Mark's truck, Rocky couldn't blast eighties rock from the speakers.

She was happy that, with Mark driving, Rocky couldn't exceed the speed of light with her car or drive like she wanted to be in the trunk of the car in front of them.

She was happy that they were making progress on the case.

And she was strangely happy to be wedged in between them in the truck. If Rocky wasn't there, Valerie wouldn't be sitting nearly this close to Mark.

*Oh, my God, that means I'm actually glad she's here,* Valerie thought, followed quickly by, *No, never.*

Their destination was Larrabee's, located, not surprisingly, in a strip mall. Mark pulled a guitar case out of the storage space behind the driver's seat in the cab and headed into the store, with Valerie and Rocky trailing him.

The store was a simple oblong room with about two-thirds storefront, one-third workshop space. The walls lined with guitars were lit with small spotlights. Valerie could feel their warmth when she moved closer to the wall. Some stools, tops emblazoned with the names of guitar or string companies, dotted the floor, along with the boxes that she recognized as amplifiers. There was one glass case with strings and picks and other small pieces of equipment, another with the colorful metal boxes lined up in a neat row that Mark explained could be hooked up to guitars to give them different voices. He called them "effects pedals" and told her they were sometimes referred to as "stomp boxes," from the way guitarists stepped on them to operate them.

Jim Larrabee put down the guitar he was working on and met the trio as he came out of the workspace. He wiped his hand on a cloth before he shook hands with Mark. "Hey, Mark, how are you?" He was sixty-ish, paunchy and balding, with silver-rimmed glasses that had gone out of style long ago. His shoulders slumped under the checked shirt he wore tucked into dark blue pants, the look of a man permanently hunched over a table.

"Jim," Mark nodded his head and introduced the women. Larrabee didn't shake hands with them, but nodded his head in acknowledgement. He seemed more interested in the case that Mark carried.

"Is this the one?" Jim asked.

Mark hoisted the case up onto the countertop, and opened it. "Yeah."

Larrabee looked at the instrument inside, then pulled it out and examined it, front and back. He strummed it, played a riff. "Nice. What are you looking for?"

"Fifteen hundred," Mark said.

Larrabee considered, then said, "I can give you five and trade you a nice bass." As Mark chatted with Larrabee about making the trade, Valerie moved further into the shop, looking at the other guitars. Rocky took up a guard-like stance by the door, her arms folded. She even kept her shades on, as if she was some sort of federal agent from television. The whole picture looked funny to Valerie, especially since Rocky wore a peach-colored dress with green heels and she still had that pink-streaked hair.

Rocky yawned. It appeared that she was not interested in much that was happening here.

When Valerie heard Mark change subjects and say something about answering questions, she pulled out her new investigator credentials, the ones Rocky had printed for her on card stock and laminated the night before. She flashed the card to Larrabee.

"I'm an insurance investigator, Mr. Larrabee. I believe Rocky called you yesterday afternoon and asked if you were at the show at the Marriott."

"That's right. I was there with Finn, my son." Larrabee's eyes didn't make contact with hers. He was looking at Mark.

"Did you talk to a man selling a 1958 Gibson Les Paul Standard while you were there?" She walked around the room, slightly away from him, pretending interest in the equipment but wanting to give

Larrabee a little space since he seemed to be so uncomfortable talking with her.

Still looking at Mark, Larrabee said, "No, I was away from the booth, but Finn talked to him. He told me about it. The guy thought we were going to give him three hundred thousand dollars for it. Finn told him to take a hike."

Mark pointed toward Valerie. "Miss Sloan would like details. Can you describe what happened, or should we wait for Finn?"

Larrabee's face locked into a frown, but he finally turned his head and directed his comments to Valerie. "Finn said the guy was either obnoxious or stupid, he didn't know which. He really didn't understand how dealers operate. Thought we would buy something like that outright. He got angry when my son told him no. I guess the other dealers weren't very helpful, either."

Valerie made a note. "What makes you say that?"

"He said something to Finn about being blackballed. Finn never saw the guy before, and neither of us recognized the name, so how the hell could we be blackballing him?"

"Did your son mention the guy's name?" Valerie asked.

Larrabee thought for a moment. "His last name was Cafferty. His first name was R-something. Not Richard, but... Randolph? No, uh..."

"Reuben?" Valerie suggested. "Like the sandwich?"

Larrabee nodded. "Maybe. Sounds right. You'd have to ask Finn to be sure."

"Is your son around?" Valerie asked.

"No, he's in New York City this week, looking at some guitars, but he's also visiting friends. He won't be back for a few days."

"Maybe I could call him?"

Larrabee frowned again, but grudgingly wrote his son's number down on one of the business cards on the counter.

"Thanks," Valerie said, picking up the card from where Larrabee left it on the counter. "Did your son say anything else?"

"Finn told him we weren't interested. He asked the guy to move on, so that real customers could shop, and the guy told Finn to go fuck himself, pardon my French." A fleeting look of embarrassment crossed Larrabee's face.

"Does that kind of thing happen often at a show?" Valerie asked

"No. But believe me, if I was able to blackball him, I would."

"Do you know if he talked to anyone else?"

"Finn said he was cruising all the tables. I was back at the booth by then, so Finn pointed him out to me. He and a dealer were looking over the guitar. Don't know what happened, but I didn't hear any yelling. I was busy talking to customers."

Valerie wrote a few more notes in her notebook, then said, "So you didn't actually see the guitar yourself?"

Larrabee shook his head. "No, but my son did. He said it was a nice piece, good shape. It might even be worth what the guy's asking, if he found the right buyer. But he shouldn't be expecting dealers to pay that kind of money." He was back to looking at Mark. "That guy was nuts."

# CHAPTER TWENTY

*Norristown, PA*
*June 13, 2009*
*4:30 P.M.*

**JEREMY WAS HUFFING AIR** by the time he got to Chad Reck's third floor walkup. *I can hardly breathe,* he thought. *I need a cigarette.* He took a moment to catch his breath. When he could breathe again, he knocked at the metal door with his special knock, two raps, followed by four faster raps. He knew that Chad would be on the other side, peering through the little peephole as best as he could, on tiptoe.

Chad opened the door and stood back a little to let Jeremy slip by him.

"Hey," Jeremy said, by way of greeting.

"Hey." Chad closed the door and made a production of throwing the lock. His hands shook as he tried to grasp the knob, but he finally did it.

Jeremy looked around the room for a spot to sit down. Bottles and cans littered every flat surface, toppling off the cardboard packing box Chad used for a coffee table. The orange couch spilled stuffing casually from one split side. A double-pronged antenna sat askew on top of the tiny TV. Used clothing, newspapers, and magazines covered the green plaid rocker and the beer-stained brown corduroy side chair, as well as the sagging couch. Jeremy had spent more than one night on that couch in the past, lying atop the assorted reading materials, covered with one of Chad's ratty blankets. This was no better than the room he occupied at the YMCA. In fact, the Y was cleaner. But Jeremy couldn't have visitors there.

In his effort to sit on the couch, Jeremy knocked some magazines to the floor. The sound of something heavy hitting the carpet got his attention.

"What is that?" Jeremy said, flipping through the magazines. "Is that a gun? What are you doing with a gun?"

Chad snatched up the magazines and held them close to his chest. Then he released his arms and laid the magazines down on the packing box. He pulled the gun from its hiding place. The gun looked tarnished and old, but Chad handled it like it was solid gold.

"It was my grandfather's," Chad said.

"Relax, dude, I don't want your gun. Does that thing even work anymore?"

"Of course it works," snapped Chad, waving the gun at him. "That's why I keep it. Protection. In case."

"In case of what?" Jeremy asked.

"In case someone breaks in."

"Dude. We are the guys that break into places. What the hell are you worried for? Think you're going to break into your own apartment?"

Chad picked through the magazines and found one that suited him. He put the gun inside it. "That doesn't mean someone couldn't break in on me," he said. "Those people? The ones we took stuff from?

What if one of those people came after me and broke in here?" His high voice was plaintive.

"I doubt that's going to happen."

"You don't know that for a fact."

"Oh, for cryin' out loud," Jeremy said, annoyed. "Do you want to hear about the job, or not?"

"I want to hear."

"We're supposed to steal a guitar from a guy's car."

Chad looked blank. "Why?"

"Because he's paying us to."

"Okay." Chad still looked puzzled. "But..."

Jeremy could see Chad wasn't going to give up on this. "He's gonna get money from his insurance company for it. Then he wants me to give it back to him," Jeremy said.

"The money?"

Jeremy glared at Chad. "No, you idiot, the guitar. But I think maybe we should keep it."

"Why?"

"Are you totally stupid? The guitar is valuable. The guy insured it. It's worth money, more money than he's paying us to take it. We could sell the guitar and get more money that way."

"What's he gonna do to us when he finds out?" Chad gripped the magazine with the gun even harder and started tapping his fingers on the magazine that covered the gun.

Jeremy thought a moment. "How's he gonna find out? Austin? All Austin has is my phone number, and I'll dump my phone after we take the guitar. He won't be able to call me. All he's gonna know is that I didn't bring it back. He doesn't know where either of us live, so he'll never find us."

"Oh. Okay." Chad continued to tap his fingers, fast, an arrhythmic staccato.

"Stop doing that, would ya? You're driving me nuts."

"Can't help it. You know I can't help it."

"Yeah. I know." Jeremy heaved a sigh. Sometimes Chad could be a burden.

"Where's the money?" Chad shook a little, his whole body full of energy he couldn't control. He started doing his little shuffling dance, a sure sign that he was about to freak out.

Jeremy fished in his hip pocket for the money. He turned away from Chad a little and counted off some bills. He handed them to Chad and quickly stuffed the rest of the wad back in his pocket. "Five hundred. Like I said."

Chad grabbed the bills and held them, no longer shaking or doing his little dance. He looked unsure what to do with the money since he was still holding the gun. He pulled the gun out of the magazine again and waved it in Jeremy's direction. "It looked like you had a lot more than five hundred dollars," he said.

"Hey, I set up the job."

Chad looked from the bills in his hand to Jeremy and back again. "All right." He clasped the gun and the bills to his chest.

Jeremy watched Chad, but in his head he could see a whole other scenario, one in which the guitar was in their hands. His hands. "If we play this right, we can make a lot more than a few thousand bucks. We're definitely going to keep the guitar."

Chad was still holding the cash and the gun, gathered in his arms like he was holding a child. He shoved the cash in his pocket, then put the gun in the waistband of his pants. He kept one hand on the grip, like he was ready to pull it at any moment.

"Watch what you're doing there, Cowboy. You could shoot yourself in the leg, like that football player." Jeremy said

"I've got to keep it handy. For protection. In case," Chad said.

*Great,* thought Jeremy. *Maybe using Chad isn't such a good idea. But I've already paid him. It's too late to go back now.* "All right. But leave the gun here when we go to the job. I don't want anything to go wrong. All we have to do is go there, grab the guitar, then get the hell out of there." Jeremy said. "Do you understand? No gun."

"I understand."

It was then, and only then, that Jeremy saw Chad relax his hold on the gun.

———————

Reuben waited until 9:30 to drive back to the Dutchman. He perched again at the bar, sipping a shot of watered-down whiskey and staring at the worn wood under his elbows. The bartender recognized him from earlier and tried to chat, but Reuben rebuffed his comments. The last thing he wanted to do was get involved in a conversation with someone. He needed to watch the time. He looked at his watch over and over. *A shrink would call me compulsive,* Reuben thought. *What the hell am I doing here? I have a nice life, a good life. If only that damned Alice didn't want the money so fast.*

At 10:15, he went to his BMW. The parking lot was lit with one overhead lamp that gave off enough light to see the outlines of vehicles, but not enough to see their true colors. Reuben popped open the trunk of his car, and made sure the guitar was inside. He turned and was about to go back to the bar when a high-pitched voice said, "Hey, Mister."

Reuben turned to see a small figure in dark clothes standing a few feet from him, close enough to make him jump. The figure's hood was up and he had his hands in his pockets. He was jittering from side to side, like he had to go to the bathroom. "What do you want?" Reuben asked.

"The guitar." Even though it was high-pitched, the voice was male, but not one Reuben could place.

"What?" Reuben was puzzled. *Who is this guy?*

"The guitar. I want the guitar you have in the car."

"No, I... I can't give it to you. I need it."

"I have a gun."

Reuben stepped back. *A gun?*

The small guy pulled his hands out of his pockets and used them both to steady what looked like a long pistol aimed at Reuben's chest.

"You're kidding, right?" Reuben said.

"I never kid about guns." The voice shook as much as the hands.

Reuben knew he shouldn't argue, but he couldn't help himself. "I can't give you the guitar. Someone else is coming for it."

"I warned you. You can't say I didn't warn you. I warned you," the guy sputtered, then pulled the trigger.

Reuben could hear the click, but nothing happened. He laughed in relief.

From two cars away, Jeremy said, "Chad, what the hell! I told you not to bring that thing. You're not supposed to shoot him, just get the guitar."

Chad jittered some more and whined, "You told me he'd give it up. He won't. He won't listen to me. People never listen to me."

Chad kept pulling the trigger and the repeating click, click, click unnerved Reuben. Jeremy came out into the dim light of the overhead and tried to grab the gun from Chad. Chad squeaked and lurched back.

"That's my grandfather's gun! You can't have it!" Chad shouted.

Reuben reached forward and grabbed Jeremy by the chest of his dark hoodie. "What are you doing!" he hissed into Jeremy's face. "This isn't what we planned!"

Jeremy grabbed Reuben's upper arms and held them to keep him from punching out at him. The two of them danced in a circle for a few moments.

Too late, Reuben realized that Jeremy was much stronger than he looked. And that Chad had disappeared from his line of vision.

With a distinct thump, the gun hit Reuben's head. Hard.

# CHAPTER TWENTY-ONE

*"Music Town"*
*West Norriton, PA*
*June 17, 2009*
*1:30 P.M.*

BAKER'S TOP GUITARS IN WEST NORRITON TOWNSHIP was a ten-minute drive from Larrabee's. Valerie liked the look of the area. Mark mentioned that this was a music hub, with a number of music shops lining the streets. She even saw a sign referring to it as "Music Town," although it was not officially a town, but a neighborhood. In addition to the music shops, she saw a florist, a bakery, several small restaurants as well as a cafe, and a convenience store flanked by a pharmacy and a bank.

West Norriton was what Valerie thought of as a typical middle class neighborhood, except for all the music stores. She saw signs for "Clef," "Great Guitars," "First Bass," "Planet Music," and "Instruments of Destruction." The "Harmony Hut" chain had a small storefront there. She even spotted "Whalen Strings," a luthier she had talked to on several occasions.

Located on a side street, Baker's was on the ground floor of a small, two-level business complex flanked by an off-street parking lot. Other businesses on the bottom floor included a computer shop, a Korean restaurant, and a financial planner. The upper level was completely occupied by one business, Ballinger Dynamics.

Pausing in front of the store, Valerie looked in the storefront windows. They were lined with see-through yellowish sheets. "What's that for?" she asked.

"Keeps the sun from destroying the display pieces," Mark explained. "But it's pretty unnecessary since there's nothing to protect," he added, gesturing at the empty windows.

Valerie opened the shop's door and heard the tinkling of a bell above her head. Mark and Rocky followed her in.

There was a dusty, dry smell to the place. *Fresh air does not enter here often,* Valerie thought. Oriental carpets lined the floors and hung on the walls. Although they looked clean, Valerie suspected they were old, contributing to the smell. A handful of guitars were positioned around the room, several inside glass cases. The cases looked like very old department store display units. Unlike Larrabee's, there were no lights in these cases.

Mark pointed to one guitar and said, "That's a Martin. A Pennsylvania-made piece. Probably made in the mid-thirties. Not quite as valuable as the Gibson we're looking for, but darned close."

Valerie leaned over to look more closely at the guitar. She still couldn't quite see where the value was in it.

"This is why I wanted you to talk to this dealer. This is one of the few dealers that I thought might seriously look at the Gibson. They have several instruments here that are on that level. That's why they're all in these cases. See the sensors on the sides?"

"Yes," Valerie nodded. "Security?"

"No, that's up in the high corners." He pointed to the small black buttons with wires attached. "These are for humidity control. It's awfully dry in here, so I'm betting these cases have some sort of humidifiers in the base."

"What's that?" Rocky asked, pointing to what looked to her like a slim oblong box with strings on it.

Mark bent slightly to look at it, then straightened, putting a hand to his back. "It's a lap steel. You hold it on your lap and play it with a metal bar. Some people call them Hawaiian guitars because they were so popular there in the twenties and thirties. From the looks of this one, it's a pretty early model. It might be from around that time."

"You're right," a smooth voice interrupted Mark, and all three of them turned around to see a young man with rumpled brown hair in jeans and a blue checked shirt. His hands were in the pockets of his brown suede vest. He pulled his right hand out and offered it to Mark. "Caswell Baker the third. Please call me Cas."

"Mark Patton."

"From Phoenixville."

"Yes."

"I thought I recognized you. You rebuilt a broken Strat for me a few years back."

Mark nodded. "I remember. Nasty accident."

Cas smiled. "Yes. I still have that guitar, though. It was one my father gave me when I first started playing. Even damaged, I couldn't give it up. Thanks for putting it back together."

"How is it holding up?"

"I get it out of the case every so often and play it a bit, but as you told me then, it will never be the same. Still, I enjoy the memories it brings. I used it when Dad and I played together, and I'll always remember that."

"Your dad's not around?"

"Died in oh-seven. Cancer. Left the business to Mom and me. She died last year."

"I didn't know. I'm sorry to hear that. Your dad was a good man. He knew his guitars. When did he open this shop?"

"Seventy-five. My grandfather died and left him enough money to quit his job and start the business. I wasn't even born then."

"When did you get into it?"

"Dad brought me into the business to help him when I started playing guitar. I guess I was about ten. That's when he gave me my first guitar lesson."

"Wow."

"The business has been good to me." There was a long moment of silence, then Cas asked, "Is there anything you want to take a look at? I'm particularly fond of that Martin. It has a real sweet sound."

"I'd love to, but actually, I'm here with my friends Valerie and Rocky," Mark said, indicating the two women. They shook hands all around. "Valerie is looking for some information on a Les Paul Standard. A fifty-eight."

"They're around. I hear about them every so often. Are you looking to buy? A few days ago I talked to a guy who was trying to sell one at the King of Prussia show."

"Really?" Valerie perked up. "Did you see the guitar?"

"Yes. It was in outstanding condition. A couple dings on the bottom front bevel, some buckle scuffing on the back, but nothing that would impact the value. It plays great.

"I don't see it here, so I suspect that you didn't make a deal with him. Am I right?" asked Mark.

"Yes, you are. He was in too much of a hurry to sell it through me. I tried to talk to him, to explain that a good deal, especially for the money he wants, takes time. I didn't have any buyers for him that minute, but if he had let me make some calls..." Cas shook his head. "I probably could have helped him."

"Did he tell you why he was in such a hurry?" Valerie asked.

"He said he needed to pay his ex-wife money to buy out her half of his house. She was in a hurry, so he was in a hurry."

Valerie and Rocky exchanged glances.

"It's always a bad idea to expect instant money for these things," Cas went on. "Plus, he seemed to have a slightly inflated idea of the value. People aren't going to drop that kind of money without taking time to research the piece and ask some questions."

"Did he give you any indication that he might do something untoward with the guitar? Illegal or... let's say, stupid?" Valerie asked.

"No. But he thought a buyer owed him that much money, and right away. Impatient sort of guy. If I compared him to my average customer, I'd call him an asshole," Cas said with a smile.

"We've gotten that impression," Valerie said, smiling back. "You've been a big help. Thanks. If you think of anything else, let me know," she added, handing him one of Harry's cards with her name written on the back.

———•◦•———

Valerie and Mark, with Rocky trailing behind a couple steps, left the shop. They walked across the open parking lot to go back to Mark's truck, which he had parked on the street. They were almost through the lot when Valerie heard a loud backfire and felt air whistle to the left of her head. Rocky yelled "Get down!" and pushed her and Mark to the ground.

Valerie tumbled onto the ground and heard Mark squawk in pain beside her. She lay very still, listening, her eyes scanning as much of the terrain as she could see. After a few seconds that felt like an eternity, she heard the gunning of an engine and the squeal of tires some distance away. As she tried to get up, Mark moaned. He was sprawled out, half on top of her legs, trying to right himself. Valerie extricated herself from him, but saw how white his face was.

"Are you okay?" she asked, worried, trying to help him sit up.

"I think so." He pushed her hands away. "I just need a moment." He lay there with his eyes closed.

Rocky crab-walked to where Valerie sat next to Mark. "Are you guys alright?"

"Mark's back..." Valerie said, gesturing, then added, "What the hell was that?"

"I think someone shot at us," Rocky hissed between clenched teeth.

"Shot at us?" Mark's eyes opened and this time he accepted Valerie's help so he could sit up. "We ought to get out of here."

"Tell me about it," Rocky grumbled. "But I think whoever it was is gone."

"I heard a car peal out," Valerie said.

"You didn't get hit, did you?" Mark asked, his eyes on Valerie.

"No, I'm fine."

Inside, Valerie wasn't fine and she knew it. She was scared out of her mind. But Rocky was there and she wasn't about to show Rocky how scared she was. Plus, there was Mark, too. She felt responsible for him being there and she was not about to show him her fear, either. *No, there is no weakness in me,* she told herself. *I am tough.*

Valerie carefully half-stood, peering around. "What on earth happened?" she asked. "Who is shooting at us?"

"Let's get back to the truck," Rocky said, tugging her arm. "It's not safe here. Mark, can you still drive?"

"Yeah."

Rocky led them back, moving fast. Valerie had to jog to keep up. Mark hustled unevenly, swearing softly as his feet hit the ground and jarred his back.

Inside the truck, her breath coming in large hiccups, Valerie noticed a piece of paper under the windshield wiper on the passenger side. She pointed it out to Rocky, who slipped out, pulled it away from the wiper, and got back into the truck. Mark turned the key in the ignition.

"How are you doing?" Valerie asked Mark.

"I'm okay. My back hurts like a b... well, it hurts, but I'll be okay." He rubbed it to ease the pain. "I'd really like to know why anyone would shoot at us. It doesn't make sense."

Rocky unfolded the paper in her hands and gasped. In the center of the sheet of paper were two Japanese characters.

"Kanji," Valerie muttered, looking at the paper in Rocky's hands.

"Kanji?" repeated Mark.

"Oriental characters used for words."

"What does it say?"

"I don't know."

Rocky said, "Damage. Or loss. Harm."

Valerie stared at Rocky for a moment. "And you know this how?"

"I used to date my aikido teacher."

"Of course you did," Valerie muttered.

Rocky ignored her and went on. "He taught me how to read kanji. Looks like someone is not happy with you."

"Understatement of the year."

"Have you pissed off anyone recently?"

"Not that I know of."

Rocky checked all the mirrors and windows. "We should get out of here," she said. "I don't want to give anyone another shot at us."

Mark gunned the engine and took off, glancing from the rearview to the side mirrors the whole time. Valerie, haunted, searched the cars that followed them or went by them, watching for guns. They went ten miles before her heart slowed.

"Just take us back to the shop to get Rocky's car," Valerie told Mark. To Rocky she said, "I want to get back to the office."

Mark looked disappointed. "Can I go along? I can help."

"You should take care of your back," Valerie said. "Rocky and I can handle it," she added, hoping she sounded positive.

# CHAPTER TWENTY-TWO

*Paoli Pike*
*East Goshen Township*
*June 13, 2009*
*10:30 P.M.*

**WHEN REUBEN OPENED HIS EYES,** he thought he was dead. Then the headache hit and he wished he was. His head throbbed and his eyes felt like they would explode. It took a few minutes for him to become aware of the car next to him, then the cold seeping into his body from the ground. He moved one arm, then the other. He maneuvered his body until he could sit up and prop himself against a tire.

The world around him came into focus. He remembered Jeremy holding his arms, the thickness of the sound of the gun hitting his skull. He remembered that little guy, dancing back and forth. *He must have been the one that hit me,* Reuben thought.

In a few more minutes, Reuben remembered the guitar.

Pulling himself up slowly, he stood next to the car. The trunk was wide open, illuminated by the lamp in the parking lot and the little light inside the trunk itself. Reuben knew what he would see, but he looked anyway. The case was gone. Reuben sank down to the pavement again. He wanted to cry, but his head hurt too much and his eyes were dry.

After a few more minutes, Reuben looked up the insurance company's number on his cell phone and called. In halting words, he gave them as much information as he could, then hung up.

"Hey, Buddy, are you okay?"

A guy in a cowboy hat and leather jacket was about to get into his truck, but stopped when he saw Reuben.

Reuben tried to think quickly, but couldn't.

"Buddy?"

The cowboy was coming closer.

"Someone hit me," Reuben said, his tongue still thick in his mouth. It was as much as he could put together after all the effort he used to talk to the insurance company. He felt all scrambled. "They took my guitar."

"Yeah?" The cowboy was standing over him now. From Reuben's vantage point on the ground, he looked about twelve feet tall. "How about if I help you back inside? You don't look so good."

"I don't feel so good." As soon as the words were out, Reuben leaned over and vomited, barely missing the cowboy's boots. The cowboy jumped back to give him more room, but Reuben was finished.

"Come on, let me help you," the cowboy said.

Reuben held out a shaky hand and the cowboy helped him to his feet.

"Thanks," Reuben said.

The bartender was pretty nice about it, Reuben thought later. He gave Reuben some ice for his head and called the police for him. Even though Reuben couldn't tell the police much, and wouldn't tell them what he did know, they wrote a report and locked up his car. Then an ambulance came and took him to the hospital in order to have his head checked.

During the ride to the hospital, Reuben annoyed the paramedics until they let him call Tammy.

"Reuben! Where are you?" She sounded frightened. "I've been trying to call you for an hour!"

"Tammy, listen to me. I'm on the way to the hospital. I stopped for a drink and..." his voice cracked, "and someone stole my guitar."

"The hospital? You're going to the hospital? I thought you were headed home. I thought you were bringing me a present."

Reuben, conscious of the paramedics, hissed into the phone, "Listen, Tam! I got hurt. I'm going to the hospital."

"Yeah?" Tammy didn't sound very sympathetic, Reuben thought.

"I got hit on the head. Someone called an ambulance. That's where I am now. They're gonna check me out and then I'll come home. We're gonna have to go back and pick up my car tomorrow, okay? Do you understand me?"

There was a long moment of silence on her end of the line. Finally she said, "Okay."

"Good. Wait until you hear from me. I don't know how long this is going to take."

"Call me as soon as you can," she said.

It took hours for the doctors to check him for a concussion and observe him. The hospital called Tammy to take Reuben home about three in the morning, at Reuben's insistence.

"I was supposed to sell my guitar to Jeremy, this guy Austin told me about," Reuben told Tammy. "Instead some guy with him hit me on the head in the parking lot where I stopped for a drink. I'm gonna have to track Jeremy down if I want my guitar back. I've been calling his cell phone, but he's not answering."

Tammy had been quiet for the entire story. Now she asked, "How are you going to find him?"

Reuben frowned. "I'm gonna call that bastard Austin. And if it's the last thing I do, I'm going to find Jeremy and nail the little rat that almost killed me."

# CHAPTER TWENTY-THREE

*Chestnut Hill*
*Philadelphia, PA*
*June 17, 2009*
*4:00 P.M.*

**WALTER ANSWERED HIS PHONE** on the second ring. "Valerie, I'm so glad you called. I wanted to talk to you about something. I thought…"

Valerie was in no mood for Walter's small talk.

"I got another one of those papers with kanji on it."

"Really? Do you need me to translate it for you?"

"No. The one I got this time was the symbol for 'harm.' Rocky knew what it was."

"Rocky?"

"She works with me."

"She?" Walter sounded confused. "She's Japanese?"

"No, but she knew what it was." Valerie steeled herself to ask, "Walter, do you know where these things are coming from?"

"You think it was me?" Walter's voice cracked. "It wasn't me, Valerie. I have no idea where they're coming from."

Valerie stared at the wall of her office, cradling her cell phone against her ear. "Someone shot at me today."

"What?"

"Someone shot at me," she repeated. "I think whoever is sending me these messages is shooting at me." She could feel fear shift in her chest. She was on the verge of crying and she hated herself for it.

"Are you okay?"

"Yes, I'm fine." Defiant now, tears pressed down. Angry. Back in control.

"Why would they do that?"

"That's what I'd like to know."

"What can I do to help?"

Valerie sighed. Walter seemed genuinely shocked. He was so concerned, and so reasonable, the steam was seeping out of her.

"I'm not sure," Valerie said. "Keep your ears open, let me know if you hear anything around the Center."

"I will do that for you."

"Thank you." Valerie pushed the memory of lying prone in the parking lot away. She was good at that. She had had lots of practice ignoring things that upset her. "Did you say you wanted to talk to me about something?"

"Yes. Uncle Min stopped by the Center to see me this morning. He asked if we would like to have dinner with him tonight."

Electricity shot through Valerie. Uncle Min. Why hadn't she put it together sooner? She thought of her mother and the fact that Walter's uncle had known her.

"Tell him yes," Valerie said.

Walter was quiet on the train ride to Chinatown. Usually, he liked to gossip. He liked small talk. But tonight he was tense and silent.

Once they were on foot, Walter practically pushed Valerie through the diminishing crowds in Reading Terminal Market until they got to Arch Street. They turned sharply to the left on the corner where Fung Insurance Company had a large storefront. Valerie tripped slightly and Walter caught her, apologizing.

"Sorry. Are you okay?"

"Fine. What's the rush?"

"I want to get to Uncle Min's. I know he's waiting for us."

As they turned the corner, Valerie gagged. Overwhelmed by the sound of voices and traffic and the smell of raw fish and vomit, she was glad that Walter was moving fast. She wanted to get out of there, to find cleaner air. Instead, Walter stopped in the middle of the block.

"What?" she asked, pressing her hand over her nose and mouth and talking through her fingers.

"This is it," he said, his lips close to her ear.

The house was inserted between a coffee shop and a clothing store. The clothing store was the kind of shop where the mannequins in the window and the customers who shopped there wore berets and scarves all year long. It catered to young, upwardly mobile Asian youth, some of whom hung about its front doorstep and patronized both the coffee shop on this side and the tea shop on the opposite side of the street.

Walter steered Valerie through the loiterers. They jostled against her and she pulled her jacket closer around her. Walter yanked her up the steps to the door of Min's house, away from the other people.

Walter rapped at the painted door sharply. The door opened a tiny sliver, and Uncle Min's eyes and part of his nose were visible to them.

"Uncle, it's me. I've brought Valerie."

Min pulled open the door enough to let them pass. He closed the door fast, and the only sound was a faint whoosh as if the room was hermetically sealed.

A thin veil of incense hazed the room, obliterating the reeking stench from the street outside. Valerie recognized the scent as jasmine and saw the burner emitting trails of smoke on a low table in one corner of the room. Grateful for the more pleasant scent, she turned her attention to their host.

Min looked like he had just gotten home from work. He wore his white shirt with a dark tie. His pants looked like the shiny suit he wore at Twist. The jacket was gone, though, replaced by an ornate silk robe tied at the waist with a long silk sash that coordinated. A large dragon snarled fire on the back of the robe, its puffed cheeks pulled back from long, glistening fangs. Two lazily undulating designs decorated either side of the front.

Min stood in the center of the room, in the dim half-light of one lit floor lamp, as though not sure what to do next.

Two things occurred to Valerie simultaneously. One, Min was a man who rarely had guests. Two, he was more comfortable in the dark than in the light.

"Uncle?" Walter asked.

"This way," Min said, and led them to the kitchen.

He gestured for them to sit at the table under the garish light of a fluorescent bulb. They were knee to knee, uncomfortably close together. Min offered them tea and allowed Valerie to serve herself from the pot. She set it down and was startled when he held out his cup to her.

To Valerie, Walter said, "Women usually serve." To Min, he said, "She is my guest, Uncle. I will serve."

Walter filled Min's cup, then his own. They shared the tea in silence, then Walter rose to get the food from the stove.

"We will eat first," he told Valerie. "Then we will speak of your mother."

Anxious to hear what Min knew about her mother, but also conscious that Min might be the person trying to harm her, Valerie fought the urge to ask questions. Instead, she studied the food. Min had prepared an aromatic fish soup and tender rice balls that put Valerie in mind of her grandmother's cooking. Even her mother sometimes made dishes like this. There were also crispy meat strips that she didn't recognize. The food was not extravagant, but she recognized the flavors that spoke to her of her distant past. It was all very, well, Japanese, to her.

Herbs from her childhood, long forgotten, stirred her memories. Her grandmother, bending over the stove, inhaling the fragrance of a simmering pot. Her mother, chopping vegetables at the table. Her father, sitting at the table across from her mother, reading the newspaper aloud to her mother and grandmother. Valerie playing with some toy on the floor, something carved from wood, a tiny instrument of some sort. *A piano,* she thought. *Wooden keys.* She was by her father's feet, half under the table.

Valerie blinked and the tableau disappeared. She was left with Walter and Min, both looking into their soup bowls, slurping the soup noisily. She spooned some into her mouth, careful not to spill the thin broth.

Walter finished his soup and slid his bowl to one side. He chewed one of the strips and swallowed. A long period of silence followed before he said, "Uncle, you said you knew Valerie's mother."

"Yes." Min pushed his bowl away and smiled slightly. His eyes sought Valerie's. "Mai and I were children together. In California. In the camp."

"The camp? The internment camp?" Valerie asked.

"Yes," Min said. "My family and your mother's family were friends, from before. Everyone had to go to the camp. They traveled there together with all their possessions, as much as they could carry, in bags or suitcases." Min rose from the table and went into the other room. When he returned, he held a black lacquer box with golden cranes painted on the lid. "This is one of the few things I have from the camp. Your mother gave it to me."

Valerie felt faint. The finish on the box matched her scrapbook. It could have been an accompanying piece. Maybe they were part of a set. She started to reach out to touch the box, but Min pulled it closer to himself and set it on the table.

He lifted the lid and pulled out a photograph and showed it to Valerie. It was a picture of Min and Mai as children, linked arm-in-arm, staring at the camera with goofy smiles on their faces. Young Min held a ball in his free hand.

Min held out the photo to Valerie. She took it, holding it with the tips of her fingers, and studied it. She had a similar photo in her scrapbook at home. This was definitely a picture of her mother.

"Our families shared a house in the camp. Your grandmother ruled your family, as did mine. They bossed everyone around. Our grandmothers fought sometimes, but they agreed that they knew what was best for the rest of us. Mai and I tried to follow their rules. But we were kids and able to slip away. We ran and hid behind other buildings, looking for each other, playing that we were hiding from the soldiers."

"Were the soldiers mean to you?" Valerie asked.

"No. Most of them ignored us and went about their business." Min took the photo back from Valerie. "When our families were released, we went to San Francisco. My family and your mother's. One of the soldiers took this photo of us before we left. He liked us, I think. He gave me the photograph as a gift."

"My mother was in the orchestra in San Francisco when she was young," Valerie said, as much to herself as to Walter and Min. She felt linked to the photo.

"Yes. Our families went there together." Min handed the photo to Valerie. "I saw your mother learn to play the the violin in camp. By the time we left, she was wonderful. She could bring tears." Min used his fingers to make trails on his cheeks. His eyes were glazed and Valerie sensed that he was hearing music that neither she nor Walter could hear.

"We were very young. Eight, I think," Min said. "Your grandmother knew that your mother was talented beyond her years. She looked for ways that Mai could perform for money. Your grandmother arranged for her to play at restaurants, at parties. Anywhere, everywhere. Your grandmother was able to make contacts with white people through Mai. It took time, but eventually Mai came to play with a small orchestra." Min shook his head. "I try to remember the names of the orchestras she played with, but I cannot. I was working by then. I only saw your mother play twice with the orchestras. Once in San Diego, once in Los Angeles. We were older, probably fifteen or so. My mother thought it would be good for me to see her play. It was free to go, the public could watch. Even us."

Walter nodded. "It was unusual for Japanese to be accepted at many functions for Caucasians. Most Japanese couldn't afford the cost anyway, even if they were allowed in."

"Mom was asked to play with several orchestras, according to the articles that she kept. She had a scrapbook," Valerie said. "I still look at it sometimes."

Min nodded. "That's good. You honor her."

"When did your mom move to Philadelphia?" asked Walter.

"After she graduated from high school. At least, that's what Dad said."

"Yes." Min flipped to another photo, this one of a gangly teenage girl with a face like Valerie's. She wore a gown and cap in pale blue. "I had a camera of my own for this. It was a graduation gift from my parents. Naturally I took a picture of your mother. Mai and I were still close then. She was not spoken for. I wanted to marry her, but I had no money of my own. All I earned went to my family."

"You wanted to marry her?" Walter's mouth hung open in surprise.

"Yes. I loved Mai. It broke my heart when her family moved east. But I had nothing to offer. Certainly nothing like Philadelphia had."

"And she moved to Philadelphia and met my father," Valerie said. "But you came here later?"

"I had business here."

"Business?"

"My organization sent me here to work. I was obliged to come here. It was not my choice, but I was glad for the chance to find Mai again."

"And you found out that she was already married to my father," Valerie guessed.

"Yes." Min studied the photo in his hands.

"Did you talk to her?" Walter asked.

Min hesitated. He fidgeted with the photo and shuffled it back into the pile in the box. His eyes were still on the photos. "Yes.

The questions spilled out of Valerie. "What did she say when she saw you? What did you say to her? Was she upset?"

"She was happy to see me, but sad, too. I think I reminded her of the past. She was a grown woman. She had a husband, a child. You. I was not a part of her life anymore."

"Were you angry?" Valerie asked.

Min placed the photo back in the box and closed it. He folded one hand over the other on the box. "No. But I had regret. I think she did, too." His eyes remained on the box.

"Did you see her often?"

Min hesitated. He appeared to struggle with the answer. Finally he said, "Yes. She and I... I involved her in some business."

"What business?" Valerie asked.

"I should not have. I saw her from time to time, right up until..."

"...the accident," Valerie finished for him. "But my father never mentioned you."

"Your father didn't know."

Valerie sat back, staring at Min. "You had an affair with my mother!"

Min shook his head violently. "No! I would never bring shame to your mother."

"Then why didn't my father know? Why were you hiding this?"

"You don't understand. I couldn't tell anyone."

"But why not?" Valerie leaned forward and stood as if to grab Min's hand, but Walter grabbed her first.

"Valerie, don't!"

Walter held back one of her arms, but the other broke free and Valerie wrapped her fingers around Min's wrist and jerked his hand. "Why didn't you..." she started to ask, but then she saw the tattoos, brightly colored and ornate, peeking from beneath Min's white shirtsleeve.

"Yakuza!" Valerie dropped his wrist as though it burned her fingers.

Min pulled his arm back and jerked his shirtsleeve down to cover the tattoos again. His face contorted.

Valerie didn't know much about Japanese culture, but she knew about the Yakuza. They were the lowest of the low, the users, the violent, the criminal element. The worst of Japan, now come to America. She always thought they were a myth. And now the myth appeared in the flesh in front of her.

*Yes, he was in Philadelphia for business, all right. Yakuza business.*

Min grabbed the box of photos and held them to his chest.

"Get out," he said. "I wanted to help you, Mai's daughter, but you betray her memory. Get out!"

"How? How did I betray her memory? By asking questions? By wanting to know?" Valerie shouted at him. "What about you? Were you with her when she died? Did you betray her?"

"That's not how it was!" Min shouted back.

Valerie narrowed her eyes. "Did you kill her?" she asked, her voice dangerous.

Min turned to Walter. "Go! Get out! Take her out of my house!"

# CHAPTER TWENTY-FOUR

*Norristown, PA*
*June 13, 2009*
*10:30 P.M.*

JEREMY CLUTCHED THE WHEEL as he drove from the Dutchman back to Chad's place in Norristown. His stomach churned. He looked into the rearview mirror and saw the black lump that was Chad, huddled in the back seat.

"I didn't want you to hurt him!" Jeremy said through clenched teeth while he drove as fast as he dared on Goshen Road. Not only was he not very familiar with this part of Route 30, he was concerned about drawing too much attention to their car by speeding. The last thing he wanted was for some over-eager local cop to find Chad's gun stashed under the driver's seat and a stolen guitar in the back seat. The first thing he wanted was to put as much space between the Dutchman and them as he could, as quickly as possible.

"We got the guitar," Chad said, patting the guitar case beside him. " like you wanted."

"Yeah, we got the guitar. But I hope for your sake that guy's not dead. If he is, it's all your fault, you know."

Chad went quiet. Jeremy knew Chad well enough to guess that Chad didn't want it to be his fault. He probably simply wanted to go home and watch TV.

"Look, he's probably okay. But you've got to listen to me when I tell you stuff. You can't just do whatever you want. You hear me?"

Chad's head popped up next to Jeremy and startled him. "Jesus, Chad!" he said.

"I'm sorry," Chad said. He sounded like he might cry. "I thought the gun would help scare him."

"It worked," Jeremy said. "It scared us all."

Jeremy remembered the gas station on his left and the feed store at the next curve, so he relaxed his grip on the wheel and eased off the gas. It wouldn't be long until he would be on familiar streets again and the knot in his stomach would go away. He could stay at Chad's for awhile until he figured out what happened to that Cafferty guy.

*I wonder if Cafferty will send the cops after me?* he thought. *I don't want to go back to jail. Maybe I could dump the gun and find a buyer for the guitar. With that kind of money, I could get away, go anywhere. And what if that Reuben guy is dead? I can still dump the gun and find a buyer for the guitar. I'll just have to go further away.*

In his ear, Chad said, "Hey, Jeremy, are you still mad at me?"

# CHAPTER TWENTY-FIVE

*Chestnut Hill*
*Philadelphia, PA*
*June 17, 2009*
*7:30 P.M.*

**THE TRIP HOME FELT LONG.** Valerie was familiar with every footstep, every connection, and every turn, but Walter's anger made him silent and sulky and her own anger kept her from attempting conversation. Although Walter accompanied her to Allen Lane, she rode the last few blocks to Highland on her own.

Valerie arrived home to find the house empty. Her father left a note on the kitchen counter saying he was going out for dinner. She figured some of his Orchestra friends were hanging out together and invited him along.

Valerie was glad he was out because she was concerned that her face would give away her guilt, now that she knew her mother had not been the pure, perfect mate her father thought. The fact that her mother was involved with someone from the Yakuza shocked Valerie.

Thinking about Min with her mother upset her. No, that was too mild a word. It scared her.

The Yakuza were criminals who sported whole-body tattoos hidden under their suits and ties. They talked about their gangs as though they were their families. They had come to California with other Japanese immigrants in the thirties and forties, and they managed to remain viable through the internment camp years. From there they spread east.

Valerie suspected that they were part of almost every large Asian community. Even knowing that, even being warned of that by her grandmother and then her mother—her mother!—until today she believed she had nothing to do with them, that they didn't exist in her world.

Now she knew better. Her own family was tainted, defiled by this man Minaru Nakamura.

Recalling the night she and Walter had dined at Twist, she thought perhaps Akio was a victim, too. She thought about the dark-suited men who surrounded Akio that night, and the fight that broke out. Walter's uncle had been one of those men.

*What did they have to do with Twist? Financial support? Protection? Probably both. At what cost to Akio?*

*And what about Walter?*

Walter was so straight-laced, Valerie couldn't imagine that he knew that his uncle was Yakuza. There was no way Walter was involved in that life, and until now he probably had had no clue that his beloved uncle was a criminal.

Valerie went to her bedroom and sat down at her desk, the desk where she had done homework as a child and paid bills and wrote reports for her job as an adult. She leaned down to the bottom drawer on the left, the one lockable drawer, where she kept her valuables.

She pulled out her mother's scrapbook, the one her mother had given her when Valerie turned thirteen. The cover was lacquered black and gold, two graceful cranes winging their way across the top, over a stylized river with a sampan afloat.

*Just like the box in Min's hands.*

A slot on the front of the scrapbook held a small picture of a young couple that Valerie had always assumed were her mother's grandparents, but she couldn't remember anymore if her mother told her that, or if she had made it up to give herself more family.

Her fingers stroked the smoothness of the cranes.

She didn't spend much time with the scrapbook these days, because it no longer offered her the comfort it once had. Now every time she looked through it, she thought of her mother and Valerie's heart hurt a little more. That was never going to change.

Inside, pages of thick, black construction paper displayed photos tucked neatly into gold photo corners. The first portion of the book contained pictures that Valerie remembered as always being there, pictures of her mother's parents, cousins, and friends. Some had captions her mother had written in white ink.

Valerie stretched out across the bed on her side and flipped slowly through the pages, looking at the boy who appeared in almost all the photos of her mother as a young girl, a boy whom she had never noticed before but was so obvious to her now. *So the boy was Min,* she thought. *He had a solid build, even as a child. He had a round face and looked more Chinese or Korean than Japanese.*

All these years Valerie considered the boy to be someone her mother played with, a forgotten street child. So focused on her mother,

Valerie hadn't realized it was the same boy in every photo, growing up with Mai, gazing at her with adoration, losing her to her East Coast life as surely as Valerie had lost her in the accident.

*Did Mom love him? She must have, to meet with him secretly after she married another man.* Valerie tried to remember what her mom and dad's relationship was like before her mother died, but only came up with dinners at the dining room table where their discussion was formal, with only the occasional tiff over small details of their days. *Had Mom thought her marriage was a mistake? Why had she seen Min more than once? What business of his was she involved in? And what about the accident? Had Min been involved?*

Valerie flipped to the later pages of the scrapbook where she kept the newspaper account. At the time, the accident garnered a certain amount of attention because Mai played for the Philadelphia Orchestra. The Orchestra was beloved there, and by extension, so were their members. A loss for the Orchestra was a loss for the community, for the entire city.

Valerie lay back against her pillows. Unbidden, her mother's funeral popped into her thoughts. Being moved around by her father's sisters because his grief was too great to take time for her, his daughter. His sisters took Valerie by the arm like an invalid, even though at fifteen she thought of herself as adult. Her aunts showed her where to sit and told her what to do.

Stay. Wait. Go see for herself the shell left of her mother.

The pain of remembering the moment she looked into the coffin would remain in her heart forever.

Valerie's father buried her mother following American traditions. She was sure that would have been her mother's wish, because her mother had talked often about wanting to be American.

*Why did my mother dislike being Japanese so much?* Valerie wondered. *Why didn't she talk about the camp, or her parents, or her cousins?*

Once, when an opportunity presented itself, Mai had refused to go to Japan. Valerie remembered her mother saying to her father, "I won't go. I don't care that they want to pay my way. I won't go. They can't make me go." Valerie never learned who "they" were, but she remembered the fierceness in her mother's voice.

Valerie was equally sure that the Japanese community that her mother shunned also gossiped about the choices her father made for the funeral. Valerie heard the words that the Japanese relatives only half-heartedly tried to hide. They called her mother "disobedient" and "rebellious." They pitied Mai's mother, who lost face for having such a willful daughter. They said it was a disgrace that Valerie knew nothing of Japanese ways and couldn't even speak the language.

Valerie was so numb, their words pelted her but caused no real damage. Or so she thought at the time.

Valerie remembered staring at her mother's face in the casket. When mourners came to pay their respects to her mother and comment on how lovely she looked and pray over the body, Valerie had turned away. The face was not her mother's, though it was still beautiful in death. It had a plastic quality that Valerie found distressing.

*It's a fake. My mother is somewhere else, on vacation maybe. She'll come back with presents for me and for Daddy.*

But in her heart, she knew with sickening certainty it wasn't true. There would be no presents. Her mother wasn't coming back.

Valerie sat up on the bed and looked at the newspaper clipping again. The article said that there were no witnesses. Even though she memorized the text long ago, she re-read the article to be certain.

*No witnesses.*

*Lost control of the car.*

*The day after a major rainstorm.*

*A winding road off the Main Line.*

*Rain-swollen creeks.*

*Rising flood waters.*

*Flooded and rutted roads.*

*No witnesses.*

*Except one, perhaps. One that was still alive, still carrying his own guilt, but refusing to speak because of his criminal life.*

A rap on the bedroom door startled her. She flipped the scrapbook closed, feeling guilty.

"Valerie?" said her dad, poking his head inside, his gray hair mussed. "Are you okay? I've been calling for you since I got home."

"Sorry, Dad. Guess I was preoccupied." She shook off the sense of surprise. "Did you have a good time?"

"Yes. My friend Barbara offered to make me dinner."

"Barbara?"

"From cooking class."

"Oh." Valerie tried to remember if he had ever mentioned Barbara before.

Her father nodded at the scrapbook. "You haven't had that out for awhile. What's up?"

"Thinking about Mom."

"Missing her?"

"Every day. Don't you?"

Her dad came in and sat down on the bed across from her.

"Yes, I do." He took the scrapbook from her and held it in his lap, running his fingers over the glossy finish. He studied the cover for a while before he said, "Sometimes I think maybe we should have sold the house and moved away, started over. But I couldn't do it. I couldn't leave the orchestra. They were my family. And I couldn't leave this house. It was our home. You can't change everything at once and I thought that with your mom gone, it would be too hard to bear. I told myself, 'Maybe next year.' But the longer we stayed, the more impossible it was to leave. So here we are, living in the same house," he sighed, "with your mother's ghost."

"I was thinking about how she grew up," Valerie said. "She didn't talk much about her life as a kid. Sometimes I wonder if she had other boyfriends when she was a girl. Do you think she did?"

Her father took a long moment before he answered. "Maybe. Probably. But that was before she met me. We didn't talk about it. We were too busy planning for our future." He handed the scrapbook back to Valerie. "It's natural for you to wonder, I guess, but try not to put too much time into looking back."

*Why not?* Valerie thought. *Why don't you want to look back? What do you know that you're not telling me, that you never told me?*

She couldn't find the voice to ask him, not after all these years. Instead she said, "That's probably good advice. I'd better get some sleep, Dad. Another big day tomorrow."

"Something special going on?"

Valerie decided her dad was better off not knowing the details of her day. "Lots of interviews," she said.

"It sounds like TransReliable all over again."

"It's not. In fact, it's quite a bit different."

"Different, but good?" he asked.

"Yes. At least, I think so," she said.

"Well, don't let the past keep you up too late," he said, nodding at the scrapbook. "Get some sleep, honey."

She gave him her best smile. "Goodnight, Dad."

After he closed the door, she looked through the scrapbook again, flipping the pages slowly. It was a different experience now than before she talked to Min. She stared at the photos and their captions, trying to read into her mother's handwriting. Something didn't feel right.

*What am I missing?* Valerie wondered.

# CHAPTER TWENTY-SIX

*Bryn Mawr, PA*
*June 14, 2009*
*11:00 A.M.*

REUBEN WAS LYING IN BED, BARELY AWAKE. His head was throbbing again. He needed more painkillers. Where had he put them last night when he got home?

"Hey, Sweetie." Tammy was standing over him, wearing nothing but a short, sheer nightie, one of his favorites. "Can I get you something?" she asked.

"A glass of water," he moaned. "And more of those pills they gave me."

Tammy flounced out of the room to the kitchen. He guessed that she expected a different reaction from him. Reuben pushed himself upright and the room spun around him. He waited until it came to a halt, then reached down to get his pants, pooled on the bedroom floor. He dug his cell phone from his pants pocket and punched in a number. When he heard Austin's voice, he said, "Austin, you dirtbag! Who was that guy you hooked me up with? He double-crossed me."

"What? Reuben? What are you talking about? What did Jeremy do?"

"He stole my guitar, that's what."

"I thought that's what you wanted him to do."

"I didn't pay him to get his hyped-up little friend to crack me on the head and send me to the hospital."

"Jeez, Rube, I didn't know..."

"Who is this guy? And how can I find him? He's not answering his phone."

"Hey, I don't know him real well. You said you needed someone to steal the guitar and that's what you got, right?"

"Jesus, Austin! Are you listening? I've got to get that guitar back from him and I have no idea where to find him. Where does he live?"

"I don't know, Rube. He used to live near me, but then he moved to Norristown with his buddy, Chad. Chad Reck."

"Little guy? Blond hair?"

"Yeah. Has some sort of problem, can't sit still."

"That's the little shit that hit me." Reuben said.

"Probably." Austin agreed. "That little shit managed to get the two of them arrested a few years back. Minor stuff, but they spent time in jail."

"Great. Where can I find these guys?"

Reuben waited while Austin looked for Reck's address. Tammy returned with the water and a prescription bottle. She wore a very short silk robe over the nightie. "Here you go, honey," she said, handing him the bottle and a frosty glass of water. "Who are you talking to?"

"Austin. He thinks he might know where the two guys are that jumped me."

"Austin? How does he know..."

"Get dressed. We've got to go get my car."

"Are you sure, Reuben?" Tammy frowned. "The doctors said you should rest for at least twenty-four hours."

Reuben waved her off. "I'm fine. I'll be even better if I can get my hands on those guys."

---

The car was right where Reuben had left it the night before. The trunk was closed, and the car locked. He seemed to remember the police taking care of that for him. He had had the keys when he went home from the hospital, and now, seeing that the car was okay, he felt better. Even though the trunk had been popped, it was intact, as though Jeremy had used a key of his own. The guy was good, even if he was stupid.

*Not that stupid. He's got my guitar.*

"Thanks, Tam. I'll see you later, okay?"

"What are you going to do, Reuben?" There were storm clouds in Tammy's eyes and her mouth turned down around the edges. "I should go with you. The doctors said you need someone to keep an eye on you. Besides, you can't go after these guys by yourself..."

"I can't very well ask anyone to help me, can I?"

"I can help."

"That's a really bad idea, Tammy. Let me take care of this."

She jutted out her lower lip. "I should take care of you."

Reuben leaned into the window and kissed her. "Go home. Wait for me there. That's the best thing you can do."

Tammy glared at him. *God, she was so stubborn!*

"Go on, now." He nudged her arm. "I'll call you."

She sighed. "Okay."

Reuben watched her drive away, then got into the BMW and switched it on. The initial fury he felt for Jeremy and that blond maniac Chad had depleted on the drive here and now, deflated, Reuben's thinking cleared. He wanted desperately to go directly to Norristown to look for the assholes who were responsible for his headache and his missing guitar, but he also knew he had patients waiting for him at work and a meeting with that insurance woman scheduled. He could cancel the patients and reschedule them, but he needed to get the insurance issue off his back. Maybe he could talk to her quickly and then go.

A quick check over the car indicated to Reuben that it was safe to drive, so he turned into the street and headed for his office.

# CHAPTER TWENTY-SEVEN

*Chestnut Hill*
*Philadelphia, PA*
*June 18, 2009*
*8:30 A.M.*

**VALERIE FELT THE CAR'S THUMPING** before she opened the car door. Opening it didn't make things better. Music flooded out of the car, setting Valerie's teeth on edge. To make matters worse, Rocky's fluorescent orange pants and floral print tank top were enough to set off a migraine. She had topped off the outfit with a pair of bright turquoise blue sunglasses with cat-eye frames. Valerie wished she could borrow the sunglasses so she wouldn't see all that orange so clearly.

As usual, Rocky sang along to the music. "Morning, Boss," she said as the verse ended.

"Turn it down!"

Rocky scrunched up her nose, but turned off the song. "Gee, I thought you'd appreciate this one. Duran Duran. 'Hungry Like the Wolf.' 1982."

Valerie pursed her lips and slid into the passenger seat.

"Ooh, you don't look so good, Boss. Long night?" Rocky asked and clicked off the song.

"I'm not your boss," Valerie snapped, then added, "I talked to Walter last night."

"Is he our mystery man?"

"He says not."

"Of course he says not. Do you believe him?"

"I do. He's not the one sending those messages to me, and I certainly don't believe he shot at me."

Rocky slid her sunglasses down her nose. "Are you sure? Why not?"

"Because I know Walter. I've known him for a lot of years. He's a stand-up guy."

"I'd like a little proof of that."

"Why can't you take my word for it?"

"Because he looks like the most likely candidate, to me."

"Well, he's not," Valerie said. "You don't understand."

Rocky took off her sunglasses. "Enlighten me, oh Not-My-Boss."

"There's nothing to enlighten you about. My relationship with Walter isn't any of your business." Valerie ran her fingers through her bangs and said, "Look, Rocky, don't take this personally. Generally, I don't confide in people. It gets you into trouble. People have big mouths and tell secrets, sometimes even when they don't intend to."

Rocky pouted a moment, then said, "I do understand, Boss, but this *is* my business. They're not only shooting at you, y'know. I may be quick when I need to be, but I can't move faster than a bullet. If I'm gonna get shot, even if it's only because I'm standing next to you—*especially* because I'm standing next to you—I wanna know why, and who's doing the shooting."

"Well, for starters, you make an easy target. Look at you!"

Rocky stuck out her tongue. "Leave my wardrobe out of it."

"All right." Valerie sighed. "Walter has a pretty good alibi, and you can check it out, if you want to. He works at the Cultural Center. His uncle, on the other hand, might be our man."

"His uncle?"

"Yeah. Walter and I went to see him last night so I could talk to him." Valerie paused, frowning. "But I found out he's Yakuza."

"What? I thought he was a friend of your mom's."

"Yeah, he was. My mom and Walter's uncle and the rest of their families were in an internment camp in California during World War II."

"Huh?" Rocky looked vacant. "An internment camp?"

"After Pearl Harbor was attacked in 1941, the U.S. government relocated all people of Japanese descent to camps designated around the country so that soldiers could watch them for signs of disloyalty. Most of the people, more than 60 percent, were U.S. citizens. Many were born in the U.S. and had never even been to Japan or knew anyone there. But the government thought there was a chance they might try to undermine the war effort."

"Wow," Rocky said. "How did that affect your mom? Did she talk about it much?"

"No. In fact, she *never* talked about it at all to me. My dad told me after she died."

Valerie paused, seeing Rocky's eyes go even wider.

"Mom died in a car accident when I was fifteen. She met a friend for dinner that night. She was driving home after a bad storm. She was on a rural road and missed a turn."

"Wow," said Rocky.

"They said she lost control and drove into a ditch, a deep one," Valerie said. "After the funeral, I couldn't even get into a car. Even now, it still makes me queasy.

"That's awful," Rocky said. "And that's why you don't drive, huh?"

"Right."

"So, your mom was raised in a camp, but she didn't talk about it. What about your grandparents? Didn't they talk about it?"

"My grandfather died before I was born and Grandma died a couple years after my mom. All I remember of Grandma is that she spoke Japanese and Mom would ask her to speak English." Valerie frowned. "I don't remember what they talked about."

"Why did your mom ask your grandmother to speak English? I mean, my nonna talks in Italian all the time and I understand most of what she says. Why did it matter?"

"I think Mom didn't like being Japanese very much. I guess living in the camp had a lot to do with that. She tried really hard to be very American and discouraged me from learning Japanese. I mean, I recognize some words, but I wasn't allowed to speak it, that's for sure."

"Okay," said Rocky. "This is all really interesting and now I understand some of your weirdness, but I still don't get why you think Walter's uncle would shoot at you?"

Valerie paused for a moment, then forged ahead.

"What do you know about the Yakuza?"

Rocky frowned. "They're the Japanese version of the Family. Sort of."

"The family?"

"With a capital F. You know, the Mafia."

"Right." Valerie squinted at Rocky. "Don't tell me, let me guess. One of your boyfriends was a Yakuza."

"Uh, no. I've seen movies."

"Okay, then I guess you know that generally they're into guns and drugs, but what they are really big into is protection rackets. The night I went to Twist with Walter, I saw these guys in dark suits hanging around, giving Akio, the owner, a hard time. I think they were shaking him down for a payment on opening night."

"Yikes."

"Walter's uncle was there that night. He appeared to be part of the action."

"Double yikes. And you went to visit him?" Rocky asked.

"At his home, yes. Before I left, I saw his tattoos. Oh, and did I mention that most of his little finger was missing? I always thought that finger thing was a myth."

"Yuck," Rocky said.

"It's a bit old-school, but I understand that can happen if someone screws up. They offer up part of their finger to remain in the family, to atone. I don't know why, but that's what they do," Valerie said.

"It has to do with holding a sword properly. It's harder to do when you're missing most of your little finger. You have to depend more on your family for protection," Rocky said.

Valerie stared at her.

"And how do you know that?"

"Movies, remember?" Rocky said. "But what does this have to do with you? Why would he shoot at you?"

"I thought about it all night," Valerie said. "I don't think he's trying to kill me, because he's had plenty of opportunities to do that."

"Right. Like in Music City. We were pretty good targets. If he was the shooter, he needs to have his eyes checked," Rocky said.

"That's what I thought, too. Heck, if he wanted me dead, he could have poisoned my dinner last night. I don't think he's trying to kill me," Valerie said.

"If he's not trying to kill you, what is he trying to do?"

"Maybe he's trying to warn me away from something," Valerie said, pushing her bangs out of her eyes.

"Do you think he might be the one sending those messages? The kanji?" Rocky asked.

"I think it's a pretty good possibility."

"So, what is he trying to keep you away from? And what does this have to do with the Yakuza?"

"Good questions. And I don't know the answers. I can't ask Min because I offended him last night and he threw me out of his house."

"Wow, you must have been a great dinner guest to get thrown out. What did you do?"

"I accused him of having an affair with my mother."

"You did what? Really?"

"Really."

"Is it true?"

"He says not, but I'm still not convinced. I want to ask him more questions, but that's not going to happen at this point. Normally, I would ask Walter to intercede, but Walter is barely speaking to me because I offended his uncle. I consider myself lucky that Walter escorted me home. Well, to the train, anyway. We went our separate ways after that. I've never seen him so angry."

"You know you're going to have to apologize," Rocky said

Valerie bristled. "To who?"

"Walter. Then his uncle."

"Why?"

"Val, I can't believe I have to tell you this, because this is your culture, not mine. You should know this. Walter's a Japanese man, right?"

"Yeah, even though he was born in the US, he acts all Japanese."

"Right. He feels wronged, and by a woman, a Japanese woman, no less. He brought you there and now he's lost face in front of his uncle. You've got to apologize to Walter if you want to get more information. And then you have to find some way to get back into his uncle's good graces."

"Did you get all this from the movies, too?" Valerie threw up her hands. "Look, this isn't my culture. I've never been a part of it. For that matter, neither has Walter!"

"Oh, yes, it is your culture, honey. Yours and his. You should realize that every time you look in the mirror. He certainly does."

Valerie was quiet for a long time. Finally she said, "I hate this. It's everything I have tried so hard to rise above. If my mother saw me do this..."

"What would she do? Disown you? I doubt that," Rocky said.

"No, but she would be disappointed in me."

Rocky reached over and touched Valerie's arm. "Newsflash, Boss: she's dead. And you're not. Let's try to keep it that way."

# CHAPTER TWENTY-EIGHT

*Norristown, PA*
*June 15, 2009*
*2:00 P.M.*

"WHERE HAVE YOU BEEN?" Chad whined as he let Jeremy in. "And where's my gun?"

Jeremy glared at Chad. "The gun is somewhere safe, where you can't do any more damage with it."

"I thought you wanted me to protect the guitar," Chad said from his chair. "I thought it was worth a lot of money." He was watching his ancient TV, fuzzy as it was, clicking through the channels as he got bored. There was a lot of clicking. He got bored easily.

"It is worth a lot of money," Jeremy said. "Too much. Everyone thinks it's hot."

"Good guess, huh?"

Jeremy threw Chad an ugly look. "I thought it would be easier than this. That Reuben guy seemed to think the money was going to fall in his lap after we took the guitar." Jeremy said, then added, mostly to himself, "I wonder if it did?"

"What are we gonna do?" Chad asked.

"You know that place on Cuthbert Street?"

"Those Chinese guys?"

"Some kinda Asian guys, Chinese, Vietnamese, Korean, whatever. I heard they might be interested."

Chad perked up. "Great! When are we going there?"

"*We* aren't going anywhere," Jeremy said. "*You* are going to stay here and stay out of trouble. I'm going to take care of selling the guitar."

"Oh." Chad stuck out his lower lip. He went back to clicking through the TV channels. In a moment, discussion forgotten, his face smoothed and he watched the flickering of the channels with the eyes of a child.

———————————

Filtered light fought its way through the grime-layered windows. Roller shades at half-mast covered the upper panes. The shades gave the room a yellowed look, like stained parchment. A simple, strong wooden table dominated the room, the top covered with distress marks. A few metal folding chairs were scattered about. Two chairs were drawn up to the table, one on either side. On one sat an old Asian man with his arms held near his body and his hands tucked inside the sleeves of his loose-fitting jacket. His head nodded as though he was about to drift into sleep. Jeremy sat on the other side.

A group of five young, beefy guys stood slightly behind the old gentleman, watching Jeremy the way cats watch mice, a pretense of disinterest covering their extreme tension. Their identical black shirts and pants made them seem nearly interchangeable. They stared at him until he looked back at them. And when Jeremy's attention drifted elsewhere, they looked ready to pounce.

Jeremy shifted his weight on the metal chair. It was uncomfortably small for his rangy frame, but he was too scared to say anything about it. He put one hand down beside him, feeling for the guitar case on the floor by his side.

The old man opened his eyes and looked at Jeremy. His left eye was filmy, like the half-cooked white of an egg. "What is it you wish?" he said, his voice thin and tired and higher than Jeremy expected.

"I was told you buy things." Jeremy stared at the old man's ugly eye.

"What is it that you have?"

Jeremy pulled the case in front of him and opened it. "A guitar," he said.

The old man's right eye flickered. "Let me see," he said, holding out a clawed hand with long, pointed nails, in the empty air between them.

Jeremy's instinct was to pull the guitar back to his chest. His hand tightened on it, but he felt it twist out of his possession, courtesy of hands from behind him. Sudden pressure on his shoulders held him in the chair.

The old man caressed the guitar. He examined it with his fingers, searching every curve, careful not to catch his nails on the finish or the strings. "What do you want for this?" he asked.

"$50,000." Jeremy's voice wobbled.

The old man considered, then said, "No. Ten."

Jeremy attempted to stand, but the hands held him still. "It's worth much more than that."

The old man laid the guitar on the table, shrugged, and said, "Twenty."

"Not enough." Jeremy said, emboldened by the haggling.

"That is my offer."

Jeremy shook his head. "Thanks, but no thanks."

He tried to stand, but he could feel hands on his shoulders ready to push him back into the chair. The old man waved off Jeremy's captors.

"You are free to go. When you find no other buyers, come back and we will complete our negotiation."

Jeremy stood and laughed at the old man. His bluff was shaky, but he was determined to see it through. "I won't be coming back," he said and left the room.

The old man closed his eyes, as if ready to return to his nap. The room was still, dust motes floating in the dim light. Eyes still closed, he turned his face slightly so that his soft voice would carry to the group awaiting their orders.

"Follow him. I want the guitar."

# CHAPTER TWENTY-NINE

*Overbrook Farms*
*Philadelphia, PA*
*June 18, 2009*
*11:00 A.M.*

"MS. SLOAN..." DARRYL—OR WAS IT DELMAR?—said, sitting down in his upholstered chair.

"...we are disappointed. We expected that you would have this task..." Delmar—or was it Darryl?—huffed as he stared out one of the windows, cup of tea in his hand. He turned his head toward his brother.

"...completed by now."

"I haven't been able to talk to Dr. Cafferty yet," Valerie said. "I'm headed to see him after I leave here. I promise I'm working on this as quickly as I can."

Their tandem stares now trained on her, Valerie felt her chest constrict. She knew that she had disappointed them. She was glad that Rocky had opted to stay with the car, and not only because Valerie was embarrassed by her own lack of success. It would also make a fast getaway that much easier.

"What is your next step? Do you have any idea..." asked Darryl.

"...where the guitar might be?" finished Delmar.

"I have some leads. Plus, as I said, I plan to interview Dr. Cafferty in person."

Tandem nods as they both considered this.

"See that you get..."

"...this done quickly."

Both brothers turned their gaze to the gardens outside the office window. Hanson appeared at the door, so she knew her meeting with the twins was over and that she was being silently dismissed. She followed Hanson out into the hall.

When they got to the front door, Hanson opened it and said, "Your car is waiting, Ms. Sloan."

Valerie stepped out of the door, then turned and looked back at Hanson. "Are they as hard to work for as I think?"

Hanson raised his eyebrows slightly. "No. Not once you understand that you work their way, and in their time frame, or not at all. Good day, Ms. Sloan."

Rocky revved the engine slightly as Valerie slid into the passenger seat.

"Well, that was unpleasant," Valerie said. The radio was mercifully silent.

"Took you to the woodshed, did they?" Rocky grinned.

"More like being called to the principal's office."

"Ick. Hanson came out to tell me to start the car," Rocky said. "He knew when you were coming out. He said I should be ready to leave quickly."

"How could he know that?"

"Maybe the office is bugged?"

Valerie laughed, but to her own ears she sounded uneasy. "You think?"

"Well, I was kidding, but it *is* sort of spooky, the way Hanson seems to know everything.

"I know." Valerie said. "But that's not our problem. We've got to find that guitar. Now. Because if I don't, I'm not sure what the Lamberts will do. Or what Harry will do."

*And I can't afford to lose this job.*

# CHAPTER THIRTY

*Bryn Mawr, PA*
*June 18, 2009*
*1:00 P.M.*


**DR. REUBEN CAFFERTY'S OFFICE OF DENTISTRY** was surprisingly pleasant, Valerie thought, with feminine touches in the decor: flowers in vases, frilly mauve curtains on the windows, and family-friendly magazines in the magazine rack. The magazines were neatly arranged, not simply thrown on a table in a haphazard fashion. The décor was a bit dated, 90s-era perhaps, but tasteful and calming. Appropriate for the families who made up the clientele.

Valerie, with Rocky behind her, went to the receptionist's window inside the front door. A little plaque on the sill of the window identified the receptionist as Gloria Robards.

"Hello, Ms. Robards. I'm Valerie Sloan, and this is my associate, Raquel Russo."

"Yes, we were expecting you. Let me take you to Dr. Cafferty's office," Robards said.

She opened the door leading to the hallway that connected the inner rooms of the office. The three of them made a right turn and went into an office with a massive wooden desk with a large leather chair and two upholstered chairs in front of it. A small couch covered in a mauve print of tiny flowers dominated one side of the room and framed photos covered the walls. From the size of the outside of the building, Valerie guessed that this room took up about one-third of the square footage. Another third went to the waiting room, so the final third must be the receptionist's office space and the rooms where he saw patients. She visualized them as cramped little boxes, packed with equipment, lights, and exam chairs.

Valerie examined the photos on the wall of Cafferty's office. "Who are all these people? Dr. Cafferty's patients?" she asked.

Robards chuckled. "No. These are people he admires. I don't know all of them, but this is Bob Dylan, and that one is Eric Clapton. The pictures over here are some of his friends. I believe they were his band maybe twenty years or so ago. They recently got together again. The big poster is Dr. Cafferty back in the eighties, when he was in the band."

"He talks about this with you?"

"He talks about them with everyone," Robards said. "He was really proud of his band."

A very young, busty blonde stuck her head and chest in the door and paused until everyone looked at her. Valerie suspected that this was her usual way of entering a room. She seemed to have the technique down pat. Valerie put her in the late-but-still-young-looking twenties, with tanning-bed skin that would not age well.

The blond stared at Rocky for a long moment before she said, "Are you coming back to the desk, Gloria? There are patients waiting." She jutted out her lower lip.

Valerie thought she was trying to look disgruntled or sexy, but it was hard to tell which.

"I'll be right there, Tammy," Robards said.

"Okay." The blonde stormed away, but not before she shot Rocky one last look.

Rocky gave Valerie a "what's her problem?" look, then went back to examining the photos on the wall.

"I'd better get back to my desk," Robards said. "Would you like something to drink? I can offer you some water."

"No, thanks, we're fine. I have a question, though. How many people work here?"

"There's two of us in the office, me and Eileen, she's our clerk. She mostly does the filing. Then there's Tammy, who you saw, and Jen. Tammy and Jen are Dr. Cafferty's hygienists. They do the info updates and clean teeth. Also, there's Dr. Cafferty's assistants, Dawn and Bonnie, who help with the more complex tasks, fillings, dental impressions, those sorts of things."

A masculine voice in the hallway caused Robards to pull herself upright and head for the door. The voice said, "It's good to see you. I'll be with you shortly."

Outside the door, Robards conferred with the voice. "I was making them comfortable," Valerie heard her say. "They just got here."

"Thanks, Gloria. I'll be in my office for a few minutes, then."

Reuben Cafferty was stocky, thick in the neck, but not like a weightlifter, thought Valerie. He was a normal-looking, slightly heavy guy with a dense head of hair and overly white, too-even teeth.

Valerie sneaked a glance at Rocky, who was looking Cafferty over thoroughly, as well. Valerie was curious to hear what Rocky would say about him later.

Cafferty shook hands with each of them as Valerie made introductions. She noted that he took a long time to take in the vision that was Rocky. And no wonder. Before they came into the office, Rocky had added a very snug tailored jacket that matched her skin-tight pants. Buttoned, it gaped over her ample chest. Also, she had replaced her sunglasses with a pair of large horn-rimmed glasses. Since Valerie had never seen Rocky wear glasses until that day, she assumed that they were for effect only.

Yes, Cafferty had plenty to look at. He started with Rocky's breasts, looked her up and down, then settled back on her twin assets. He paid very little notice to Valerie. Taking a seat behind the desk, he propped his elbows on the glossy wooden surface and tented his hands.

*He looks,* thought Valerie, *like a man who likes being in charge.*

Still staring at Rocky, Cafferty said, "So, ladies, what can I do for you?"

Valerie glanced again at Rocky, who, in all her fluorescent glory, ignored Reuben and assumed the persona of a secretary, tablet and pen at the ready.

"I would like to go over the details of the loss of your guitar," Valerie said. "Could you start with a bit of history? How you got the guitar in the first place?"

"Sure. I assume that you know the guitar is a 1958 Les Paul." Cafferty came across as haughty, as if he thought a great deal of himself for owning the guitar.

"Like this one?" Valerie asked, pulling out a photo of the instrument.

"Yeah, that's it. I recognize the number." Cafferty pointed to the guitar's registration number at the bottom of the sheet. "I gave this information to the insurance guy when I insured it in 2006."

Valerie heard the scratching of Rocky's pen.

"But you owned it before that."

"Yeah. I bought it from a guy in 1989."

"A guy? Who?"

Reuben shrugged. "I don't remember his name. He was in a band I went to see."

"That seems odd that you don't remember, since the guitar is so valuable."

Reuben frowned. "The Rays—that's my band—played a lot and things were a little crazy. I bought and sold a lot of equipment back then. Mostly keyboards." He pointed to the poster of himself on the wall. "But I picked up this guitar because it had a lot of cred."

"Cred?"

"The model is pretty famous in the world of rock," he said. "It has a great sound, distinctive. I liked the idea of having it in my collection. I didn't play much guitar at that time. I picked that up later."

"So, you bought this guitar in 1989 from a guy whose name you don't remember and you didn't insure it until 2006. What made you decide to insure it after seventeen years?"

"A friend of mine mentioned it was valuable. Guitars are funny like that. You buy them cheap, and sometimes they become collectible. I found out I was sitting on a gold mine."

"And this friend happened to mention that you might want to insure your gold mine."

Cafferty grinned. "Well, the friend was the lead guitarist for The Rays. He was pissed because I bought this guitar out from under him.

He didn't quite have the money to buy it and I did." He warmed to the story. "I think it chafed him that I had it. A few years ago he mentioned it to me. I think he was surprised that I still had it. He said I should take better care of it than he figured I did."

When Cafferty looked away, Valerie guessed he was replaying the conversation in his head.

"It was sour grapes," Cafferty said. "He didn't know I was really careful about taking it out. I didn't play it much."

"What made you take it out to play now?"

Cafferty seemed surprised by the question. "I've been playing a bit more lately, trying to get back into the guitar. The Rays played in Atlantic City last weekend."

"And you decided to take it there to play."

"Well, no. I used a different one."

"So, you took it out now because..."

Valerie stared at him, waiting. She could see Cafferty trying to come up with a reason. His lips gaped, fishlike.

"I... I took it out because I was thinking about selling it. I took it to the guitar show in King of Prussia."

"I thought you said you really liked having it?"

"I did. I do. But... well, sometimes life circumstances intervene."

"You need money." It wasn't a question.

Rocky's scratching stopped. Valerie saw out of the corner of her eye that Rocky held her pen steady in mid-air.

A bit of dampness appeared on Cafferty's brow. "My wife and I are splitting up. I need the money to pay her off."

"I see. If I may ask, how much were you planning on selling the guitar for?"

"That really isn't any of your business."

Valerie feigned a smile. "Humor me."

"The guitar is worth at least three hundred thousand. I was willing to sell it for two fifty."

"About what the policy would pay."

Cafferty swallowed hard.

"You played in Atlantic City, but you didn't use this guitar."

"I'm primarily a keyboard player," he said.

"Then you came home, unpacked everything, and picked out this specific guitar to sell at the show."

"That's right. The show was the next weekend. On Saturday."

"You took the guitar to the show that Saturday. You stopped at a bar on the way home, the Dutchman. And the guitar just happened to get stolen from your car there."

"Right."

Valerie stared at him long enough that he finally looked away again, his color rising. "All right. We'll come back to that," she said. "Let's talk about the night of the attack. You were at the Dutchman Bar and Grill."

"Well, it's not much of a grill these days, but yeah, that's right."

"The Dutchman seems pretty far afield from both the guitar show and your neighborhood. Why were you there?"

"Meeting a friend."

"Who was this friend?"

"A friend. Look, I told the cops all about this. He has nothing to do with it."

"Did you meet this friend both times?"

"Both times?"

"Yes. The bartender said you were there earlier in the day, around four or five. The same day as the attack which, I believe, occurred after ten."

"Oh. Oh, yeah, right." Cafferty pulled a cloth handkerchief from his pocket and pressed it to his brow.

"Did you meet this friend both times?"

"Well, I... No, actually. My friend didn't show up later."

"Really?" Valerie drew the word out as though she was fascinated. "Did he explain to you why?"

"No. But he had nothing to do with me getting beat up."

"Are you sure? I'd like to ask your friend about that."

"Well, you can't."

"Why not?"

Reuben did the fish thing again. Finally he said, "Because I've been trying to find him and I can't seem to track him down."

"That's quite a coincidence. Does your friend have a name?"

"Jeremy."

"Does Jeremy have a last name?"

Cafferty seemed to think hard to remember the last name. Valerie waited him out.

"Walters. Jeremy Walters."

"Do you have an address for this friend?"

"Ah, no."

"I see."

Rocky's pen scratched away. *She's probably making a note to track down the elusive Mr. Walters,* thought Valerie.

Cafferty shifted in his chair. He avoided Valerie's eyes for a long moment. Finally he asked, "Do you have any other questions? I have patients waiting."

# CHAPTER THIRTY-ONE

*Bryn Mawr, PA*
*June 18, 2009*
*1:45 P.M.*

"WHAT A JERK," ROCKY SAID after they got into the car.

"I think we can make that unanimous," Valerie said. She put her hand on Rocky's arm as Rocky reached for the gearshift. "Don't go yet."

"No?"

"Let's give Dr. Cafferty a little time."

Rocky looked puzzled.

"Cafferty must be worried about his friend Jeremy, the guy who disappeared, especially if he's the guy who took the guitar and bonked him on the head. If Cafferty doesn't know where Jeremy is, he's going to want to find him, and soon, before Jeremy sells the guitar out from under him," Valerie said.

"And he's not going to be able to concentrate on patients while he's worried about where his buddy went. You think Cafferty's gonna go looking for him?" Rocky said.

"Exactly," Valerie said. "Let's see what he does next."

Rocky leaned her head back on the headrest. "Ah, the best part of investigating. Relaxing."

"Not for long," Valerie said. "There goes the patient that was in the waiting room."

Rocky sat up.

"Wow," she said. "Fastest teeth cleaning on earth. He should advertise."

# CHAPTER THIRTY-TWO

*Norristown, PA*
*June 18, 2009*
*1:35 P.M.*

**JEREMY PARKED NEAR A NEIGHBORHOOD GROCERY** on his way back to Chad's from Oriental Exchange. He bought some iced tea and a bag of chips, and sat on the stoop of the house next to the store to enjoy his purchase, the guitar in its case at his feet. He watched the traffic for awhile, then stood up, picked up the guitar case, and continued to walk back to the apartment.

He didn't notice the blue car double-parked across the street, or that the driver shadowed his movements.

Jeremy adjusted the guitar's weight in his hand. The guitar seemed much heavier now, not helped by the added weight of his disappointment.

*I'm never going to be able to get rid of this damned guitar,* Jeremy thought. *I'm going to have it forever and it will be worth nothing. I can't even play the stupid thing.*

He maneuvered the case up the four floors to Chad's apartment and rapped his knuckles on the door in their special code. Chad let him in.

"What happened?" Chad asked, nodding to the case.

"He offered me twenty thousand dollars," Jeremy said, putting the case down.

"And you didn't take it? You should have taken it!"

"Yeah, maybe. But Reuben said it's worth more. I've got to keep trying." Jeremy flexed his fingers. "I'll find someone to take it off my hands."

Chad danced back and forth in front of Jeremy. "What about my gun?" he said, his voice whiny and pleading. "Where's my gun?"

Jeremy huffed. He went to the kitchen, Chad scurrying behind him. Jeremy reached into the little space above the refrigerator and pulled out one of Chad's worn sweaters folded into an oblong package. When he undid the folding, he revealed the pistol.

"My gun!" Chad grabbed it and cradled it in his arms.

"Yeah. Don't kill anybody else with it."

Chad frowned, but continued to clutch the gun to his chest.

A knock at the door made them both jump. Jeremy hustled back into the living room and grabbed the guitar. He hauled it into the kitchen, while Chad answered the door. From Jeremy's vantage point, he could see a large boot blocking the door open.

*Damn*, thought Jeremy. *Chad never put up the chains.*

Two hundred pounds of muscle pushed through the door and knocked Chad to the floor.

Jeremy pulled his body back from the kitchen's door jamb, hiding, then peeked around the corner and saw the face of the man who had pushed his way in. Jeremy recognized him as one of the gang members from Oriental Exchange. The man pulled a knife from somewhere hidden, blade glinting slightly in the late afternoon light. The man's head swiveled in Jeremy's direction.

*Oh, God,* Jeremy thought, *a Ninja.*

The Ninja saw Jeremy and lunged for him, missing him, but Jeremy pulled the guitar case up and between the two of them. The knife glanced off the case, making a scraping sound. The case clattered out of Jeremy's hand and onto the floor and the Ninja leaped onto it. Jeremy bolted for the window, where he knew the fire escape would take him down a couple floors and he would have an opportunity to get away.

Before he got to the window, Jeremy heard Chad coming around, moaning. The Ninja turned back to Chad, the easier prey. Jeremy followed far enough to see Chad hold up the pistol and point it at the Ninja. The Ninja pointed his knife at Chad and the two faced each other in a standoff. Then Chad pulled the trigger, making the clicking noise, and the Ninja plunged the knife deep into Chad's side.

Chad fell to the floor grunting a single low "unh." He laid there, holding his side, blood seeping through his fingers.

The Ninja straightened and looked at Jeremy. Jeremy turned and leapt for the window.

———————

Jeremy waited a few minutes before he sneaked back to the apartment. The door stood wide open, and Chad lay on the floor. Blood soaked into the carpet around him, a wet-looking, dark circle. Jeremy gasped.

"Chad! Chad!"

To Jeremy's great relief, Chad's eyes flickered open. "I'm hurt," he said, his voice barely audible.

"I know, I know. I'll get help," Jeremy said and pulled out his phone. He didn't really want to talk to the police, but...

# CHAPTER THIRTY-THREE

*Bryn Mawr, PA*
*June 18, 2009*
*12:15 P.M.*

*SHIT. THINGS ARE NOT GOING ACCORDING TO PLAN.*

Reuben waited until Valerie and Rocky left the building to ask Gloria to cancel his remaining patients for the day. He shut himself in his office and stared at his hands, flattened on his desk. He needed to do something and do it fast. There was no point in waiting.

———————

"There's Cafferty," Valerie said. "Must be a short workday."

Cafferty's BMW pulled into traffic. A few cars passed, and Rocky pulled out to follow. Cafferty took Montgomery Avenue to Henderson Road, then turned onto Dekalb Pike to go to Norristown. As he turned off Arch Street in Norristown, Cafferty slowed down and turned onto Elm, looking for parking.

"What the hell?" Valerie said when Rocky pulled over near where Reuben parked in front of an apartment building. "What is he doing here?" She watched him get out of his car and, after looking around, lock it.

Rocky settled low in her seat and scoped out the scenery. "Pretty transitional area," she said. "Apartments and closed businesses mostly. No restaurants, if we're here for the long haul. Gonna be hard to find something to eat or take potty breaks."

Valerie called up a map of the area on Rocky's GPS, a handheld unit which had been sliding back and forth on the floor. "There's food within walking distance, a block or two away," she said. "A sandwich shop. Means there's a bathroom, too."

"Can I turn on the radio?" Rocky asked. "Some really great guitar would make this a whole lot more interesting. That's what they do on TV, right? Play a little music to keep you from going to sleep during the investigation?"

"Rocky. No."

"You really are taking all the fun out of this job."

"That's why they call it a job. Fun is not the operative word."

Rocky stuck out her tongue.

"Mature," Valerie said. " be patient, would you?"

———————

Reuben stood outside the apartment door and rapped on it sharply. The unlocked door drifted open and, still standing in the hall, Reuben assessed the room. The air smelled musty, as if no one ever opened the windows. In addition to the room's general disarray, a broken chair lay on its side. Reuben wasn't completely sure, but it looked as though someone might have broken in and thrown things around. A dark stain on the floor grabbed his attention.

"Shit. Someone else killed him before I got the chance," he muttered aloud. He stepped into the room and made his way to the kitchen, careful not to touch anything. There was nothing much to see. No people, no explanations. Worst of all, no guitar.

"Shit," he repeated, and returned to the hall. He pulled the door closed behind him and looked at the two other closed doors in the hallway. He made his way to the first one and rapped on it. "Hello?" he called.

The door opened a tiny crack and an eye looked out at him. He could see that a chain was still across the slit that the door created.

"What do you want?" a creaky voice asked. The sound reminded Reuben of someone who was recovering from serious illness. High-pitched. Thin.

"Do you know where the neighbors have gone?" he asked.

"Don't know. Don't want to know."

The door clicked closed again. Reuben heard the latches, several of them, being thrown. He sighed and moved to the next door.

"Hello?" he said, rapping on the door. *Why don't these places have doorbells?* he wondered.

The door opened a bit. Scared eyes inside the door. Again the chain still hooked across to the door. Even with this tiny sliver of a view, Reuben could see it was a woman.

"What do you want?"

"The guys next door... Do you know them?"

"No, I don't know them." There was a pause while she looked Reuben over. "Why do you want to know?"

"I loaned them my guitar. I'm trying to get it back."

Another pause. Then she said, "There's a blond guy that lives next door. I see him sometimes, but I don't really know him."

"That's the guy. He isn't home right now. Do you know where he is?"

She opened the door a little further, to the chain's furthest extension. Reuben could see a lamp and part of a stuffed easy chair through the wedge of doorway. The chair was sagging. But the carpet on the floor was clean and the room was brighter than Reck's apartment.

The woman hesitated again before she spoke. "I... I think he might have gotten beat up. I heard some thumping, and then later, an ambulance came."

"An ambulance? Where did they take him?"

"I don't know."

Reuben frowned. "Where's the nearest hospital?"

"Methodist?" Her answer was more of a question.

"Thanks for your help, Miss..., uh, Miss...?"

Reuben instinctively reached out a hand as if to shake hers, then realized the door was already closed.

———————

Rocky stared at the building where Reuben disappeared.

"Do you think we should follow him?" she asked.

Valerie frowned. "Not yet. Let's see what happens."

"How can we see what happens from here?"

"Patience, please." Valerie gazed out the window, doubting her own decision. *What if he doesn't come out? Should we go in after him? How long do we give him?* She was still mulling the questions when Reuben came out of the building at a run and, after juggling his keys, got into his car, slamming the door. He pulled out, tires squealing.

"Go!" said Valerie.

# CHAPTER THIRTY-FOUR

*Johnson Memorial Hospital*
*Philadelphia, PA*
*3:30 p.m.*

**REUBEN HAD TO ASK A FEW QUESTIONS** to find Chad Reck in the hospital. According to the receptionist, Reck started out at the emergency room at Methodist Hospital, the victim of a knife wound, but they sent him on to Johnson Memorial for treatment. Reuben parked in Johnson's high-rise parking garage and made his way to the emergency room entrance. Two cops were there, chatting with the woman behind the admissions window. None of them noticed Reuben, so he poked his head into where the patients were waiting for attention.

A nurse bumped into him. "Oh!" she said. "Can I help you? Are you looking for someone?"

"Yes," Reuben said. "My cousin came in with an injury. His name is Chad. Chad Reck."

"Oh, yes, he's here. Let me take you to him," she said, and showed him to the curtained area where a small blond man was curled into the fetal position under a blanket. "Chad? Chad, how are you feeling? Your cousin is here for you."

"Cousin?"

Reuben would recognize the thin, reedy voice anywhere. "Hello, Chad," Reuben said. "How are you doing, Cuz?"

The nurse disappeared, letting Reuben alone with his attacker. Chad's eyes went wide. "Who... who are you?" he asked.

Reuben leaned close to him. "I am the guy you hit over the head the other night," he hissed into Chad's face.

Chad squeezed himself even more tightly into a ball, his arms protecting his midsection. "Don't hurt me," he bleated. "I didn't mean to hit you. I was scared, that's all. I thought you were going to take the guitar away from us."

"You and Jeremy,"

"Yes." His voice penetrated the air like a blade, high and keening. "Don't hurt me!"

Reuben wanted to punch him, but seeing how small Chad was in the light of day, and knowing that he was already hurt, took the pleasure out of it. Instead, Reuben said, "Your neighbor told me there was a ruckus in your apartment and the ambulance came for you. What happened?"

"Me and Jeremy were just sitting around. Then some guy knocked on the door and when I saw who it was I tried to keep him out, but the guy got in and tried to kill me. He had a knife. He... had a knife."

Chad was crying now, real tears, and shaking horribly. Reuben actually felt sorry for the little guy. But it crossed his mind that Chad was like Reuben's mother's chihuahua, tiny and trembling, but not afraid to bite you when you glanced away.

"Where's Jeremy?" Reuben asked.

"I don't know. I haven't seen him since the ambulance came and picked me up."

Reuben thought about the apartment building he'd been to. He remembered seeing an open window in the kitchen and figured there must have been a fire escape there. That must have been how Jeremy got away. "Does he have the guitar?"

"I don't think so," Chad said, hiccoughing between words. "The big Chinese guy took it."

"Big Chinese guy?"

"The guy that broke in."

"Okay," Reuben said. "If you see Jeremy, you tell him to call me. I'm not pissed or anything. I just want to get the guitar back."

"Okay,"

Reuben slipped out of the curtained area and headed for the exit. As he stepped out, Reuben saw Jeremy heading into the Emergency intake area.

Jeremy's eyes bugged out when he saw Reuben. He turned and ran across the access road to the parking garage, but Reuben was right behind him and running faster than even Reuben thought possible. Reuben grabbed Jeremy's arm and let gravity throw him to the ground.

"Where the hell is my guitar?" Reuben yelled.

Jeremy popped back up again and threw a punch at Reuben's face. Reuben ducked and lunged for Jeremy's midsection. The two went down together, Jeremy trying to find purchase to hit Reuben, Reuben using his weight to hold Jeremy down. When Reuben got the opportunity, he clobbered Jeremy on the nose, and Jeremy let out a high-pitched whine.

Jeremy collapsed in on himself, rolled into a ball, and wrapped his arms around his head to protect his nose. Reuben grabbed Jeremy's shoulders and shook him over and over, shouting, until he realized that Jeremy was either too hurt or too terrified to talk. Reuben shoved Jeremy away from him, hard, and pulled himself upright, straightening his clothes.

"Get up," he growled at Jeremy.

Jeremy peeked through his arms. When he was sure Reuben wasn't going to punch him again, he struggled to stand.

"Where is it?" Reuben asked.

"I don't know."

"What do you mean, you don't know?"

"Some guy broke into my friend's place and took it. He stabbed Chad."

Reuben's eyes narrowed. "I heard. So, someone else did me the favor. Who was it?"

"I don't know."

Reuben grabbed the front of Jeremy's shirt and pulled him close. He pulled back a fist as if to strike Jeremy again.

Jeremy, still holding his hands over his nose, turned his face away from Reuben, eyes closed, waiting for the blow. "I think I know who he works for. Oriental Exchange. I talked to them about the guitar. They buy stuff all the time."

"A pawn shop?" Reuben still held Jeremy's shirt in his fist.

"They don't call it that. They're a shipping company."

"They ship guitars?"

"I guess. I know they buy them."

"You're sure that's who has it?"

"Yeah. Well, pretty sure."

Reuben's cell phone jingled with the song "Brick House," and he pulled it out of his pocket muttering, "Not now." He shoved it back in his pocket, grabbed Jeremy by the arm, and said, "Let's go, asshole, you have work to do."

⁘

Outside Oriental Exchange, Reuben pulled Jeremy close to give him instructions. The blood had congealed around Jeremy's nose thanks to repeated applications with a paper towel from the trunk of the car. Only one of his eyes was starting to bruise.

"Okay, when we go in there, you do the talking," Reuben said. "You tell them we want the guitar back, and if they comply, we won't talk to the police."

"The police? Are you gonna call the police?" Jeremy's eyes went wide.

"No, you idiot. I just want them to think I will."

"Oh," Jeremy said. "Oh, okay."

Reuben shoved Jeremy. "Get going. Let's get this done."

Jeremy gulped audibly, but pushed through the front door of the warehouse. The hallway led to the right past one office, then left past two more offices off a long hall. At the end of the hall a set of steel double doors with rubber-gasketed upper windows opened into the main area of the warehouse. A stairway to the second floor rose to the left of the doors.

In the warehouse, the second floor was open to the first, finished with a rim of flooring that could hold materials for storage. The second floor was low, half the height of the first floor, a simple mezzanine. Skids of boxes shrink wrapped for shipping were stacked on the second floor, skids with loose boxes sat on the first floor near a wrapping contraption loaded with frosty-looking heavy plastic on perpendicular spools. Off to the far right were two loading bays, with thick plastic sheets covering the opening inside large garage doors.

The doors themselves were closed. In the far left corner of the warehouse was another small door, leading to a room that could be used as an office or a storage area.

Their footsteps muffled in the dusty warehouse, Jeremy led Reuben to the extra room where earlier Jeremy met with the milky-eyed Asian about the guitar. The room was deserted now. Jeremy stopped in front of the table where his discussion with the old man with the funky eye took place earlier.

"Where is the guy you told me about?" demanded Reuben.

"I... I don't know."

Reuben grabbed Jeremy's arm. "What kind of fool do you take me for? You'd better come up with that guitar real quick, asshole."

A voice behind them said, "Are you looking for Mr. Itoh?"

Reuben and Jeremy whipped around to see who was talking. It was a young girl who looked about 16 years old, her dark hair woven into long braids. She was dressed in a red knitted dress with black tights and boots that came up to her calves. She carried a black backpack in one hand.

*She looks like she's coming home from school,* thought Reuben. The students who came to see him after school often carried their backpacks that way, using the handle instead of the straps.

Her dark eyes stayed on them. "Mr. Itoh isn't here. He went to the docks to check on a shipment."

Reuben elbowed Jeremy, and Jeremy said, "We have some business with Mr. Itoh. When will he be back?"

"I don't know. Maybe in an hour or so."

"Do you know which dock he went to?" Reuben asked. "Maybe we could meet him there."

The girl cocked her head slightly. "I don't think he'd like that."

"Are you his granddaughter?"

She laughed. "No. He works for my dad."

"Did your dad go to the docks with him?"

She nodded. "He said I should wait for him here."

"What about your mom?"

"She's working." The girl's eyes shifted from Reuben to Jeremy and back again. "My dad will be here soon," she said.

"I see." Reuben stepped toward her.

She pulled the backpack up, closer to her chest. Reuben took another step, and she backed through the doors and disappeared.

"Shit," Reuben spat out. "We should've grabbed her."

Jeremy looked at him as though he was crazy. "You don't know what you're getting into," he said. "If her dad is Mr. Itoh's boss, you could get yourself killed."

"Not if I have his daughter. Let's go see if we can find her."

Jeremy shook his head. "I didn't sign up for kidnapping," he said.

"It's not kidnapping. I'm not taking her anywhere. I just need to find her and hold onto her."

Reuben was already looking around the doors to try to find the girl. A movement above his head caused him to crane his neck. He saw a puff of dust and heard a footstep.

He knew where she was.

"Wait here," Reuben told Jeremy, keeping his voice low.

Reuben stepped out into the hallway, looking for the door to the second floor. Finding it, he scaled the steps as quietly as he could. It opened into the area above Jeremy. The girl was across the open space, behind a full skid, against the outer wall. Her eyes followed Reuben's every move.

"What's your name?" he called across the open space. He could see Jeremy craning to look for the girl.

"Suzume." Her voice was so soft, Reuben could barely hear her.

"That's a pretty name. Suzume, you don't have to hide from us. We are going to wait for your father, too. Why don't you come downstairs and sit with us?"

"No, thank you."

*Well, she's polite,* Reuben thought. He shifted his weight and started to move to his right. First one step, then a second. She skittered away into the darkness behind the skids.

"Jeremy!" Reuben hissed between clenched teeth.

Jeremy moved further into the center of the room and leaned back so he could look up.

"Come up the stairs. Stay by the door. I'll steer her in your direction."

Jeremy nodded and Reuben heard him move up the stairs. When Jeremy's shadow became visible at the door, Reuben went toward Suzume again. By staying against the wall as Suzume had done, he was able to negotiate a path around the skids. He had to be careful of his head because he was much taller than the girl, but the skids were placed near the inner edges of the upper deck floor, and he was able to move around them.

Reuben saw Suzume watching him. She skirted the edges of the skids, then paused to check his progress. Jeremy still blocked the door, the only door to the first floor. When Suzume got near Jeremy's spot and Reuben closed in on her, she huddled near the wall. Reuben smiled to himself. She was all but in his hands.

He reached out to grab her, aiming for her arms. She scrambled around him, a skid still blocking Jeremy from her path, and leaped from their level to the first floor. She landed in a rolling tumble, using the backpack to help break her fall, kicking up dust in airy swirls around her. She scrambled up and through the door to the hallway before Reuben could react.

"Imbecile!" Reuben barked at Jeremy. Reuben cracked a knee on one of the skids as he went for the door. He fell over Jeremy hurrying down the stairs to the hallway. When they got to the street entrance and looked for the girl, she was gone.

"Shit." Reuben whacked Jeremy on the shoulder. "It was easy. It was all you had to do. Just grab her."

"She jumped! What was I supposed to do? Jump after her?"

Reuben was about to answer when he saw the six young Asian men in black clothes coming toward them. They moved together, eyeing Jeremy and Reuben. The speed of Reuben's heart increased exponentially with each of the thugs he counted in front of him.

———————

On the street, next to a fire hydrant, Valerie and Rocky parked so that they had a full view of the Oriental Exchange parking lot and the door that Cafferty and the scruffy young man with him had entered.

"I've heard of these guys," Valerie said. "I can't believe that Cafferty was idiotic enough to work with them. They'll never give him that much money for the guitar and if he tries to borrow any money from them, they'll charge him interest forever."

"Hey, what's that?" Rocky pointed in the direction of the building's entrance. A young girl raced out, followed a few seconds later by Cafferty and his ragged companion.

A black SUV with tinted windows pulled up in the parking lot and six young men looking to be in their twenties got out. The young girl ran to them, pointing and yelling in a shrill voice. Valerie didn't understand a word of what she said, but she saw guns being drawn.

"Boy, is she upset," said Rocky.

"No kidding. I don't know what she's saying, but I know it's not good."

Valerie's eyes were trained on the group in the parking lot as though if she could see them better, she could hear them better, too.

"What are you doing here?" one of the young men asked in forced English.

"Waiting for Mr. Itoh," Cafferty replied.

"What is your business?"

"Guitars."

Their leader, smooth-cheeked and beefy, looked at Reuben strangely, then looked more closely at the scruffy guy with him. The leader conversed with the other men in another language, then pointed Cafferty and his sidekick back into the building.

The girl stood between the last two men to enter the building. She was not frightened now, she was angry. Valerie could see her glare, even at this distance. Her eyes glittered.

"Hey, Suzume? How are you doin'?" Reuben called to her.

In a string of high-pitched, unintelligible words, Suzume rattled off a stream of what Valerie guessed were epithets. *Jeesh. What's her problem?* Valerie thought. The two guys beside the girl actually had to hold her back from attacking him. Reuben and his friend were hustled into the building ahead of the young men and the girl.

"Ooh, that wasn't good," Rocky said. "They tried to kidnap her."

"They what?"

"That's what the girl was saying. They were trying to pick her up and take her away."

"How do you know that?"

"I speak a little Japanese."

Valerie slapped her forehead with her palm. "But *of course* you speak Japanese. The aikido boyfriend?"

Rocky tried to look innocent, but she nodded. "And I guess you weren't kidding the other day when you said you don't know Japanese, were you?"

"No. I was not kidding," Valerie said and waved a hand at the retreating group. "Let's go see what we can do about this."

Valerie and Rocky let themselves into the building, the door sliding noiselessly into place behind them. The latch caught with a slight click. They could hear voices down the hall, so they moved cautiously, looking around every corner and into every window as they went. At the end of the hall, outside the doors to the shipping floor, they paused and listened to the conversation.

"But we didn't want her! We wanted to get the guitar back and get out of here. That's why we were waiting to see Mr. Itoh," Cafferty shouted as though the men couldn't hear him.

The leader looked at his phone. "He should be here soon. Why don't you sit down while we wait?"

One of the young men dragged two folding chairs out of the corner to the center of the room. Cafferty and his sidekick sat down on the chairs, eyes flicking from side-to-side as they tried to watch everyone at once. The sidekick started to say something, but Cafferty told him to shut up. The two remained silent while the gang conferred a distance away from them.

Rocky motioned to Valerie that she couldn't hear and that she was going up the stairs to the second level. Valerie followed her. They sneaked through the upper doors into the storage level. The gang's voices penetrated the gloom.

Rocky leaned over to get close to Valerie's ear. "They're talking about getting rid of the doctor and his friend."

"Getting rid of... like, killing them?" Valerie felt her chest constrict when Rocky nodded.

"They're not going to wait for Itoh."

Rocky moved to the other end of a skid, then came back.

"Go downstairs. Stay by the door. I'm going to distract them. You get Cafferty and his buddy out of here and meet me at the car."

Valerie looked at Rocky as if she'd gone mad, but Rocky was already positioning herself by a small shrink-wrapped skid of metal boxes. Valerie crept down the steps and waited.

# CHAPTER THIRTY-FIVE

*Oriental Exchange*
*Philadelphia, PA*
*June 18, 2009*
*5:00 P.M.*

**SHINY SILVER BOXES EXPLODED** and thin metal tubes shot through the air and rolled around the floor of the shipping area. The gang members scrambled to avoid the projectiles and fought to keep their balance. Cafferty grabbed his sidekick and headed for the double doors to the hallway, which Valerie conveniently opened for them. Cafferty's eyes went wide when he saw her, but she hissed, "Follow me!" and to her amazement, they did.

Valerie pushed through the front entrance of the warehouse and ran down the block to the car. She propelled herself into the car as Rocky opened the driver's door. The guys whipped open the back door and jumped in, falling over each other. The engine was already running. Rocky jammed her foot on the gas.

As they drove away, Valerie swore she saw the angry glitter of the young girl's eyes as she stood shaking her fists in front of the warehouse.

Rocky drove like an even crazier woman than Valerie had ever seen before. She zoomed down alleys and side streets until she was blocks away from the warehouse and positive no one was following them.

"We've got to get back to the office," Rocky said. "Harry needs to know about this. I don't want that gang to find out where we are. Harry can find us a place to go."

"Really?" Valerie squeaked.

"Yes." Rocky threw her an annoyed look. "Pull yourself together, Val. We got them out of there. Safe."

Valerie took a moment to breathe, then turned around to face their passengers. "What the hell was all that? Who has the guitar? And who the hell are you?" she added, pointing a finger at Jeremy.

He looked shaken. "Jeremy Walters. Who are you?"

Cafferty glared at her. "She's the insurance investigator who has been following me."

"Yeah, the insurance investigator who pulled your butt out of a very bad place, Bucko. You should thank her," Rocky growled, eyeing him in the rearview mirror.

"I was negotiating."

"Yeah, right. Negotiating yourself right into the river. Those guys had no intention of waiting for Mr. Itoh. You're freakin' lucky Valerie was following you."

"When did you start kidnaping kids?" Valerie asked.

"Huh?"

"That's what they were about to kill you for. What did you do to that kid?"

"Nothing! Honest! She happened to see Jeremy and me there. I was trying to talk to her."

"Yeah, right," snorted Jeremy. "You wanted me to grab her."

"I wanted to have some leverage." Cafferty had that look on his face again, the one that said "I'm in charge," even though he wasn't.

"Instead you almost got yourself and your buddy killed." Valerie turned around and closed her eyes. She didn't know which was worse, scrutinizing Cafferty and Walters, or watching Rocky drive.

"What about my car?" Cafferty whined. "My car is parked back there."

"Oh, for crying out loud," Rocky grumbled.

———— ⚬⚬ ————

At the office, Harry opened the door and let the quartet in, locking the door and closing the blinds behind them. "How's the job going, Valerie?" he asked as she passed him, and winked.

"We have a few wrinkles to work out." Valerie said and recounted how they had followed Cafferty, how the situation at the Oriental Exchange developed, and how Rocky pushed the skid down onto the lower floor to divert the attention of the gang from Cafferty and Walters. She finished with, "And now we need someplace to stash these two until we can deal with the guys at Oriental Exchange."

"I'm not sure we can do that," Harry said, unfolding a couple of chairs that he kept for unexpected visitors.

"*This* is your office?" Cafferty asked. "I thought you'd work out of some high-falutin' lawyer's place. Or some high-rise. Not some hole in Philly's back alleys." He started to laugh. "What crap." Then, almost as an afterthought, he added, "I want to get my car back. You have to take me back there."

"We're not taking you anywhere," Rocky said.

"Sit down," Valerie said.

"And shut up," Rocky added.

"You can't force me to stay here," Cafferty said, but grudgingly seated himself on one of the folding chairs. Walters followed suit.

Rocky rummaged in her desk. She found a pack of gum and offered silver-wrapped slivers to their guests. Cafferty turned up his nose, but Walters took a piece. When Rocky offered her a piece, Valerie shook her head. Rocky then unwrapped and popped a piece into her own mouth. "Dinner," she said, aiming the comment at Valerie.

"Well," Harry said, facing Cafferty and Walters, "you two seem to be in a bit of trouble."

"No, we're not," Cafferty said. "You're in trouble because your employees interfered with our negotiations with some businessmen – and they forced me to leave a very expensive car behind. I fully expect you to retrieve said car and let us get back to our business."

"This business you speak of," said Harry. "Would that have to do with your guitar? The one you are trying to have the insurance company pay you for?"

Cafferty stared hard at Harry.

"Maybe."

"This is all my fault," Walters interjected. "I didn't mean to let it get away from me."

Harry's eyebrows lifted. "You let the guitar get away from you? I thought it was his guitar." Harry jerked his thumb at Cafferty.

"They came and took it."

Cafferty grabbed Walters' arm. "Shut up, you idiot!"

"Ow!" Walters said and pulled his arm away, rubbing it.

"Who came and took it?" asked Harry.

"This gang," Walters answered. "The one at Oriental Trading."

"They took it from you. How did you happen to have it?"

"I got it from him," Walters said, pointing at Cafferty.

274

"At the Dutchman?" asked Harry. "In the parking lot?"

"Yeah," Walters said.

Cafferty threw up his hands, "You are so stupid!" he said.

"Settle down," Harry said. "Let's think about this. It didn't sound like the good folks at Oriental Trading were going to cough up your guitar, am I right?"

"I guess not," Cafferty allowed.

"And you provoked them with whatever was going on between you and the girl."

"I suppose."

"It sounds to me like your best bet at this moment is to go home, get some rest, and let us continue to investigate and see if we can get your guitar back."

"What about my car?" Cafferty sneered.

"We'll work on that, too," Harry said. "You stay away from Oriental Trading. We'll handle the details. Rocky, how about if you give these guys a lift?"

Rocky frowned, but nodded.

"Come on, you two. Let's get out of here."

---

After Rocky left with Cafferty and Walters, Harry steered Valerie toward her office.

"Why don't you sit down for a moment," Harry said, gesturing to the chair behind her desk. "It sounds to me like you had a full day."

"I suppose so," Valerie said and sat down in her desk chair.

Harry sat on the chair in front of the desk, facing Valerie. He rolled his pencil between his hands for a moment.

"How are you doing with the case, Valerie?"

She could feel her energy shutting down a bit, after all the excitement at Oriental Exchange and racing back to the office. She took a deep breath.

"It's been interesting."

"I bet."

"It's certainly not exactly the way I pictured it."

"New jobs never are."

She wondered what he was looking for. "I never thought this job would be so, uh, physical."

Harry chuckled a little. "When people talk about insurance, they always think of the paperwork. But what we do is investigation. It can be simple, yes, paperwork, phone calls, internet searches, interviews. But sometimes it's chasing people across a parking lot."

"Or dropping a skid of metal cans on someone's head?"

"Well, that's a new one. But leave it to Rocky to do something I've never heard of."

"Yeah. Rocky." Valerie sighed deeply. "I don't think I handled it very well. Rocky took charge. If it hadn't been for her, I don't think Cafferty and his buddy would still be alive. And that would have been my fault."

"There's no point in playing the 'what if' game. The point is they are alive. Rocky didn't indicate there was any problem."

Valerie could feel the decompression setting in. Unexpected tears were welling in her eyes. "There were guns. We could've gotten killed."

Harry's face remained impassive. "Guns are never a good thing."

"I felt..." Valerie tried to speak, but the word caught in her throat. "I felt helpless."

"Do you want to learn how to handle a gun? I didn't expect you to need it on your first case. As soon as this is wrapped up, I'll take you to the range myself."

"I'm not sure I can do that." She leaned forward a little. "I mean, I'm not sure I can do *this*." She waved her hands around the office. "I think it may not be for me." She wiped her eyes, angry with herself, first for being weak and second for revealing that weakness to her boss.

"Valerie, listen to me. I've worked with you long enough to know that you do have it in you. You need to believe in yourself and your strengths. All you need is a little training. You'll be fine."

Valerie shook her head, not completely agreeing with him, but at least her anger at herself dried up her tears.

Harry stood up. "When Rocky comes back, have her take you home. Sleep on it. See how you feel in the morning. Things always look different the next day."

———•••———

The ride home had been quiet. Even Rocky seemed bothered by the memories of the day. They played no music and didn't talk at all.

At home, Valerie lay across her bed, staring at the ceiling. It was still fairly early in the evening. She wasn't sleepy. Sleep would be a long time coming.

Valerie wanted to get home, but now that she was here, she felt unsettled. She wanted a distraction.

She thought about the case. She couldn't think about anything else. She wished she had someone to talk to, someone who could stand outside the situation and tell her what to do.

When she worked for TransReliable, it was all so easy, so normal, so laddered. You took step one, then step two and three, and eventually you had an office and people asked for your input instead of telling you what to do. There were no decisions on who should be helped, no decisions about people with guns. You did what the corporation wanted.

Valerie was glad her dad wasn't home. If he had been, she would have talked with him, but he would be mortified that his "little girl" was in a dangerous situation. She could try talking to Walter, but he was probably still angry with her. No, thinking about the case and deciding what to do were her responsibility.

Valerie heard buzzing across the room. It was her cell phone, which she had tossed into her tote bag on the way home. It stopped buzzing. A minute later, Valerie heard the ping of a message being left on the phone. She pulled herself up off the bed and looked for the phone.

The message was from Rocky. "Hey, Val, I can't sleep. Call me."

At first, Valerie thought the last person she wanted to talk to was Rocky. After all, Rocky was the one who was the real trouper. *She was the one with the good ideas. She was the one who knew martial arts and could speak Japanese. Why didn't Harry make her his partner instead of my driver?*

Still, curiosity got the better of her.

"Hey Rocky, still awake?" Valerie said when Rocky picked up.

"Yeah. Hey, have you eaten? I finally remembered that we never had dinner. I thought maybe we could get a burger and a drink somewhere."

Valerie was about to turn her down when the picture of a sizzling hot burger and an icy cold beer leaped into her head. *Yeah. I could do that. Even with Rocky. Better than staring at the ceiling.* "I haven't eaten yet. A burger sounds good."

"I'll pick you up in ten."

———————•••———————

Valerie and Rocky sat at the bar, drinking their beers and waiting for burgers. Rocky had changed from her secretary outfit and now wore dark pants and a butterscotch sweater. She was also wearing a chocolate brown wig styled into a bob, and her bright green eyes were perfectly framed by the thick fringe of bangs. It was a dramatic improvement over her usual look. Two different guys had hit on her already. She sent them away, but they bought her drinks in spite of their frustration.

"You look great," Valerie said.

"Thanks. Sometimes I want to see what my real hair color looks like."

"Yeah, well, it's working in your favor."

*Some women have that thing,* Valerie thought, *the one that draws men. The thing I don't have. Since Rocky sent those guys away, she must be on a mission. I'm guessing that mission must be me.*

"So, what's up, Rocky?"

"What do you mean?"

Rocky looked so innocent, Valerie almost laughed out loud. "C'mon, I know I'm not your first choice of dinner date. Did Harry send you to talk to me?"

"Well, sort of, but I also wanted to talk to you about Oriental Exchange. Normally, I would do that before we got back to the office, to go over what happened, but we didn't get a chance. Before we left, Harry told me he thought you were having second thoughts about working with us. He called me after I got home to ask what I thought about working with you and I told him."

Valerie cringed inside. She knew what kind of "boss" she had turned out to be. She was rude, thoughtless, and ultimately weak. She could imagine what Rocky had to say.

Rocky took a long sip of beer, then added, "After I talked with him, he asked me to tell you what I told him. So I called you."

"Let me have it," Valerie said and looked deep into her beer, unable to meet Rocky's eyes.

"I like working with you."

It took a moment for the words to register with Valerie, but when they did, she looked up at Rocky. "You do?" And then, without thinking, she added, "Why?"

"Because you're smart. You're quick when you need to be, but you don't rush things. You look at a situation carefully before you act. And you know when to step back and let someone else do the dirty work."

Valerie took a sip of beer, letting this sink in.

Rocky went on. "Okay, you may not know everything there is to know about being an investigator, but you know a lot. You can learn the rest. Plus, you're pretty good about dealing with all that unknown stuff that comes up. I mean, how could we know how ugly the Exchange was going to get, right? Like an idiot, I didn't even have my gun on me. And I know better."

"You... you carry a gun?"

"All the time. Well, most of the time." The color in Rocky's cheeks gave away her embarrassment. "I left it in the car. Sorry."

"I didn't know."

"I should have been protecting us. I didn't do a very good job. When we got back to the office, when you were talking to Harry, you made it sound like I did good. Thanks."

"You don't need to thank me. I thought you were great. I never would have thought to do what you did. I'm not even sure I would have had the courage to go into the Exchange if you hadn't been there."

"We're actually pretty good partners," Rocky said.

"I guess so." Valerie couldn't believe she was actually saying this aloud.

"Even if I play music too loud in the car."

Valerie laughed. "Yeah."

The burgers arrived, thick, juicy patties of Angus beef, a hefty slice of tangy sharp cheddar, topped with lettuce, onion, and tomato, and a quarter section of a tart deli dill pickle on top. A long toothpick with curly cellophane frills held it all together. A little dish with pristine white mayonnaise came with it, and on the side, a salad slathered with the bar's house dressing. Between them, a huge basket of crispy hot fries drained on absorbent paper.

Although she had a tender spot in her heart for fine dining, Valerie loved the taste of a bar-room burger, hot off a fifty-plus year old well-seasoned grill.

"Oh, man, this is unbelievable," moaned Rocky after her first bite. "When you said you knew where the city's best burgers were, I thought you were kidding. If God struck me down tonight, I'd die a happy woman. I'm gonna have to hit the gym for days to undo this damage."

"I'm glad you like it. This is comfort food for me, I guess. When things went well at work, while I worked at TransReliable, my friends used to come here to celebrate."

With a jolt, Valerie wondered where all of those people were now. So many of them had been laid off before her, and she hadn't bothered to stay in touch. She wondered if she really had friends among them. She certainly didn't treat them that way.

Rocky peered at her from under the shade of her bangs and said, "So is this a celebration?"

Valerie thought for a moment before she said, "Yes, I think it is. We didn't get hurt, and we got the client out without him or his buddy getting hurt. I'd say we should celebrate. We'll deal with the rest tomorrow."

# CHAPTER THIRTY-SIX

**BY THE TIME THEY GOT TO THE OFFICE** the next morning, Valerie and Rocky had hashed out their plan. It was simple and direct: confront Itoh and get the guitar back from him.

Rocky was dressed in leather today, with her gun snug against her, hidden inside her jacket. Her streaked hair was teased into a bouffant, near-punk look. Valerie had to admit to herself that Rocky really looked badass in this outfit. As though to complement Rocky's look, Valerie had chosen to wear slim-fitting pants with a tunic top, also in black. *We look very ninja,* she thought, *except for Rocky's hair.*

Rocky called Oriental Exchange and set up the meet. They arrived at the warehouse half an hour later, parked in the lot this time, and went inside. One of the young guys met them at the door and escorted them to the back office. Valerie expected to be surrounded by gang members again, but they were not in evidence. She didn't hear anything other than the scuff of her soft-soled shoes on the warehouse floor, as well as the click of Rocky's boots and the shuffle of the young man's flat leather shoes.

As they made their way through the skids and into the back office, Valerie remembered the sound of the skid hitting the floor, scattering the wires everywhere. The wires were gone now, any evidence erased by the fresh marks of a broom. There were also tracks from what Valerie guessed was a skid truck, but these were mainly in the center of the floor. They were wide and marked a criss-cross pattern in the wood shavings and dust of the area. From the movements they outlined, it looked as though a number of skids had been shifted since yesterday's visit. In fact, the place looked a lot emptier. Valerie suspected that she and Rocky had constituted a security breach and the stock had been moved.

*So, where's the guitar?* she thought.

Valerie entered the back office. Sitting at the table in the dusty room was an old, round man with little hair. He wore a thick, plain gold kimono over dark trousers and shoes that looked like leather slippers. She could see them under the table. His belly bumped up against the table, pushing it forward when he breathed. A tea service was laid out in front of him, with three cups in a line. The only physical force in evidence was the young man who had shown them in and he looked more like a servant than a bodyguard.

The old man's eyes appeared closed, but he opened them as Valerie took the chair opposite. His left eye was a milky white color that made her recoil slightly. He coughed and the table, the tea, and the cups rocked.

The old man gestured to his teapot. "We do not often have visitors here. Would you like tea?" His voice was thin. She had to focus on his lips to understand him.

Tea was the last thing on Valerie's mind, but she thought about Walter and Uncle Min and the value of sharing tea with a possible opponent.

"Yes, please."

He poured a cup for Valerie and another for Rocky. He sat back and waited for them to respond.

Valerie lifted her cup and said, "Thank you." She sipped the tea, all the while thinking she was probably drinking poison, since she didn't see Mr. Itoh drink any of his.

Mr. Itoh watched her, then poured a bit of the tea into his own cup and drank it. It was only at this point that Rocky picked up her cup with both hands and drank.

*She's even more suspicious than I am,* thought Valerie.

"What is it you seek?" asked Mr. Itoh.

"The guitar you took from my client."

"The gentlemen who visited me yesterday? He and his friend are your clients?"

Valerie put down her teacup. "My companion and I are insurance investigators. One of the gentlemen had his rather expensive guitar stolen from him. He would like it back."

"Are you suggesting that I stole it from him?" Mr. Itoh tilted his head back and laughed. The sound was similar to his cough, and shook the table in the same way.

"I don't know how you acquired it. I do know that you have it."

Mr. Itoh held his hands palm up. "Where? Do you see it here?"

"No."

"Then how do you know I have it?"

"The other gentleman said that it was taken from a friend of his by one of your employees."

"Which one? I would be glad to let you ask him." Mr. Itoh's face crinkled up from smiling. His milky eye was barely visible, lost in the folds of flesh on his face. When Valerie didn't answer him, his smile disappeared and in a more serious voice, he said, "I think you must be mistaken. We have no guitar."

"I'm sure you could find it if you looked around. There are lots of boxes here that may be big enough to hold a guitar." Valerie paused. "Although I think there are fewer to choose from today than yesterday."

"And if we find this guitar, what are you offering for it?"

"Nothing. The guitar does not belong to you. My client has ownership papers."

"Ah. It seems to me that, if we had a guitar, it would be ours, not his. Papers? Papers mean nothing to me."

"No, but the papers mean something to the police. Perhaps you would like to explain to them why the guitar is in your possession."

The laugh crinkles left his face. "I am willing to see if I can locate your missing guitar. And if I find it, I will let you know."

"I need to know soon," she said.

"I like to be thorough."

"I like to close cases. So do the police."

"We do not need the police," Mr. Itoh said. "I'm sure that I can find this guitar and we can come to a settlement. My friends might be able to find it for you fairly quickly." He gestured to his servant, who removed the teapot from the table. "But we need to discuss the price."

"I have no money to offer you. I am merely trying to retrieve the item."

Mr. Itoh sat back, folding his arms over his belly. "I understand you are the daughter of Mai-Ling Yoshida."

Valerie started. Heat flooded her face. She caught Rocky turning toward her.

"Yes. She was my mother." *How does Itoh know about her?*

"Your mother was a lovely woman. It is too bad she died so young. You look very much like her. I wonder if you have the same skills that she did."

"Skills?"

"Yes. Your mother was, let's say, useful. Helpful. She tried very hard to make sure that information was given to the right person."

Valerie stared at him. "I have no idea what you are talking about."

Mr. Itoh nodded. "You were a child. Perhaps you didn't know. But I thought by now-" He coughed, stomach and kimono heaving in a slow, shuddering vibration. When it passed and he regained his breath, he said, "I also am looking for something. Perhaps you can help me find it."

"What's that?"

"Information. I believe your mother knew where it was. Perhaps you can find out what she did with it. Without attracting, shall we say, the attention of other parties?"

"What kind of information? What other parties?"

Mr. Itoh gazed into his teacup, then at her. "Let's call it financial information."

Valerie considered this. "So, this would be a ledger book of some sort?"

"Not exactly. Perhaps something less noticeable. Perhaps something smaller. Perhaps microfilm."

"Microfilm? How old is this information, anyway?"

"The last person to see it was your mother."

Valerie thought her heart stopped. *My mother. Microfilm. Itoh.* "If this is old information, why is it so important?"

"Like your guitar, it is a matter of ownership. The microfilm, the information on it, belongs to my family. I merely want to get it back for them. Like your guitar."

Valerie tried to put the picture together in her mind, to figure out what her mother had been doing with microfilm of a financial nature, particularly since that information belonged to Mr. Itoh.

*My mother.*

*And a Yakuza leader.*

*And a car accident.*

*And Uncle Min.*

*And Walter.*

*Oh, no.*

Valerie picked up her teacup. She could see the slight tremor of her own hands and quickly lifted the cup to her mouth to sip, careful to steady it against her lower lip. She needed to wrap up this talk and get out of the building, away from Itoh, to figure this out. She needed to talk to Harry, to Walter, to Uncle Min. She put down the cup.

"I think we can help each other," Valerie said at last.

# CHAPTER THIRTY-SEVEN

*Berwyn, PA*
*June 19, 2009*
*10:45 A.M.*

"ARE YOU NUTS?" ROCKY EXPLODED as soon as they got into the car. She accelerated before Valerie could fasten her seatbelt, shouting at Valerie the entire time. "He's a gang boss! You are crazy to think he's going to help you. What on earth was your mother doing, mixed up in all this? Why didn't you tell me?"

"I didn't know about it!" Valerie yelled back. "She died when I was fifteen. I didn't know anything more than it was a car accident."

"A car accident? She was probably knocked off by the Yamaguchi-gumi or the Goto-gumi, or some other gang. Great! No wonder people are shooting at you! We need to go to the cops."

Valerie had to concede that Rocky was probably right.

*If it was true.*

"Look," Valerie said, "I didn't know about any of this until Itoh told us. Let me think. First, there's the bit about my mother. How did he know her name?"

"She either worked for him or for someone he knew," Rocky said.

"Or he's trying to get me off his back by throwing her name around."

"Unlikely. Why would he care about you unless he could get something from you? The idea that he can use you to find that microfilm makes sense to me. That would be a good reason to make a deal. So, where is it?"

"I told you, I don't know anything about this," Valerie snapped. "I have no idea where the microfilm might be."

"Did your mother give you anything? Something she might have asked you to keep for her?"

"Good grief, Rocky! I was fifteen! Nobody trusted me with anything back then. Do you really think Mom would have given me something this important?"

"What about your dad? Maybe she gave it to him?"

*Dad. How can I bring this up? He's going to think I'm out of my mind. Unless he's involved, too. And doesn't want to talk about it.*

"I don't think so." Valerie tried to think logically. "He's never acted like he was hiding anything important from me."

"Like you would remember." Rocky's voice dripped sarcasm. "Let's ask him."

Valerie could picture Rocky confronting her dad with this, blurting out her questions. *He'll have a heart attack.*

"Let me handle my dad."

They fell silent. Valerie's brain spun wildly. All she could think about was how her mother had never wanted her involved in anything related to her Japanese heritage.

*Why? Was Mom really involved with the Yakuza?*

Valerie couldn't bring herself to believe it. It didn't make sense. *But Itoh knew her mother, at least by name. How? When did he first know*

290

*about her? He acted like they worked together somehow. And what about Dad? What did he know?*

Valerie asked Rocky to drop her off at home, suggesting they go to the office later. Valerie wanted to see her dad, talk to him, and settle this. Her mother couldn't have had anything to do with the Yakuza. Valerie was positive about that.

Her dad was out. He left a note for Valerie, saying he was having an early dinner with friends from his cooking class and he would see her later that evening. Frustrated, Valerie called Walter. When he didn't answer his cell phone, she called his work number.

"What do you want?" Walter still sounded angry. Getting his cooperation was going to be difficult.

"I wanted to ask if you would see me for a few minutes."

"That doesn't sound like a good idea to me."

"I have some questions to ask you about my mother."

His sigh was audible.

"It's always about your mother, isn't it? What makes you think I know anything about your mother? You must be mistaking me for my uncle and I doubt he wants to talk to you, either. Why don't you go ask your father?"

Valerie felt the jab. She ignored it so she could plunge ahead. "He's not here. Look, Walter, I had a meeting today with someone else who says he knew my mother. I wanted your opinion of his information."

A heavy silence greeted her. She forced herself to wait it out. At last, Walter said, "All right. Where are you?"

"At home."

"I'll come over after work. I should be finished here around five."

291

"Okay. I'll be here. And Walter? Thanks."

She jumped when the phone slammed in her ear.

---

Walter had been to the house a few times, but never alone with Valerie before. She brought him into the kitchen and offered him a beer, which he refused, or a soda, which he accepted. He didn't say much, answered her small-talk questions with one-word answers, and didn't look happy to be there.

"I know you are angry with me," Valerie said after they sat down on the stools at the island in the kitchen. "I want to apologize for not understanding your uncle's reaction to me, for pushing too hard about my mom. But today something happened that makes me think I really need to talk to your uncle again."

"You must be joking."

"No. I met with a guy today that I think was a Yakuza boss."

Walter's face went from angry to astonished to suspicious in mere seconds. "And now you want to talk to my uncle. Because you think he's Yakuza. Here. In America."

"Come on, Walter. You know he is."

"What does this have to do with your mother?"

"The guy I met knew her name. He seemed to know something about her, but it was something that I can't picture when I think of my mom."

"Like what?"

"That she was passing information for the Yakuza."

"The Yakuza don't allow women."

"And you know this because-?"

Walter's brow was still furrowed, his lips curled. "I read about it."

Valerie banged her hand on the countertop. "Come on, Walter! Get a grip! You might think you can fool yourself into believing that but you are never going to fool me. Did Uncle Min tell you that?"

"No. I really did read it."

"Good grief. Did you ever ask your uncle about his life? What he does? Who he works for?"

"No. I was told not to ask him questions like that."

"By whom?"

"My mother."

"And do you think she knows what her brother does?"

Walter gulped. "Probably. But we follow tradition. We don't ask those questions. It's best that way. There's nothing you can do about it, so you don't ask questions."

"There's nothing you can do about it? Oh, please. You might follow tradition, but the only person it's best for is your uncle. Your mother has managed to keep you quiet and out of his way."

"If I draw attention, if I ask questions, my uncle may be in danger. Have you thought of that?" Walter snarled. I'm trying to keep Uncle—and the rest of my family—safe. I don't want them to end up like your mother."

Valerie flinched.

"You knew. You knew all along and didn't tell me," she said.

"What would have been the good of that? It would have put you in danger, too."

"What about my dad? Did he know?"

"I don't know."

The doorbell rang and both Walter and Valerie jumped.

"Who's that?" Walter whispered.

Valerie checked her watch. "It's Rocky. I didn't realize how long we've been here." She went through the living room to let her in.

"Hey, Boss. Ready to go? You weren't on the curb."

Valerie pulled Rocky into the house and pointed at Walter, who was staring at the new arrival. And no wonder. Tonight's look was tacky rocker chick, with shredded jeans, a snug tee with Bon Jovi emblazoned on it, and a red military style faux-leather jacket that clashed with her hair's strawberry streaks. "Rocky, this is Walter."

"Hey, Walter, nice to finally meet you. You're cuter than Val said you were." Rocky stuck out her hand and shook Walter's enthusiastically.

Valerie glared at her. "I'll be ready in a minute. Wait here." She turned back to Walter and said, "I really need to talk to your uncle."

"Why should I help you?" he sneered. "What's in it for me?"

"The chance to do the right thing. If not for me, for my dad."

"For your dad? He may not even know..."

"And maybe you can help me keep it that way."

Walter pressed his lips together. "All right. I'll see what I can do."

---

In the car, Rocky was singing along to Bruce Springsteen's "Dancing in the Dark." She had already told Valerie that she wasn't much of a Springsteen fan, but she liked this song for some reason. When Rocky went on to explain the pros and cons of her choice, Valerie tuned her out. At some point, the explanation over, Rocky started to sing along again.

It was dusk and the streetlights were starting to come on. Valerie wondered how she could convince Uncle Min to confide in her, when her cell phone buzzed. She shushed Rocky and picked it up.

"Walter. I didn't expect to hear from you so soon."

"Uncle says he'll meet with you."

"Great. I'll give Rocky directions to his house."

"No, not there. He wants you to meet him at a place outside the city, up the Main Line. Do you know where the Wet Duck Inn is?"

"No, but Rocky has a GPS unit."

Rocky pulled the little handheld GPS unit from the side pocket of her door and gave it to Valerie. It sputtered to life and Valerie punched in the address from Walter while she held it in her lap.

"Will you be there?" Valerie asked Walter.

"No. Uncle told me not to come. He wants to talk to you alone."

"All right. And Walter? Thanks. I owe you."

"Yes. Yes, you do." The phone clicked in her ear. Yeah, he was still mad at her. But at least she was getting a second chance to talk to Min.

Valerie programmed the address into the GPS and Rocky followed its instructions. As they got further out onto the Main Line, clusters of houses replaced city blocks, followed by areas that were fenced instead of tree-lined.

Valerie noticed that Rocky was not her usual breezy self. She had stopped singing, turned off the music, and appeared to concentrate on the road. The GPS announced turns as they came to them and although she followed them, Rocky kept checking the rearview mirror. "I think we're being followed," she said.

"What makes you say that?"

"The van behind us has been making the same turns we have for the last three turns."

"Maybe it's Min."

Rocky speeded up. "And maybe not."

The GPS unit chirped, "In five miles, turn left."

Valerie glanced at the rearview mirror outside her door. She watched as the van speeded up as well. Rocky slowed down. So did the van. When the car came to a clear passing area, Rocky stuck her arm out of the window and motioned for the van to go around her. The van didn't respond.

The GPS woke up again. "In 500 feet, turn left."

As Rocky made the turn, Valerie saw that the road changed from macadam to concrete. Two lanes, yes, but the weather had been hard on it, and because it was a minor road, little repair had been done. The tires rumbled as they hit a number of small potholes in the road. Rocky maneuvered to avoid them, but the road was not wide enough to give the car much space.

Valerie tried to watch where they were going, looking at the dwindling number of houses around them. This road took them further and further away from civilization. She saw horses in a field to her left and corn in a field to her right. They passed a barn across the two-lane highway from a house, but the GPS was silent.

The van suddenly picked up speed behind them and made a run for their back bumper. Valerie could only watch as Rocky tried to outrun the van, without luck. The van's extra-wide front bumper made contact and Rocky's little car fishtailed slightly.

Valerie thought she might throw up. Instead, she said, "Let's find somewhere to turn off!"

Rocky said, "Where? There's no place to go!"

Rocky was right. A fieldstone wall was now to their left, and the cornfield had dropped down about six feet from the right side of the road, exposing a deep embankment. No side roads, no barns, no houses. The sound of the van's engine behind them increased again.

Valerie braced for the hit. To her credit, Rocky held the car as steady as she could. The GPS interrupted with "In three miles, turn right."

Valerie looked into the mirror again and saw something odd. It was another pair of headlights. She stared, trying to make out the vehicle. "Rocky! I think there's another car back there!"

Rocky craned to look in the rearview, then the mirror on her side of the car. "I see it," she said. "I hope it's the cops."

Valerie knew that, without any lights to indicate otherwise, the extra car was more likely additional reinforcements for whoever was behind them. She stared into the mirror, willing the third car to hit a siren or blinking red and blue lights, anything to scare off the van.

*C'mon, c'mon, c'mon.*

"In one mile, turn right."

"Will you turn that damned thing off?" Rocky growled.

Valerie snapped the power button to the off position and tossed the GPS aside. It slipped onto the floor. Valerie ignored it and looked into her side mirror. The van was bearing down on them yet again.

"Look," Rocky said. "Lights." Then she added, "Brace yourself."

Valerie glanced at Rocky, but rather than brace herself, she went soft and limber. Rocky started weaving the car back and forth, making it harder for the van to anticipate what they were doing. Valerie forced herself to remain limp, her eyes on Rocky, waiting for the hit.

The lights marked what looked like a large driveway. Rocky swerved sharply into the driveway at the last possible second. The van flew past them with the third vehicle following at high speed close behind.

The driveway curved up a long hill. Rocky followed the curve while maintaining speed. She found a little paved niche and pulled over. She immediately turned off the car's lights but kept the engine running.

"What the hell was all that about?" Rocky asked.

"Looks like we may not make our connection tonight," Valerie sighed.

"You think Min set us up?"

"Don't you?" Valerie was both annoyed and angry. *Paybacks are a bitch,* she thought.

Rocky picked up the GPS from the floor in front of Valerie and stuffed it into the storage bin between their seats. When she did, the thing clicked back on and blurted, "Recalculating."

Rocky gave an exasperated grunt and looked for the power switch. Before she found it, the GPS added, "Drive straight for two miles."

Valerie and Rocky looked at each other.

"We seem to be on the right road. Going in the right direction. Maybe we should keep going, what do you think, Boss?" Rocky grinned.

Valerie grinned right back at her. "Boss agrees," she said.

# CHAPTER THIRTY-EIGHT

*Goshen Road, Malvern, PA*
*June 19, 2009*
*7:45 P.M.*

**THE WET DUCK INN WAS HARD TO SEE** in the fading light. Valerie could make out a low structure, surrounded by a small parking lot crowded with cars. She could see people at the entrance, smoking, the door occasionally opening to either swallow or regurgitate patrons.

Inside the building, the bar was lit by neon lights proclaiming beer names. Two bartenders, both 30-ish and lean, worked ceaselessly to supply the jostling crowd with drinks. At the tables on either side of the bar, low lighting and faux candles on the tables attempted an intimate atmosphere. Rocky pointed to a small spot where they might insert themselves to get served, but before that could happen, Valerie felt a hand pulling her arm.

"I have a table over here," Min said in her ear. Valerie grabbed Rocky and pulled her along as they squeezed their way to a dark corner with a tiny table and two chairs. A young man waited there, holding the table for them, but Min slipped him some cash and he disappeared into the crowd. Min directed Valerie to one chair and took the other himself. He looked at Rocky, annoyed.

"I thought you would be alone," Min said.

"I need Rocky with me," Valerie said. "She's my driver. And my partner."

"I'll get us some drinks," Rocky said, and propelled herself back through the crowd to the bar.

Min and Valerie sized each other up across the table. To Valerie's surprise, Min was wearing jeans and a cotton shirt with a casual tan jacket. He looked like all the other guys in the bar but a little more substantial. No shiny suit. No ornate silk robe. He fit in, even if he was a little older than the clientele's general demographic.

*Oh, and there is that Japanese thing,* she thought. *You can never hide that face or those eyes. Or that scar.*

"You wanted to talk to me," Min said, his voice even and smooth, no residue of the anger he showed two days earlier.

"First, I want to apologize," Valerie said. "I was very rude to you in your own home."

Min shrugged. "You were shocked. I over-reacted." He waved a hand in mid-air. "It is important to forgive."

"Thank you," Valerie said.

"You have more questions."

"Many. What was my mother to you?" Valerie asked. "How did she get mixed up in your business? Who is Mr. Itoh? How does he know my mother? And who is shooting at me?"

Min shook his head and pulled a pack of menthol cigarettes out of his pocket. He lit one, and drew on it slowly, savoring the smoke. "Americans. You want everything, right away."

Valerie laughed and to her own ears, it sounded bitter. "You're the only person who has ever called me American."

"Your mother would be happy about this. She wanted you to be American."

"I know she did. I don't think she knew how tough it would be with a face like mine."

"She knew very well how difficult it would be. She spent her own life trying. I understood, but I wasn't as strong."

"When did you become a Yakuza?" Valerie asked.

"After your mother moved east. I was eighteen. I was still in California. I couldn't find a job, and the Goto-gumi used me for deliveries.

"The Goto-gumi?"

"The Yakuza family I work for. At first I didn't know what I was delivering for them, but I found out it was drugs, methamphetamine. And money. By the time I found out, it was too late for me to break away. I knew too much." Min shrugged. "I needed a job. They took care of me."

"And Mom didn't know."

"Not until I came east, years later. I made a mistake in California. It was small and the Goto-gumi sent me to Hawaii. Not for discipline, but for learning. They moved me to Japan as I proved to be more trustworthy."

"But you made another mistake, right? It must have been something big, to lose a finger." Valerie pointed to his right hand, missing most of its little finger.

Min slid his left hand over to hide the right. "Yes. I paid for my mistake. I will tell you, in due time."

Valerie didn't like bargains, but she was curious. "So, you came back to the States after you were in Japan?"

"Yes. I was in New York for a few years. Then the Goto-gumi moved part of the business into Philadelphia and I was assigned there. I learned your mother was there. It didn't take long to find her."

"But she was married. You chased a married woman."

"It wasn't like that. I knew she was married, but I needed her help."

"You needed her help?" Valerie sat back, confused. "For what? She was a concert violinist and a housewife. What could she possibly do to help you?"

"I needed her invisibility."

"To blend in? You asked a violinist?"

"Yes. She drew attention for her music, not for her other activities." Min focused on the table, unable to look into Valerie's eyes. "I asked her to keep something for me until I asked for it back."

"Drugs?"

"No," he said, and irritation showed on his face. Valerie guessed she was about to make him angry again, so she tried another direction.

"You were hiding something from the Goto-gumi?"

"Not from the Goto-gumi. From the American authorities. From the Yamaguchi-gumi, also."

"What was it?"

"Photos and paperwork that showed Goto's business involvement with the Asano-gumi. Proof that Goto was moving part of the business to America. The books showing Goto's investment in land here and the distribution of money in order to profit by that property. I had no idea that anyone would guess that she might have it."

Working with a rival family. Money-laundering. Real estate fraud. Valerie felt sick. "And you gave this information to my mother."

"Yes."

"But my dad and I went through all her things when she died. We saw no such papers."

"No papers. Microfilm. I don't know where she kept it. She said that she told no one, but that she put it where she could get it at a moment's notice whenever I needed it again. She was afraid for me."

"You said that someone guessed she had it. Who?"

"It doesn't matter who. They were doing their job. Your mother had an accident and she died." Min choked on the words, but stopped short of tears. "Because she was trying to help me."

It took Valerie a minute to register the full impact of his statement. Finally she said, "Someone in the Goto-gumi."

"I don't know."

Valerie wanted to hit him. She grabbed onto the sides of the table to keep from doing it. "She didn't lose control of the car. She was run off the road, the way Rocky and I almost were tonight."

Min stared at her. "You were run off the road?"

"Not quite, but close. You didn't send them?"

"No. Why would I do that? You might be able to tell me where to find the microfilm. Why would I take the chance to hurt you?"

As angry as Valerie was with Min, she thought he might be telling her the truth. She took a deep breath. "My mother. What actually happened? How did she die?"

"We were supposed to meet here. The Inn was called Jonah's in those days. It's nicer now than it was then. It used to be surrounded by bushes and trees. It was hidden from view of the road. Mai had a car, so she agreed to meet me here. She was going to tell me where to find the microfilm. I waited here, but when she didn't show up, I went looking for her. I saw the ambulance blocking the road and people directing traffic around it. I stopped to see why it was there and saw her car. I guessed what happened. And when I went back to the city, some of my Goto brothers, were waiting for me." Min uncovered his hand. "They wanted to know what she knew. I lied and said she knew nothing, that she was my concubine, that we were meeting to be together. They sent me back to Japan. I lost my finger there."

"You lost a finger. I lost my mother."

"I know. I'm sorry. There was nothing I could do."

"So, you saved yourself."

"What good would my death have done?"

Rocky arrived with bottled beers for Valerie and Min and one for herself. She looked for a chair, but finding none, leaned with her back against the wall behind Min, to watch the crowd and still be able to listen to the conversation between Valerie and Min.

Valerie took a deep drink from her bottle. "Why didn't you mention this to my dad?"

"I was protecting him. And you."

"Something you do so well," she said, a sour taste in her mouth. She wasn't sure if it was the beer so much as the company. "What do you want from me?" she asked.

"I want you to look for the microfilm."

Rocky's eyebrows shot up. Valerie ignored her and plowed on. "How would I find it now? It's been twenty-five years since my mother died. We didn't keep a lot of her stuff. We gave away her clothing and most of her jewelry and personal items. I kept a few things for sentimental reasons, old perfume bottles, some clothes and a couple hats, but there's no microfilm."

"Are you sure?" Min said. "Maybe not the bottles, but the clothing might have the film sewn into a hem. Or the hats, around the hatband. Will you check?"

"What good would it do all these years later?" Rocky asked.

"The information lays out the beginnings of several lines of business that the Goto-gumi would prefer to keep private. I would have peace knowing it would not fall into the wrong hands."

"Like government hands. Like law enforcement hands." Valerie tented her fingers around the sweating beer bottle.

"No," he said. "Like Yamaguchi-gumi hands. If they get it, there will be more bloodshed."

Valerie sipped her beer. "All right. I'll look. But there's something else that I want to know. Who is Mr. Itoh? Goto-gumi?"

"No. Yamaguchi-gumi."

"But he knows who my mother was."

Min stared down at the table for a long moment. "She became known. They call her the Woman of Secrets. All Yakuza know her legend."

"What legend is that?"

"How the Woman of Secrets stole the information from me while I was bewitched and took it with her to Hell. That every Yakuza who betrays the oyabun, who is our father and our leader, will see her there."

"But they must know you as the Yakuza who outlived her."

"No. I am known as the one who let her take the information because I was so blinded by love for her. I am The Weak One. The Foolish One." He bowed his head.

Valerie didn't know whether to believe him or not. She didn't feel sorry for him. Her own concerns were more pressing.

"How do I deal with Itoh?"

Min met her eyes. "He is very dangerous. He is not the leader, but a close advisor to the oyabun. There is a young girl, Suzume. She has more power than Itoh, but he watches out for her, because she is so young."

"The girl? Why is she so powerful?"

"She is the daughter of the oyabun's favorite mistress, his only child. She is spoiled by many who want to get close to her father, but she twists their words and often they lose their lives. I have heard that men die for looking at her in the wrong way. Keep away from her."

"She's a child."

"You are blinded by her appearance. She can kill with her words."

Valerie slid her beer bottle aside.

"Someone shot at me while I was in West Norriton, talking to guitar store owners. Why would the Yamaguchi-gumi want to shoot me?"

Min hung his head again.

Rocky shifted, touching Valerie's arm with her fingertips. "We have company," she said.

"Who?" Valerie asked, turning in her chair to look toward the door. Three men were moving through the crowd, looking over heads and through breaks between people. One of them caught a glimpse of Valerie, Min, and Rocky. Valerie could see a flash of recognition on his face.

Min was on his feet, moving in the direction of the kitchen. Valerie was surprised to see how fast he was.

Rocky pulled Valerie toward the ladies' room.

"Is there a way out that way?" Valerie asked.

"Window." Rocky pulled her into the tiny room and when she heard all hell break loose in the next room, she jammed her elbow into the frosted window, breaking the lower panes. She cleared the glass from the frame and pushed Valerie out headfirst.

Valerie broke her headlong fall with her hands, tucking into an awkward roll on the stones between two cars. She lay there for a moment, taking inventory of her bones and checking her hands for damage.

Rocky dove out of the window behind her, landing on her hands also, but pulling her body out and up in one graceful movement. She grabbed Valerie and pulled her upright between the cars. They ran for Rocky's car parked at the edge of the lot.

"Where's Min?" Valerie asked.

"Don't know. He headed in another direction."

They heard footsteps followed by a slamming car door. A car squealed its tires as it pulled out of the lot. A white cargo van pulled out behind him.

"There he is," Rocky said as she slipped behind the wheel. Valerie strapped herself in as Rocky gunned the engine and took off after the van. Valerie wondered what they would do if they caught up with it. There were at least three unhappy people in that van, and Valerie realized that they weren't after her.

*Min. They're after Min. But why? Isn't he working for them?*

Rocky barreled along as fast as she could, considering the age of her car and the condition of the road. Valerie felt the car slide from time to time, but she could see that Rocky was closing in on the van.

*That must be Min's car ahead of them,* Valerie thought. *Where the hell are they going?*

There were no fields of corn or fenced fields for horse farms here. No houses, no real signs of life. It was dark, though.

*I wouldn't see houses even if they were there.*

Rocky and Valerie were close enough to the van to watch it pull side-by-side with Min's car. A road sign indicated a long left-hand curve ahead. Even in the dark, Valerie could see a drop on the right, but it was hard to tell how deep. She could see a hulking stand of trees set back from the road ahead. Min's car lost traction as the van veered over into the driver's side. Min's car fishtailed, held, and kept moving. A flash came from the van and Min's car fishtailed wildly, squealing its tires. The car left the road and in eerie silence sailed into the air. As the van raced off, Min's car smashed into the trees. The nose crumpled on impact, followed by a large plume of smoke.

Rocky jammed on her brakes and pulled her car to the side of the road. "We've got to get him out of there," she said as the two of them opened their doors.

Cautiously they approached the car. The window was broken, but they could see that Min was still behind the wheel, airbag deployed.

He moaned and then he coughed. Smoke leaked into the car from under the dashboard.

Rocky tried to open the door, but it was jammed. "I've got a crow-bar in the trunk," she said to Valerie and headed back to her car.

Valerie leaned into the car to look at Min. His face was cut in a number of places, but he was conscious. "Who were they?" Valerie asked him. "What did they want?"

Min blinked, but didn't answer her. He coughed again, and this time, she saw blood.

"Rocky? Hurry," Valerie called to her.

Rocky arrived, carrying the thick metal bar, but she also had a thinner rod in her hand. Using the rod, she set to work on the door. Rocky's head bent over the window, blocking any view of progress. Then Valerie heard a pop and the door opened.

"I thought the door was bent, but it was the lock," Rocky said. "Let's get him out of there."

The car was still hissing and sputtering. They yanked Min out and jerked him to his feet. He was disoriented and hard to steer, so it took them awhile to haul him to Rocky's car. After Min fell across the back seat, Rocky leaned on the open door, breathing heavily, and said, "This is not my idea of a great date, Sloan. No wonder you're single."

Rocky turned the car around and they headed back toward the city. They had driven about a mile when Min's car exploded in the trees behind them. Valerie turned around in her seat and watched flames rise in the night sky. A few miles further and emergency vehicles passed them by, sirens blaring.

# CHAPTER THIRTY-NINE

*Paoli Hospital, Paoli, PA*
*June 20, 2009*
*10:30 A.M.*

**ROCKY TURNED OFF THE RADIO** as Valerie got into her car. "How is Min this morning?" Rocky asked.

Valerie slipped her seatbelt over her hip and heard the reassuring click. "The hospital says he's doing okay. Harry's not happy, though."

"I'm sure he didn't think this is the kind of thing we'd get involved in," Rocky said.

"Exactly. He still has friends on the force, so he's looking into it. I also called Walter and told him about Min, the gunshot wound on his forearm, the cuts and bruises. Walter's even less happy with me than he was before." Valerie sighed. "He thinks it's all my fault."

"Did you explain?" Rocky asked.

"Of course I did, not that he was listening. He went to the hospital after I talked to him. When I called this morning to find out how Min was, the nurse told me his nephew had been there. Along with the police."

"Uh, oh."

"I'm not worried. Min wasn't doing anything wrong, to my knowledge, and I'm sure he's talked to police before. Heck, maybe they'll even find out who ran him off the road."

"Sure they will." There was no mistaking the cynicism in Rocky's tone. "And how about you? Get any sleep last night?"

Valerie shook her head. "No, I was wide awake most of the night. I spent some time going through the stuff that I have from my mom."

"I take it you didn't find anything."

"No. My entire inventory consists of one perfume bottle, four dresses, one coat, two hats, one scarf, and six hankies. Then there's the scrapbook and a couple pieces of jewelry too small to stash microfilm in. That's it. I couldn't find anything in the hems or the pockets or the linings of the clothing. There was nothing inside the hats. I've been through the scrapbook a dozen times." Valerie grunted her disgust. "I keep thinking about those guys in the van. They were trying to kill Min, right? Why didn't they come back to make sure he was dead?"

"Maybe because we were there?"

"Yeah, but it wasn't like we were messing up their plans. It would have been easy for them to make us collateral damage. After all, they tried to scare us earlier."

"Maybe they were trying to scare him, too. Or keep him in line," Rocky said.

Valerie tilted her head back and closed her burning eyes. "Possibly."

"You didn't catch the license plate, did you?"

"Ah, if only. No, I managed to miss that."

"There was a lot going one, as I recall," Rocky said. "Well, I guess Min is in good hands and we are back to where we started. What's the next step, Boss?"

312

"I'd like you to set up another meet with Itoh. Let's get that guitar back."

———————◦•◦———————

The entrance to Itoh's private compound in a scenic area of the Delaware Valley was nearly hidden among some tall cedars. The driveway took them up to the top of a hill with a stunning view of green fields and horse farms. A young Asian boy showed them to a tiny formal garden, where they sat on a low bench, waiting for Itoh.

Valerie had visited very few places as quiet as this garden. She could hear wind chimes somewhere, and a pretty spillway gurgled with moving water that fed a small pond. Golden koi hung in the pond under the spillway, waving their sleek tails slowly. Occasionally their chubby faces flashed in the air, only to be lost again in the green/black depth of the pool.

A manservant arrived and bowed to them. "Please, come this way," he said. They followed him through the garden gate onto a stone path that in turn led to an ornate deck.

Itoh, wrapped in a heavy quilt of exquisite peacock satin, sat on a cushioned chair upholstered in shimmering gold and red-orange fabric. His slipper-clad feet were propped on a small tufted stool. His face tilted toward the sun, eyes closed. Two three-legged stools sat a few feet in front of him and the servant indicated with a silent gesture that Valerie and Rocky were to sit on them.

Itoh opened his eyes, his face still turned upward in such a way that Valerie couldn't see the milky one. "Welcome. I am glad you were able to visit on a day when you can be outside to appreciate the garden. It is still cool for this time of year." He let his eyes close.

"It is beautiful here," Valerie said. "I understand why you might want to spend as much time as possible in this place."

"It is my refuge," Itoh said, nodding in the way of the very old or very tired. He opened his eyes again and this time the milkiness was visible. "But solace is not what you seek. You have come for the guitar, have you not?"

"Yes." Valerie said. "May I take it with me? Or do we need to involve the authorities?"

Itoh considered. "I think we can come to an agreement without intervention," he said.

"An agreement?"

"I'm sure you have given my suggestion some thought."

"I don't have any information for you. I checked everything I have, everything I can. I don't have what you are looking for."

Itoh nodded to his servant and the servant disappeared. When the servant returned, he was carrying a guitar case.

Valerie felt her heart lurch. She glanced at Rocky, whose eyebrows were lost somewhere under the thick bangs of her wig, but whose eyes were wide.

"Please, take it. Consider it my gift," Itoh told her.

"Thank you. But I'm sure this is not a gift. What do you expect in return?" Valerie asked.

Itoh smiled. "You already know. You say you can't help me, but I think you can. I think you should keep looking," he said. "I have great faith in the daughter of the Woman of Secrets."

# CHAPTER FORTY

*Upper Darby, PA*
*June 20, 2009*
*11:30 A.M.*

**WHEN HARRY SAW THE GUITAR CASE,** he said, "Nice work, Sloan."

"Thanks," Valerie said. "I called Mark Patton to let him know that we located it and that I was bringing it here. He said he wanted to stop by and take a look at it. He hasn't seen the guitar since he appraised it."

"Good. I contacted the Lambert Brothers. They are very happy. At least, I think they are. It's kind of hard to tell, with them."

"I know what you mean," Valerie said, "but I understood completely when they were *not* happy."

"I'll bet."

Valerie heard the door open as Mark entered. He smiled broadly and leaned over and gave her a quick hug, which she pulled back from awkwardly, noting Harry's surprise.

"Congratulations! I'm so glad you got it back," Mark said. "I'm sure you couldn't have done it without your trusty sidekick." He winked at Rocky.

"Very true, but we appreciated your help, too." Valerie gestured to the case. "Take a look."

Mark took the guitar out of the case. Holding it by the neck with his left hand, his right hand traveled slowly over the body's finish with near-reverence. He sat on one of the folding chairs and strummed it softly. He was about to put the guitar back into the case when he changed his mind. Instead, he played a few bars of a tune that sounded vaguely familiar to Valerie, but she wasn't sure why. "I've heard that song. What is it?" she asked.

"'Satisfaction'," Mark said. "The Rolling Stones' Keith Richard used a '59 Les Paul to play the song in the mid-sixties."

"I'm surprised you recognized something other than Mozart," Rocky added.

Valerie made a face at her.

"Nice comeback," Rocky said.

Mark placed the guitar back in its case. "I know people talk about the Standard as a top collectible model, but not all of them bring top dollar. This is one of the really good ones, though. It's worth being insured at the level it is. Beautiful striping. Good condition. Fantastic tone. Almost creamy to play."

"Seems like a waste, being owned by Cafferty, though, doesn't it?" Valerie said.

The hint of a smile touched Mark's lips. "You could be right." He closed the case. "Sad that it's going back to him. Good job finding it, though. How did you do it?"

"It's a long story. Mostly luck."

"Maybe you could tell me over dinner."

Valerie's eyes met his and she felt her cheeks warm. "Maybe."

"All right!" Rocky cheered, but lost her enthusiasm when a sullen Reuben Cafferty arrived.

"I heard you have my guitar," Cafferty said. "Give me my property. I demand that you return it to me!"

Rocky laughed. "No way, compadre. You are in deep doo-doo with the insurance company, my friend."

"Yes, you are," Harry said. "A couple detectives should be here shortly to talk to you. Do you have your phone? You might need to call someone to bail you out."

"Bail?" Reuben said.

"Yeah, might as well get a start on that," Harry said. "Go ahead."

Reuben waffled, trying to decide if he should call Alice or Tammy. He opted to call Tammy. It didn't take long to hear that she was a bad choice.

"I knew it!" Tammy said, loud enough to be heard by the entire room. "I knew you were a loser. No, I won't be bailing you out, Reuben. Let your wife do it. Oh, and by the way, I QUIT."

"But... but..."

Reuben stared at the now-silent phone in his hand.

"At least the guitar is back," said Rocky. "At least those Asian guys didn't keep it."

Reuben glared at her.

# CHAPTER FORTY-ONE

*Overbrook Farms*
*Philadelphia, PA*
*June 20, 2009*
*2:00 P.M.*

"SO THE GUITAR IS BACK AND CAFFERTY is being charged with fraud," Valerie told the Lambert brothers over tea in their office the next morning. "I assume you will take ownership of the instrument, correct?"

"Well, technically, it still belongs..." said Darryl.

"...to Mister Cafferty. It depends on who..." said Delmar.

"...takes over his affairs while..."

"...he is in jail."

"He is still married, I understand. His wife hasn't filed for divorce," Valerie said. "Not yet, anyway. I gather she was beginning the process."

"How unfortunate..."

"...for him. I'm sure his wife..."

"...will know what to do..."

"...with the instrument."

"Yes, I'm sure she will." Valerie drank the last bit of her tea. "I want to thank you for having faith in me. In us, actually. Harry is a good investigator and I'm proud to work for him. And with Rocky."

"We're glad..."

"...to hear that. But there is..."

"...something else..."

"...you should know."

Valerie sat down again. "Something else?"

Their smiles faded into pursed lips.

"We understand that you have been..."

"...approached by some unsavory people."

"Well, it was part of the case," Valerie said.

"No. They are trying to find out..."

"...what you know about your mother."

Valerie looked from one brother to the other, trying to guess what was going on in their collective mind.

"But we know..."

"...that you know nothing."

"Make sure..."

"...that they know that."

"It would be best..."

"...if you kept it that way."

"What do *you* know about my mother?" she asked.

The brothers exchanged glances.

"Your mother..."

"...was a lovely woman..."

"...who craved excitement."

"She got involved in..."

"...things that she shouldn't have."

"Don't do…"

"…what she did."

"We may not…"

"…be able to help you…"

"…if you do."

———•••———

Rocky was rocking out, waving her arms and bellowing along to a song, when Valerie got to the car. She jumped when Valerie opened the door, and turned off the music when she saw Valerie's face.

"You look troubled, Boss," said Rocky. "What's up?"

"The Lamberts. They really bother me."

"See? I'm glad I told you I wasn't coming in. They are too weird. What did they say this time?"

Valerie told Rocky about her conversation with the twins.

"Wow. I wonder what they know?" Rocky asked.

"Good question. And why do they want me not to know?"

"How are you going to find out?"

"Keep looking, of course."

"Atta girl, Val." Rocky grinned.

———•••———

Valerie asked Rocky to drop her off at home. Her dad was not there and left no note, unusual for him. Because Valerie was thinking about the Lamberts and what they said, she was actually glad he wasn't around. She tried to figure out how the Lamberts knew about her entanglement with the Yakuza.

Valerie washed her face and looked at herself in the mirror. "If you're so smart," she said to her reflection, "tell me what I'm still missing!"

Her cell phone buzzed in her pants pocket and she pulled it out. The phone number was not familiar, so Valerie put the phone on the counter next to the sink while she brushed her hair. When the phone beeped, indicating a message, she picked it up and listened.

"I believe," the soft, girlish voice said, "that you have something that is my father's. Mr. Itoh tells me that you received payment in advance. You owe us the microfilm. Deliver it, or you will be sorry. It would be sad for you to have no family at all."

The message ended. Valerie stared at the phone.

*Suzume.*

*Dad.*

*Where's Dad?*

*Dad is in danger.*

She tried calling his cell phone, but it went to voicemail. She left a quick message, then shoved the phone back in her pocket.

*I've got to find that microfilm.*

Valerie went to her closet and pulled out the dresses, the coat, the scarf, and the hats again. She went over them, inch by inch. Nothing.

Valerie sighed and pulled the scrapbook out of the desk drawer for inspiration. She ran her fingers over the lacquer, thinking to herself, *If only Mom was here to tell me where it was.*

She leaned over to slide the scrapbook back into the drawer. The scrapbook slipped out of her hands and fell to the floor. She scrambled to pick it up, and when she did, she saw that the photo in the slot on the cover had shifted incrementally. Shocked that she had done damage, Valerie tried to slide the photo back into its slot with two fingertips.

The photo angled itself in the slot, making it difficult to move, but after a little effort to straighten the photo, it slipped out into her hand.

Valerie blew out a breath of exasperation, and bent over the scrapbook to slide the photo back in place. She picked up the photo from her palm with her thumb and forefinger, and a small glossy black piece of what looked like old projector film fluttered to the floor.

Valerie's mouth dropped open.

*Microfilm.*

# CHAPTER FORTY-TWO

*Chestnut Hill*
*Philadelphia, PA*
*June 20, 2009*
*9:00 P.M.*

**"ROCKY, I FOUND THE MICROFILM!** It was in my scrapbook."

"What scrapbook?" Rocky asked, her voice sleepy.

Valerie looked at the clock in her bedroom. It was after eleven.

*And Dad's still not home.*

Valerie explained to Rocky about the scrapbook and the phone call from Suzume. Rocky sounded more awake by the time Valerie finished.

"What are you going to do?" Rocky asked.

"Call Harry," Valerie said.

"I'm coming over," Rocky said.

———◆———

By the time Rocky arrived, Harry was there, too. He looked at the microfilm through a magnifying glass, while Valerie filled Rocky in.

"I've tried to call Dad numerous times, but the phone just goes to voicemail. I was going to track down Suzume by the phone number, but it's blocked on my phone. I don't know what to do." Valerie laid her cell phone on the kitchen counter face up, willing it to jingle with her dad's ringtone.

"Stay calm," Harry said. "We can't do anything unless Suzume contacts you again." He put down the magnifying glass. "I can't see much other than pages of squiggles. Everything is too small."

"Can we look at this somewhere?" Rocky asked.

"I can take it over to Dr. Eastlake's house. He was my mentor at Drexel. He taught criminal justice. He had a lot of forensic equipment at home—I seem to remember a microfilm reader." Harry looked at his watch. "It's late, but Dr. Eastlake is a night owl. I'll give him a call."

Harry went into the living room, leaving the women sitting at the kitchen counter.

Valerie put her head in her hands. "If Suzume hurts my dad, I don't know what I'll do." Valerie's voice cracked and she felt Rocky's hand on her shoulder.

"Hang on, Valerie. It's too soon to think like that."

The noise of a door opening, then closing, interrupted them. They heard Harry greet Valerie's dad. Valerie jumped off her stool and charged into the living room with Rocky right behind her.

Her dad looked surprised to see them all there. "What's going on, Valerie?

"Oh, my god, Dad, where were you?"

"I was at a friend's house," he said. "We went to a movie and then stopped for a drink. Till I dropped her off..." He looked puzzled. "Is there a problem?"

"Didn't you get my messages?" Valerie asked.

Liam pulled his cell phone from his pocket and said, "No, I had it turned off for the movie. I guess I forgot to turn it back on." He turned it on and frowned at what he saw there.

"Why didn't you leave me a note, Dad? You always leave me a note."

"Going out was a sudden decision. I didn't think of it. I'm sorry if I worried you, Honey."

Harry said, "Well, we're glad you are here now. Valerie, I think that takes care of one mystery for tonight."

Rocky patted Valerie's shoulder and said softly, "See, I told you it was too soon to worry."

Valerie forced herself to calm down. She was about to pocket her cell phone when she saw that she had another message waiting.

"Hey, I think this might be Suzume again." Valerie listened to the message playback using the speaker so they all heard her say, "Missing your father, bitch? Better get used to it."

"Who's that?" her dad asked.

"A gang leader's daughter," Valerie said. "She's been threatening me, but I'm not quite sure why."

"Gang?"

"An Asian gang that seems to think that Mom had something to do with them a long time ago."

"Mai? She didn't have anything to do with anybody but the orchestra."

"Then what's this?" asked Harry, holding up the microfilm.

Valerie's dad looked at the small piece of film and said, "I have no idea. What is it?"

"Microfilm," Valerie said. "It was in the scrapbook hidden behind the photo on the cover."

Her dad shook his head and rolled his shoulders, looking completely baffled.

"Okay," Valerie said. "Let's go talk to Dr. Eastlake."

They squeezed into Harry's small car and within fifteen minutes were standing in Dr. Eastlake's living room.

Eastlake was a small man with gray hair and bright blue eyes that sparkled through his glasses. He had a goatee that bounced when he talked. Valerie thought he looked a little older than her dad, putting him in his late seventies.

"So good to see you again, Harry," Eastlake said, shaking his hand.

"And you. How is retirement?"

"Full of unexpected events," said Eastlake. "Like getting your call in the middle of the night."

"I'm sorry if I disturbed you."

"Not at all. I was going over some notes on a cold case that I've been asked to look at. Seems that you're not the only person trying to untangle the past."

Harry introduced everyone to the professor and then explained their mission. "We can't read this film with a magnifying glass, so we thought perhaps we could use your microfilm reader. Did I remember correctly? You do still have a reader?"

"Yes," Eastlake said, "I do. Let me see what you've got."

Valerie gave him the piece of film. "We don't think there are a lot of pages," she said. "But we can see writing on them. It looks like there might be a few photos, too."

"Hmm." Eastlake held the film up, looking at it against a light. "Yes. Let's take a closer look."

The four followed Eastlake into a small room off the living room. Like the living room, the little office was packed with books and equipment. One wall held a built-in countertop where Eastlake set up the microfilm reader, and all of them gathered around to watch.

Eastlake lined up the film between two glass plates and clicked on the light in the machine. He fine-tuned the focus so they could see what was written.

"Even this is not going to help you read everything," Eastlake said. "You'll need to use a stronger unit than what I have. The University's library may be able to help with that."

Eastlake moved to one side so that Valerie could stand in front of the machine. She looked at the page centered on the small square of glass. "This page is dated March, 1984," she said. "It looks like account-ing of some kind. Last names and dollar figures, maybe." She stood back so that Harry could see. Rocky and Valerie's dad stuck their heads in, too, to get a closer look.

"Are all the pages this same kind of thing?" Rocky asked.

"Don't know," Valerie said. "Try another one."

Eastlake showed Harry how to move the lens in order to focus on the next image. Harry slid the lens over several pages, pausing to look at each one, then sharing them with Valerie and Rocky. Valerie's dad hovered over their shoulders.

"Yeah, they're pretty much the same thing, only different months," Harry said.

"Mostly the same names, too," Rocky said. "But the list is getting a little longer in the later months, so I guess there were new additions."

"Okay, so what are we looking at?" asked Valerie. "Names of donors to some organization? People paying for protection? What?"

Harry continued looking at pages. Suddenly he stopped short. "Photo," he said. He swallowed hard and added, "Looks like a crime scene."

"Let me see," said Eastlake. He moved the photo around, tweaking its position. It looked like he was trying to see into each corner. "Oh, my." Eastlake turned away and put a hand to his mouth. "Even after all these years, I find it hard to look at pictures of the dead. I'm not one of those people who can pretend the corpses are not human."

Eastlake closed his eyes and took a deep breath, then looked through the lens again. "Definitely a crime scene. Three bodies. Posed, I think. There's a man next to them with a gun." Eastlake shifted his glasses slightly, then moved the lens around. "I was hoping to see some of what's around them, maybe figure out where this was taken, but I can't see enough detail."

Harry moved to another photo. "Hoo, boy. More."

They all had a look at the new photo.

"Different victims," Eastlake said, tamping down a small burp. "Look at the clothing."

"Right," Harry said.

"Can we make copies of these pages?" said Valerie, straightening.

Eastlake shook his head. "This is only a reader, but I'm sure you can make copies at the library."

Harry nodded. "How about if I take this over to Hahnemann Library later today and see if their reader/printers will work with this?" he asked Eastlake.

"I'll go with you. I'd like to take a closer look at those photos myself," Eastlake said. "After I've taken some antacid, that is."

---

On the drive back to the house, Valerie sat with her dad in the back seat.

"You've been awfully quiet, Dad."

"I didn't know this was what you did," her dad said. "I thought it was all phone calls and letting other people do the dirty work."

"That's what I did at TransReliable," she said. "This is different."

"I wish I didn't know that," he said.

"Sorry, Dad. I wish you didn't have to know. The thing is, this is about Mom. Do you know what she was doing with this microfilm?"

"I've been thinking about that, trying to remember what happened back then, especially around the time of the accident. All I remember clearly is rain. For two days, it poured. And I remember that your mom said an old friend came to town and she was meeting him for dinner. I thought she meant downtown. I didn't even ask who it was. I thought it was another musician. I was practicing for a special performance with a trio I joined, and I was focused on that."

"The performance got cancelled," Valerie said

"Because of Mai's death, yes." Her dad's hands gripped his knees. "That day...." He paused, then started again. "She said you'd be okay. She said you could make yourself dinner. I went to rehearsal. It ran late. I came home and you were in bed and then the police called."

"But what about in the days before that?" Valerie asked. "What did she do?"

He shook his head. "I don't remember anything out of the ordinary. We practiced, we talked to you about school, we rehearsed with the orchestra. I worked on the music for the trio. We took care of things in the house. There were breakfasts, and lunches, and dinners. It was normal." His voice was just short of a sob. "I don't remember anything else."

Valerie patted his arm. "It's okay, Dad. That's enough. Try to put it out of your mind now."

After waving goodbye to Rocky, Harry walked Valerie and her dad to the door. Her dad let himself in. Harry tugged Valerie's arm to keep her on the porch.

"What?" Valerie asked.

"I'm afraid your dad thinks we may figure out what really happened with your mother that night. I want to make sure that *you* know we may not ever find out," Harry said.

"I know that," Valerie said. "But we've got to try. I've got to try."

# CHAPTER FORTY-THREE

*Upper Darby, PA*
*June 21, 2009*
*10:00 A.M.*

"SUCCESS! ALTHOUGH DR. EASTLAKE MAY NOT be able to eat breakfast for a few hours," Harry said when Valerie and Rocky got to the office. He handed a sheaf of papers to Valerie, along with a tiny glassine envelope. "Copies of all the pages on the microfilm. The microfilm is inside the envelope. The librarian gave it to me to protect the film a little better."

"That's great, Harry," Valerie said, pocketing the envelope. She distributed sheets of paper around Rocky's desk. "Now all we have to do is figure out what it all means."

"Dr. Eastlake thinks we had it right last night," Harry said. "Accounting, probably protection money and who paid it. Each month the number of accounts increased."

"I can't imagine why this would be important to a gang twenty-some years later," Rocky said, looking at the lists.

"Maybe that's not the important part," Valerie said. She pulled the reproduced photos from the pile and looked more closely at them. "Maybe these are what make the microfilm valuable."

Rocky looked at them over her shoulder. "Gross," she said. "Even more gross than last night."

"Murder's never pretty," Harry said. "And I think Valerie might be right, the photos make the film important. How can we find out who the victims are?"

"And who took the pictures?" added Valerie.

"How's your relationship with Walter these days?" asked Rocky. "Maybe he could suggest someone to talk to."

"No." Valerie gathered the photos and the pages of lists and made a tidy stack that she slipped into a slim messenger bag. "No, I think I have a better idea."

———————

The fetid smell in the street near Min's home enveloped them like a slimy cloak. Valerie heard Rocky gag when they made the short walk from Broad Street Market to his front door. Valerie pulled Rocky along, much as Walter had pulled Valerie the night she first went to see Min. The messenger bag's strap was set across her body so she could move fast. She took the steps up to Min's front door two at a time, dragging Rocky with her.

Min peeked through the door and when he saw Valerie, opened it enough to let the two women in. "I was surprised to hear from you," he said as the door closed behind them with its soft whoosh. "I thought you had forgotten me."

"I'm sorry if this is an imposition."

Min motioned to the couch. "Please, sit down. May I offer you tea?"

"Yes, thank you."

After Min went to the kitchen to make their tea, Rocky leaned over to Valerie and said, "Tea? I thought we were in a hurry?"

"Sharing tea is important. It shows respect. Didn't your boyfriend tell you that?"

"Well, yes."

"Besides, I know your stomach must be queasy from the smell outside. The tea will make you feel better."

Min rejoined them, tray in hand, the scent of caramel perfuming the air. *Hojicha tea,* Valerie thought. *My grandmother made this sometimes.* He put the tray on the low table in front of the couch and sat opposite them. To Valerie's surprise, Min served her first, then Rocky, then himself.

Valerie held her cup and inhaled the smoky steam. Her first sip was extraordinary, an unusual blend of spinach and walnut flavors infused with the smokiness of the roast, followed by the light caramel finish. *Coffee-like, without the coffee.*

Valerie tried to remember the formal steps of sharing tea she should follow. She had looked them up after her first visit to Min, but that felt like years ago to her now. Still, she wanted to please their host and facilitate their discussion.

"Such a lovely cup," Valerie said, holding the teacup in front of her. "Is it from Japan?"

"Yes," he said. "A cousin sent me the pot and cups."

"What does the design mean?" Rocky asked.

"Good health," Min said.

"And how is your health?" asked Valerie.

"Fine, thank you. The doctors were efficient." Min contemplated his cup, then said, "I believe I have the two of you to thank for that."

"Even if we may have been the reason for your... difficulty?" Valerie said.

They sipped for a few minutes more in awkward silence. Valerie gave up on the idea that this was even remotely close to a formal tea ceremony. She put her teacup on the table. "I am afraid we have unpleasant business to discuss."

"I'm not a stranger to unpleasant business, as you well know," Min said, pulling his lips into a thin almost-smile.

Valerie said, "Yes." She pulled the papers from her bag and placed them on the table. She flipped to the bottom of the stack. She chose one of the photographs and handed it to Min. "Do you know anything about this?" she asked, keeping her voice as neutral as she possibly could.

Min looked at the photo, then at Valerie. "Yes."

Valerie felt as though he had stabbed her. She sat up a little straighter and said, "Do you know who it is?"

"Yes. There should be more."

Valerie slid the other two photos across the table. He picked them up and looked at each one. He cleared his throat.

"When your mother moved east, I remained in California," Min said. "I lost focus without her there. I wanted to earn enough money to follow her to Philadelphia. I got involved in a drug operation, but I made some mistakes and the boss sent me to Japan to 'learn to be more respectful'."

"As you already told me," Valerie said.

Min waved away her interruption.

"I didn't know until I got to Japan that I was part of the Yakuza. They are not called that in this country. In the United States we use names that do not trace to people. 'Gold Tooth Clan.' 'Dragon Clan.' I was part of the Green Mountain Clan. In Japan, they are the Goto-gumi.

"I stayed in Japan almost fourteen years. When I came back, my family—my Yakuza family, that is, Green Mountain—placed me in New York City. We expanded our operations on the east coast, so they sent me to Philadelphia.

"It wasn't hard to find Mai. The orchestra is well known to everyone in the city. I first contacted her by telephone. She was happy to hear from me, but afraid to meet. She told me about you, told me about your father. At first, I didn't want to tell her what I had become, but it was so good to talk to her, so easy to confide in her. It was as though the years between disappeared. I told her about Green Mountain.

"She was not pleased. But she didn't refuse contact with me and we spoke several more times by phone. Then we met in person. It was very... moving. I still loved her. I believe she still loved me."

Min paused to sip his tea.

"My family collected much protection money back in those days. We kept ledgers of those we protected. Green Mountain was moving into Gold Tooth territory. We tracked which of their clients we secured."

"The lists," Valerie said.

"Yes. There were confrontations, of course, as Gold Tooth tried to stop us. These pictures show the outcomes from several of those encounters.

"We used the photos to apply pressure to new targets, to show Gold Tooth Clan's weakness. See how the shirts are arranged here, open and with coins where the heart is? The message is that they can be bought. Each of these photos shows a boss from different lines of the Gold Tooth Clan family."

"How did my mother end up with the microfilm?" asked Valerie. "Did you give it to her?"

"Yes," Min said. "After so many years, Green Mountain accepted me as reliable, safe. At the end of 1984, they gave me the microfilm to take to the Green Mountain boss in New York City, who would turn it over to his family in Japan."

"But you gave it to Mom."

"Mai wanted me to leave Green Mountain. She wanted me to take the film to the FBI, which she heard had a task force that intervened with gangs. I tried to explain to her that, just as she could never leave you or your father, I could not leave Green Mountain. The roots were too deep. You can't simply call up the authorities and have them take you in. But Mai had already contacted them."

Min sipped at his tea again. *That must be cold, by now, and bitter,* Valerie thought.

"I told her to take the microfilm. I told her what was on it, and who. I told her I would play the fool, take the family's punishment, and she could take the film to the authorities. They would protect her. She was a public person and they would protect her. They would never protect me."

"So, she took it home, but she didn't take it to the FBI. She hid it instead," Rocky said. "What about your punishment?"

"I knew the family would ridicule me for losing the microfilm to a woman. I knew I would be punished, perhaps even lose another finger. I didn't think they would kill me, though. This microfilm was just a small part of our operations," Min said. "Instead, they sent me back to Japan for 'retraining.' Since I knew that Mai would never leave you and your father, I went without regret. It was a minor punishment.

"I called her to meet one last time before I left. We had dinner. We talked. She told me she would wait until after I left to hand over the microfilm. She told me it was in a safe place that she could get to quickly. That night was so wonderful. We laughed. She cried and held me, the first time we touched since we were children. I walked Mai to her car, holding her umbrella over her head."

He put his cup on the tray.

"The rains were hard that year. We had more rain in two days than we normally have in six months. Many side roads were flooded out. I knew the roads would be dangerous. I told her to be careful."

Min took a deep breath.

"I saw the car pull out after her and I recognized the driver. I couldn't see his passenger, but I knew they would kill her. I went after them, but it was too late."

# CHAPTER FORTY-FOUR

*Arch Street, Philadelphia, PA*
*June 21, 2009*
*Noon*

**MIN'S EYES DAMPENED.** "I loved your mother, but I was also the cause of her death. My first thought was to kill myself for my part in this awful thing, but I kept thinking about Mai's insistence that I use the information I knew to get out of Green Mountain. I tried to honor her memory in the only way I knew. I went to the authorities."

"Even though you knew the family might kill you?" Valerie asked.

"Yes. I had lost Mai. I had nothing else that mattered."

"Yet here you are."

"Yes. At first, the police were quite interested in what I had to say, but I no longer had the microfilm and couldn't tell them where Mai had hidden it. They simply told me to go home. They had nothing to go on, nothing to hold me for, nothing to arrest anyone else for. They even doubted my suggestion that Mai was murdered. The conditions that night were so terrible. Her murder was ruled an accident."

"What did you do?"

Min's face was smooth, bland. "I started feeding them information. Telling them where clan events were happening, connecting specific clan members to small crimes."

"You're a snitch for the cops!" Rocky said.

"It took the police some time to accept that I was giving them good information, but after several small incidents worked out, they started coming to me instead of the other way around."

"And you're still alive, all these years later?" Valerie asked. "The family never figured out that you are a leak?"

"I'm good at what I do."

Valerie let the information filter through her mind. She asked, "Why would the family care about information from twenty years ago?"

"Family oppositions never die. Alliances are short and uneasy. Rivalries fester and old wounds bubble up into new battles." Min picked up the photos on the table. "These pictures prove that Green Mountain killed captains from Gold Tooth many years ago. It is enough to start another gang war, even today." Min picked up his cup as though he was going to take another sip, but seemed to realize it was empty and put it back down on the table. "I'd like to keep that from happening. Do you still have the microfilm?"

"Yes. In a safe place."

"If you turn it over to me, I can give it to my contacts with the authorities."

"Let me think about that," Valerie said.

Min started to say something more, but then seemed to think better of it. He stood, and Valerie and Rocky followed.

"Thank you for the tea," Valerie said. She moved to shake Min's hand. He gave her a small, polite bow instead. "You didn't have to meet with me again," she said. "I'm sorry for the pain I caused you last time."

Min shrugged. "I owed you for taking me to the hospital. Also, I met with you to honor your mother. She would say you deserve an explanation."

As they headed for the door, Valerie thought of something else. "Were the kanji from you?" she asked Min.

"Kanji?" he asked.

"I got several warnings in kanji."

"No."

Valerie frowned. "Did you shoot at me? In Music City?"

"Music City? Where is that?"

"West Norriton."

"No. It was not me."

———————

Harry suggested she take Sunday off to relax, but Valerie used the afternoon to prepare for a meeting with a possible customer for a violin. To Valerie, that was relaxation. She was excited to have a customer, her first since Mark's sister, and she found herself daydreaming, gazing at the beautiful instruments she positioned around her workshop.

Valerie kept her workshop pristine, her tools placed neatly in drawers, oils, alcohol, and varnishes lined up on small shelves and carefully labeled. She thought about the differences between her workshop and Evan Eastlake's office and it made her smile.

Valerie's customer was thinking about purchasing a hand-made Cioata violin, but Valerie selected a few others to give her a choice in the matter. As Valerie shifted cases onto the room's central table, she thought about Min.

Min's love for her mother and his desire to do the right thing for her memory moved Valerie, yet made her question his ethics.

As for Walter, his ability to look the other way where Min was involved seemed both weak and tacitly supportive.

Then there was her mother. The Woman of Secrets, indeed. Her mother's affection and respect for a man other than her father, and a Yakuza at that, astonished her. *I can't decide if I admire her, or am angry with her,* she thought.

She pulled out the Cioata that she was sure the customer would like and stroked it. She picked up one of her favorite bows, checked the tuning, and played Handel's "Bourrée," a song from her grade-school years when she was attempting to learn the instrument that eventually defeated her. *I'm a violin mechanic, not a musician,* she thought, hearing her own clumsiness. But the familiarity of the song allowed her mind to wander and the music to fill her.

Valerie finished the song, satisfied that the instrument was as she remembered the last time she had worked on it. As she positioned the violin on a stand near one of the large windows of the workshop, she shivered. Was she being watched? It certainly felt like it.

Suzume's looming presence threatened her family, her friends, and her peace of mind. Itoh's patient waiting for the return of the microfilm underscored his knowledge that it had been somewhere in Valerie's hands all these years. How would he know, if he didn't watch her? And Walter, always pursuing her yet keeping his distance, stalking her.

*Or maybe not. What did Walter really want?*

———•••———

The bus dropped Valerie less than a block from the Japanese American Cultural Association. Valerie entered through the imposing doors and in the cool hallway, found the elevator. A placard outside the elevator showed the floor where JACA occupied office space.

Walter was in his office, reading, when she poked her head in his door.

"Valerie!" he said. "What a surprise. And on a Sunday afternoon. Are you here for the program?" He pushed his glasses up his nose.

Valerie sat in the straight-backed chair opposite his desk. "No, not today. But I wanted to ask you about the classes you offer here."

"Great," he said. "Do you want a schedule of what's coming up?"

"No, this has to do with a class offered here awhile back. A class on kanji." Valerie was guessing, but she wasn't about to tell Walter that.

Walter nodded. "Yes. That was last year, actually."

"Who taught the class?"

"My cousin Arthur." Walter's face changed then, a startled look that he quickly removed. He dropped his eyes to the papers on his desk.

"So, the kanji on the table..."

"Could have been from anyone in the class."

"Oh, Walter."

"I can give you a list of their names."

"Walter, look at me."

He lifted his eyes.

"It was you, wasn't it?"

Walter hesitated, his eyes dropping to the desk. In a tiny voice, he said, "Yes."

"Why, Walter?"

"I wanted to protect you," he said. "You were so bent on finding out about your mother, about her accident. Tell me the truth, Valerie, isn't that why you work in insurance investigation anyway? To find out about your mother?"

"I don't think so..."

"And there were people who knew you had a piece of information so important..."

"You knew about that?"

"Of course. My uncle..."

"Who you conveniently failed to tell me was involved with a gang," Valerie said.

"You found out anyway," Walter said, pushing his glasses up his nose, "putting yourself in even more danger. Why did you take that job?"

"What job? The search for the guitar?"

"No, the job with the guy who used to work with you."

"Harry?"

"Yes, Harry."

"I took the job because he asked me to."

"But he got you in trouble with TransReliable."

"He got himself in trouble at TransReliable. I was collateral damage."

"How can you work with him?"

"I can work with him because it's the best job I've been offered since I got laid off. The violin business won't support me."

"Your dad takes care of you," Walter said.

"When he retired, I was still working for TransReliable. I had a good income and things looked great. But Dad didn't think much about his retirement years. Living only on Dad's retirement income... let's just say I need to work. For Dad and me."

"I could take care of you," Walter said. "I could take care of you both."

*And there it is,* Valerie thought. "No, Walter. You want to own me. You want me to think like you, act like you, be like you. I'm not about to do that."

They glared at each other over the desk.

"Did you shoot at me, too?" Valerie asked.

Walter looked shocked. "I told you before, Valerie. I had a luncheon to attend. How could I shoot at you?"

# CHAPTER FORTY-FIVE

*Berwyn, PA*
*June 22, 2009*
*11:00 A.M.*

**"IT IS GOOD TO SEE YOU AGAIN, MISS SLOAN."**

Itoh, wearing a supple robe the color of spring grass, was ensconced on a divan piled with luxurious silk pillows before a large window in his retreat.

"It is good to see you, as well."

Valerie turned her attention to the view through the window. As on her previous visit to the garden, the scene thrilled her. In the foreground, a low fountain bubbled a constant stream of water. A boxwood hedge trimmed in a neat row edged this angle of the garden. Behind it, the rolling hills and valleys were bathed in golden sunlight, suggesting warmer temperatures were on the way. Thin clouds streaked the sky.

In the city, Valerie barely noticed the weather, but out here, where the sky was so big and the clouds so low, she felt the pressure to get things done before the full heat of summer arrived and made taking a breath difficult.

Itoh's servant pointed her to a low cushioned stool. Valerie was conscious of sitting where Itoh looked down on her. It didn't bother her. Had they been standing side by side, she would have towered over the squat old man.

*He needs to feel like a big man,* Valerie thought. *I can't believe that he feels the need to do that with me. His servant could carve me into little bits and feed me to the wild animals.*

"You have something for me?" Itoh asked, turning his milky eye to her.

She fingered the microfilm in its envelope in her pocket. Against every instinct in her to do it, she pulled it out. It lay like a glittering minnow in the palm of her hand.

"Yes."

Itoh nodded to his servant, who stepped forward and took the envelope from her hand.

"I knew you would find it." Itoh relaxed onto the cushions again. "You will be quite an asset for us, like your mother was."

"No." Valerie said. "I'm finished here. But I have a request."

"You have already been paid." Itoh rearranged the heavy folds of his robe. "Handsomely, I might add."

"Tell Suzume to stay away from my family."

Itoh's milky eye rolled in her direction. "Young Suzume does not like you very much, I think."

"She tried to shoot me," Valerie said.

"Yes. She is quite jealous. She knows her father is interested in you. She has known about you for some time. You were of little concern to her father while you worked for that company."

"TransReliable?"

"Yes. You drew attention to yourself when you left."

"It wasn't my choice," Valerie said.

"No, but while you were with them, you were not a threat. You were immersed in your grief. You did not look at anything except what was put in front of you. But when you left there, it was as though you woke up. You could see the whole world. Your attention went to your mother."

"It's always been on my mother," Valerie said.

"It's different now. You were grieving then. Now you are angry. You are searching for someone to blame."

Valerie couldn't fault Itoh. He was right about that.

"Now Suzume's father wants you close, to work with him," Itoh said. "Suzume believes that she will lose her place in the family."

"That's not up to me. She should talk to her father," Valerie said, then added, "Call her off.

"I have no jurisdiction over her."

"Then tell her father to call her off." Valerie seethed. She added, "Threatening my family will not convince me to help you."

A small smile crossed Itoh's lips. "You have already decided to help us."

"Not if I feel as though someone is endangering my family. Call her off."

Itoh folded his hands on his lap.

"I'll make a request."

"Thank you." Valerie rose and started for the door. She paused as she was stepping over the sill and turned to look at Itoh. "As long as you protect my family, I will protect yours."

She could feel Itoh's eyes on her back as she left.

# CHAPTER FORTY-SIX

*Upper Darby, PA*
*June 22, 2009*
*5:00 P.M.*

**MAGGIE'S PUB WAS BUSTLING** during happy hour, filled with workers finished for the day. Alcohol flowed freely. Harry had to raise his voice to be heard over the crowd.

"I went over all the paperwork. Your report looks good, Valerie," Harry said between sips of beer. The beer's head spread itself on his mustache and he brushed it away with his fingers. "The rest is up to the authorities. I talked to one of the officers that's working on this case and he told me that Cafferty was able to scrounge together the money for bail. I gather his buddy Jeremy was not as lucky."

"I bet not," chuckled Valerie.

"I'm glad we were able to resolve this case," Harry went on. "It was a bit more complex than I thought it might be. The Lambert brothers called to thank me for your services. We really need to celebrate this one. Especially since it's your first closed case."

Rocky grinned and held her glass up for a toast. "To our new guitar expert."

Harry clinked her glass and turned to Valerie. Valerie shook her head. "I'm no guitar expert. That was Mark."

"I know. But it was your work that got the guitar back and the criminals behind bars," Harry said.

Valerie touched her glass to his, then Rocky's. "I guess I can toast that.

"So, we know that Jeremy is still incarcerated," Rocky said. "What about Chad, the guy that knocked Cafferty out?"

"He's in jail, too," Harry said. "Cafferty made sure Chad was arrested for assaulting him."

"Seems like it ought to be the other way around," Rocky said, sliding her glass forward for a refill. "Cafferty was the brains of the bunch."

"Relatively speaking, perhaps," Harry said. "I don't think there were a whole lot of brains to go around. The officer I talked to told me that Cafferty's going to try to prosecute that other guy, the one from his band. What was his name?"

"Austin. Austin Barclay," Valerie said.

"Yeah, him," Harry said. "Mr. Helpful. I don't see how Cafferty can do anything about Barclay. It was Cafferty's fault for listening to the wrong guy."

"He made bad choices all along," Valerie said. "He really should stick to dentistry."

Harry took another sip. "Valerie, I know this has been a trying time for you, getting used to the job and all. This was not a typical case, in my experience."

Valerie shrugged. "I got through it."

"You did well," Harry said.

"I don't know, Harry," Valerie said. "I'm still not sure I'm the right person for this job. You should have someone with more experience in real-world detective work. I'm a paperwork kind of person."

"You're wrong about that," said Rocky. "You're the kind of person we need. You're fluid. You think as you go. You understand that things aren't always black or white. That's what Harry needs. What the business needs."

"What she said," said Harry, tilting his bottle against Rocky's in a toast.

Valerie smiled at Rocky's enthusiasm. *Am I what they need?* she thought. *Can I do this job and still do what I promised Itoh?*

"Come on," Rocky whined. "You know you can't live without eighties rock and roll blasting in your ears! Let me pick some out now!" Rocky hopped off her seat and headed for the jukebox.

"All right," Valerie said, clinking her bottle against Harry's. "Let's have another round."

*The End*

# AUTHOR BIO

**SANDY NORK IS A WRITER, LIBRARIAN,** and musical tourist who lives in New Cumberland, PA, with her musician husband and his collection of guitars. Recently she vacationed in Nashville, the home of country music. She plans to include anecdotal souvenirs from that trip in her next book, Flood Risk.

For more information, visit sandynork.com.

# ACKNOWLEDGEMENTS

**I'VE HEARD MANY WRITERS SAY** that it takes a village to write a book and this one is no different.

Huge thanks to Bill Nork, my husband, for the idea, the in-depth guitar knowledge, and the continuing support. This book belongs as much to you as to me.

Thanks to all our musician friends who provided stories and background.

Thanks to the Pennwriters 4th Wednesday Writers Group from Area 5. Tough love from an inspiring critique group can only help and you folks helped a LOT. Hugs to Don Helin and Dennis Royer, and special shout-outs to Tina Crone, Gina Napoli, Janet Cincotta, David Tamanini, Bill Peschel, and Carrie Jacobs.

Thanks also to the Soft Addiction Round Table: Ann Kemper, Jane Smith Stewart, Kathy Hale, Barb Miller, and Sharon Anderson. Not only do you know your wine and chocolate, you are all so patient! You're the best cheerleading squad I could have.

Thanks to Susan Roller, my initial reader and editor, who helped shape the book.

Thanks to Beth Dorward, my editor at Reedsy and the reason this story makes sense. Thanks for rescuing me at a critical point. Several critical points, actually.

Thanks to Tara Mayberry at Teaberry Creative, for creating a great cover and designing the beautiful interior.